Stone, Paper, Boml

©Neil Hallam 2017

Published by Lauman Media and Publishing

Other titles by Neil Hallam

The Nev Stone & the Watchers novels

Between stone and a Hard Place

Stone, Paper, Bomb

(Coming soon) Breath becomes Stone

Loxley: modern day Robin Hood tales

Loxley: a dish served cold

Chapter 1

Nev Stone was living the dream. The ex cop powered his big adventure motorcycle along Portugal's Algarve coastal motorway towards the international airport at Faro. As he rode, Stone's thoughts drifted to the complicated turns his life had taken since resigning from the police.

The surfer community on Europe's South Western tip had become Stone's home since he left the British Police in disgrace over the shooting of a terrorist suspect. Stone's athletic appearance had helped him fit in with the surfers. A cop for most of his life, Stone had never been in the Army, but his appearance suggested otherwise. His neat haircut and a physique honed by years of police firearms duty, gave Stone a military bearing. Stone had expected to miss being part of the Midlands Counter Terrorism Unit. But his life in the Algarve National Park had been far from dull. Stone lived off the grid in a yurt among the temporary encampments of surfers and hippies. His 20 years in the police had taught Stone all manner of surveillance, firearms and special operations skills. But with a manslaughter conviction, all that experience was useless to him in the British marketplace, where a Security Industry licence is needed.

Stone had settled into his eco friendly lifestyle, riding his motorcycle and enjoying the area's impressive surf. Sports photography and the occasional paparazzi assignment were enough to fund Stone's low budget life.

Surfing and motorcycling were giving Stone all the adrenalin he needed and he had to work very little to sustain himself. Despite his thoughts occasionally straying to chasing terrorists across Britain, Stone was content in his new life.

Then Stone's life had taken the latest in a succession of dramatic turns. Stone had interrupted the kidnap of nine year old Lucy Varley. His attempt to rescue the young girl failed, leaving him with one dead kidnapper. He was sure that his previous manslaughter conviction for using excessive force would land him back in prison.

Stone's search for Lucy led him across Europe and North Africa, into the murky worlds of narcotics and sex trafficking. Freeing the girl from a former spymaster turned gangster saved Lucy from a life of sex slavery, but also saved Stone from a second prison sentence.

An unexpected result of his search for Lucy was falling for her mum, Trudy. Brought together by a desperate need to find Lucy, the two tried hard to continue a cross Europe relationship. But, Stone had the MC and Trudy would not leave her daughter's side. So in time, they parted as friends.

Returning his thoughts to the present and his ride towards Faro, Stone looked around him at the group of hard looking outlaw bikers who surrounded him. Riding with him were men he had come to accept as brothers.

A chance incident in prison led to Stone saving

the life of the biker leader Skull Murphy.
Fanatically anti drugs since his brother died of an
overdose, Skull did what he could to disrupt the
drugs trade. The prison drug dealers had brought
makeshift knives to end Skull's interference in
their business. Stone's opportune arrival saved
the biker's life and began what would be the
strongest friendship Stone had ever known.
Skull was the founder and International President
of the Watchers Motorcycle Club. His unusual
nickname had come from the skeletal appearance
of his head. Tim Murphy had lost his hair while in
his early twenties. A lifetime of body building had
pulled his skin tight, giving his head a skull like
appearance.
More than just a club, the MC members
considered themselves family. But, they also
considered themselves outside of society, part of
the 1% of bikers who rejected many of societies
stricter rules and conventions. Initially brought
under the MC's wing through obligation, Stone
had won the bikers trust and confidence and was
treated as one of their own.

The man they were riding to meet was not a biker,
but had become closer to the MC than any
outsider had ever got before. Tony "Jonah" Jones
had been a Detective Inspector in Special Branch
throughout his long career with the British police.
He was the Ops Commander on the fateful
operation that led to Stone's imprisonment. For
decades Jonah had been considered the best of
the best among terrorist hunters, but the new
breed of political bosses viewed him as a

dinosaur and forced his retirement.

It was Stone's search for young Lucy that earned Jonah the respect of the MC. He had effectively run their investigation and had joined the bikers on their dangerous mission into Morocco. The ageing detective's bravery and loyalty to his younger protégé had impressed the Watchers and brought Jonah into their world.

Jonah had become a regular visitor to the Watchers' Lagos clubhouse. He had come to value the friendship of the bikers and to enjoy the warmth of the Algarve sun on his ageing bones.

Jonah's arrivals at Faro airport had come to warrant the ceremony usually reserved for MC members. A convoy of 10 gleaming customised motorcycles led the van in which Jonah would ride. At the airport the small convoy pulled straight into the busses and taxi area outside the arrivals hall. Most people would be quickly moved on by the airport police. But there was always a reluctance to take on a group of bikers.

Throughout the search for Lucy, the senior officer Chief Inspector Ricardo de Sa had an all consuming hatred for the bikers. But most of his junior officers had developed a grudging respect for what Nev Stone and his friends had achieved in damaging the gangster O Lobo's stranglehold on the Algarve.

Before long Stone spotted his former DI through the crowd of tourists. Jonah always stood out from a crowd. Throughout his police career Stone had never seen his boss without a dark business

suit. In retirement Jonah had adopted the image of an English country gent. The checks, tweeds and earthy colours suited retirement in the English Shires, but made Jonah easy to spot amongst the Algarve's mix of surfers and golfers. As always, Jonah greeted Stone with a loud "Morning Nev lad". Then the influence of his time with the MC took over as he greeted the bikers with their almost ritual hugs and back slaps.
Before the airport police patience ran out, the bikers mounted up and rolled out of the arrivals zone. Whenever the Watchers rode together, they always had a van in support to carry tools and luggage. Usually one of the prospects, or probationary members drove the van. But Jonah had become used to the van during the Watchers' Moroccan adventure and eagerly took the wheel joining the back of the bikers' convoy.
Jonah made small talk with the Prospects in the van. Serious conversation would have to wait until they reached the Watcher's club house in Lagos. None of the full members of the MC would willingly give up their motorcycles to ride in the van
Like his protege Nev Stone, Jonah occupied an unusual place in the MC's otherwise rigid hierarchy. The path to club membership always began with someone becoming either an associate of the club, or an employee of their legitimate businesses.
With full membership of the Watchers MC came directorship in their international security business. So it was not something they gave away lightly.

All true 1% MCs assess their prospective members through a long period of probationary membership. During this six to twelve month Prospect stage, the aspirant member is virtually a slave to the MC while they prove their worth. Stone and Jonah had earned the MC's trust many times over in Morocco searching for Lucy Varley. So much so that the members accepted them into almost all levels of club business. They could not become full members without Prospecting, and the club could not treat them as servants.

It took a good hour for the convoy to reach its home in Lagos. Stone never tired of riding into the ancient walled town amongst the convoy of bikers. He loved the contrast of old and new. Lagos' heyday was in the days of Prince Henry the Navigator sailing off to discover new worlds. The fortified harbour and town walls stood strong against the old days of high seas piracy. The bikers' highly customised motorcycles brought the new part of the contrast to Lagos. The roar of so many exhausts echoing off the old town walls was like music to Stone's ears.
Despite some of today's Lagos residents wishing the defences would keep out the bikers, they had made their home within the old town walls, where most locals accepted them.

The Watchers' began their security business working in bars and nightclubs. The building which was now their clubhouse had once been a nightclub for which they provided bouncers. The owner had gone bankrupt owing the Watchers money, so they converted the building into a home for their growing Algarve chapter.

Set above a car repairs garage, the building provided a perfect home for the MC. The secure ground floor garage kept their motorcycles safe, and the upstairs became their bar and meeting rooms.

Stone's life in Portugal had begun with living in the MC clubhouse. In time he found the perfect spot in the surfer community of Ingina to pitch his Mongolian yurt. Much as Stone loved the eco friendly lifestyle in the Costa Vincentina National Park, the Watchers' clubhouse still felt like home. The Watchers were always conscious of security around their clubhouse and a prospect would always be on duty watching the CCTV monitors. So it came as no surprise to Stone when the roller shutters opened on their approach. Two armed prospects were on hand to welcome the bikers home and quickly park their motorcycles safely away. With their bikes secure, the ten bikers climbed the stairs to their bar, catching up on Jonah's news from home.

The Watchers MC was founded by Skull Murphy in England's rural county of Derbyshire. A fanatical body builder and motorcyclist, Skull used his size and image to build a successful bar and nightclub security business. But Skull was an educated engineer and his company quickly diversified into all aspects of physical and technical security.

Skull's life was inseparable from motorcycling and his company and his motorcycle club became one and the same.

Success carried the Watchers away from Derbyshire into many of Britain's biggest cities, before eventually becoming international. The full members, as directors of the business were now moderately wealthy men, but they all still enjoyed the grass roots of the business they ran.

Since Jonah's retirement from the British police he had put his decades of experience to work in service of the Watchers's English Chapters. His almost 40 years in Special Branch had taken him from being a spy catcher during the Cold War, through hunting the IRA during Ireland's Troubles, to tracking Islamic fundamentalists in the post 9/11 world.

With Jonah's worth proven in their Moroccan adventure, the MC were quick to secure his skills for their surveillance and investigations section. It was Jonah's English caseload that provided Skull with much of his early conversation with Jonah.

As International President of the Watchers, Skull had to keep a keen interest in all aspects of the MC's business. But he was always most interested in home. Skull's convictions for beating up drug dealers cost him his British security licence and caused his exile to the Algarve. But Skull's heart remained riding his motorcycle around the peaks and dales of Derbyshire.

As soon as the bikers reached their first floor bar, they heard the hiss of the steam and smelled the rich roast as prospects prepared good quality coffee for their senior members.

Some might be surprised at ten bikers walking into a bar and drinking coffee. The group would later party to welcome Jonah to his second home. But first and foremost they were businessmen and they needed clear heads to get though their business.

Jonah's biggest case was a large British pharmaceutical company, worried about corporate espionage. His team of retired undercover cops were tasked with infiltrating the company at all levels to test their security. The Watchers could then sell the company solutions to all their vulnerabilities. So, the more areas Jonah could penetrate the more money the Watchers could make.

This was the main focus of Skull's discussion with Jonah. All the members present had read Jonah's reports, but there is no substitute for a personal briefing.

"So, here it is from the horse's mouth Skull lad", began Jonah as he started to take the members through his many months of work on their behalf. "What horse Jonah?", asked Joao Alva. The English Watchers were used to Jonah's quirky mannerisms and colourful speech, but often their Portuguese brothers were caught out by phrases like "straight from the horses mouth".

Joao Alva was the Lagos chapter's Sergeant at Arms. The giant man took charge of the chapter's own security and looked after the fairly small stock of weapons they occasionally needed.

In a truly "outlaw" motorcycle club, the Sergeant at Arms also deals with discipline. The mature professionals within the Watchers' membership never warranted any discipline. But the nightclub bouncers and uniformed guards at the bottom of their organisation were often a different matter. One sight of the enormous biker was usually enough to calm the most argumentative of men. Rarely did Alva have to prove the power of his huge body.

After pausing to satisfy Alva with an explanation, Jonah continued his briefing. The old detective took the members carefully through everywhere he thought there was money to be made. He had identified weaknesses in; physical security, CCTV cover and quality of guarding. But most of all, in cyber security. Jonah took pride in his work and was thorough in his briefing, but all the time the real reason for his visit was burning inside him.

"I need some Church time with the Officers Skull lad", said Jonah. "I've a little job I need to bring to the table". The bikers did all their formal business in private meetings they called Church. Even 1% MCs with very chaotic lifestyles were strictly democratic, always conducting business in accordance with Roberts' Rules of Order.

"I think for this client, we might need Nev lad too", he added. Jonah was asking for a private meeting with the most senior of the Watchers, those holding official office. It was a big ask to exclude any full members from a Church. But it was an extraordinary thing to also bring in Nev Stone, who although trusted was not an MC member. Skull considered Jonah's request, then replied "it's unusual Jonah, but I trust you man. You had better convince me quickly though".

11

Joao Alva gathered together the officers present and led the group into the comfortable Board Room they called their Church.

Alva's first task, as always, was to sweep the room for bugs. While he worked, the others took their seats at the table. Skull Murphy took the head of the table. On his right was Vice President Miguel Cuba, one of Skulls oldest friends. Portuguese born he was raised in an English Catholic boarding school with his sister Barbara. Miguel's family obviously had more than their share of Moorish DNA. His dark colouring and the confident mannerisms from boarding school, always reminded Stone of Zorro.

Completing the group were Paulo and Pedro Da Costa. The identical twins were respectively Secretary and Treasurer of the Chapter.

"Ok Jonah, the gang's all here", said Skull. "Who's your mysterious client?"

"Well Skull lad, you're going to love this one", replied Jonah. "Her Majesty is in a bit of a pickle".

Chapter 2.

Mention of Her Majesty brought a stunned silence to the normally extrovert bikers.

"What does the Queen want of us?" asked Stone when he regained his composure.

"Actually, she wants you Nev lad", replied Jonah. He went on to explain that the Queen wanted to Knight Nev Stone for saving Prince William and Prince Harry during the terrorist operation which ended his career. Stone's conviction for shooting the terrorist prevented the Queen from publicly honouring him, but she maintained an interest in Stone's career through her weekly meetings with the Prime Minister.

"It's nice to be appreciated Jonah", replied Stone. "But what does she need doing? and how are you involved?"

"Well Nev lad, I spent half a lifetime in Special Branch. I might have retired from the police, but the Service still has its hooks in me." The Service Jonah referred to was Britain's Security Service, which is often incorrectly called MI5. Because the spy catchers have no police powers, they rely heavily on officers from Police Special Branch to support them when arrests are needed. Over his 30 years working with the spooks they had learned everything there was to know about Jonah. This gave them influence over him, but more importantly meant they trusted the old detective implicitly.

Jonah continued his story, "we've rather

carelessly lost a nuclear weapons engineer Nev lad". The group of bikers were still lost for words. Only Stone, who was used to Jonah, seemed to be processing any of the information. "But how does that involve us Jonah? We did a half decent job in Morocco, but the spooks have greater reach and much more clout than us".

"That's the thing Nev lad", replied Jonah. The Security Service's hands are tied on this one. They can only operate in the UK and they think their man is abroad. SIS could pick up the trail, but they would embarrass us with the cousins."

Stone had to translate the police speak into something his biker friends would understand. He explained that all overseas covert work was handled by the Secret Intelligence Service, or SIS. This is the organisation made famous through the James Bond movies and usually referred to as MI6.

The cousins were the Americans. Stone had made the connection that Britain's nuclear deterrent actually uses US technology. So the loss of one of our weapons engineers would be highly embarrassing to the Crown and could set NATO cooperation back years.

"So Nev lad, we needed some damage limitation without involving the Yanks. Then it turns out that our man is a regular visitor to the Algarve. So, her Majesty pushed the PM into contracting out to the Watchers. They were impressed with what we did in Morocco, and using you gives deniability."

"I'm in", said Skull. "But we need to vote it". The Watchers always operated democratically. Any decision, whether to do with the MC or their security business, needed a majority vote of full members. Skull went on, "some of this has to be kept need to know, but we need club approval. I propose we vote taking on MI5 as a client, then keep the detail within an operational team". Jonah had already worked out the same strategy, but it was good to let the Watchers' International President come up with the idea. "Sounds dandy to me Skull lad. Can I suggest we bring Steve Butler into the Ops team? He knows the UK end and he was very useful in Morocco."

Steve Butler was a member of the Watchers' London Chapter. He also held office as International Sergeant at Arms. The former Royal Marines Commando was a key member of the Watchers' search for Lucy in Morocco.

"Agreed", replied Skull. "Let's get the other guys in to vote the contract. Then we'll work out the details".

Despite the need to keep some of them in the dark about all the details, the members voted unanimously to take on the Security Service as a client. Knowing the request came directly from Queen Elizabeth II made Jonah's sales pitch unnecessary.

Soon the core group of Watchers were gathering together personal kit for the flight to London. They also loaded one of their vans with the more bulky kit they might need on an operation. Prospects would drive the van over to London, allowing the more senior members to fly.

While two Prospects started driving the van

towards the Channel Tunnel, another Prospect collected a mini bus for the airport run.

Skull, as President would lead the team. Jonah, as conduit to MI5 was an essential team member. Nev Stone went along with Royal approval. The other members were Miguel Cuba and the giant enforcer Joao Alva.

The five of them, together with Miguel's sister Barbara had taken on the whole of O Lobo's Moroccan operation and come out on top. They were confident of handling a missing person investigation without great difficulty.

Twin brothers Paulo and Pedro Da Costa stayed behind in Lagos while the others drove to the airport. As the only other Watchers with full knowledge of the contract, they would be needed to direct investigations into the missing engineer's Algarve visits.

Their first task was to arrange motorcycles for the Watchers travelling to London. Each chapter of the Watchers maintained a motorcycle dealership as one of their legitimate businesses. This provided income for the chapter and a ready supply of loan bikes for visiting members.

"What goodies will London have for us this time Nev?" asked Skull.

"Who knows", replied Stone. I quite like the surprise though".

For their personal machines, the Watchers insist on a European only policy. This is to counter the more famous American clubs, who allow only Harley Davidsons.

The Watchers' bike dealerships stock mostly

European models, such as Triumph and BMW. But trade-ins produce a huge variety of used machines, and it is from the used stock that the loan bikes come. The visiting bikers could be sure of getting the best of their bikes, but they could be of any make or style.

Steve Butler arrived at London Heathrow Airport to collect the visitors in a company mini bus. He had little trouble in getting close to collect Stone and his group, as one of the London Chapter's security contracts was with the airport.
Before long they were turning onto London's North Circular Road and heading towards the London Clubhouse. Each of the Watchers' many Chapters maintained its own clubhouse. These doubled as a base for the motorcycle club to meet and party, but also as head office for the Watchers' business activities in that area.
The London Chapter had chosen to convert a former tyre and exhaust centre on the North Circular Road. One of the location's most attractive features was being close to the famous Ace Cafe.
The Ace has been a biker meeting place since the early days of the British Rockers in the 1950s and 1960s. After sampling mugs of Ace tea, the Rockers would head for Brighton to take on the Mods, or alternatively they would race to the nearest roundabout, returning before a juke box record ended.
Today, the Watchers appreciated it as a place to meet like minded bikers, as an excuse to party and often to make new business contacts.

Historically, motorcycles were the transport of the workers who could not afford cars. Today's biker is much more likely to be successful in his area of business.

A visit to the Ace Cafe would have to wait for Stone and his team. They had business to deal with at the London clubhouse. Butler pulled his mini bus into the fenced car park, as Prospects opened and closed the huge gates for him. The visiting Watchers soon made it inside the clubhouse, to be greeted by the London Chapter's Officers.

Jack Tate, the London Vice President led the welcoming committee. Tate was the Watchers' leading computer expert. Stone and Jonah had worked with Tate before, during their search for young Lucy. His computer skills would no doubt be useful to them in hunting for their missing nuclear engineer.

Next to great the visitors was Jim Reynolds. As the London President he was expected to be present to meet the Watchers' International President on a visit to his clubhouse.

Reynolds was brought up in Derbyshire. He met Skull and Cuba bouncing in Derby's night clubs and helped found the MC. As the Watchers' influence grew, he looked after some of their new London contracts. Eventually he founded the London Chapter, building it into one of the Watchers' most profitable chapters.

Biker greetings always seem over the top to outsiders and the meeting of the London and

Lagos Chapters was no exception. They gripped each other in tight bear hugs, followed by rounds of vigorous back slapping.

Despite Jonah not being one of the bikers, his help to the MC in Morocco was well known throughout all of the Watchers' Chapters and he was always treated as one of their own.

"Ahoy Jim lad", said Jonah as he hugged Jim Reynolds. "On Treasure Island again? said the London President. Jonah had taken to using the Long John Silver quotation whenever he met Jim Reynolds.

Once the ritual greetings were over, the Watchers quickly morphed into the professionals that they are. The Lagos visitors joined the three London Officers and Jonah in their Church.

Each MC Chapter had a conference room which was traditionally called their Church. Just like the room in Portugal where Skull's Chapter agreed to take the MI5 contract, the London Church was secure and swept regularly for bugs.

Jonah and Skull had already agreed to bring Jack Tate and Jim Reynolds into the operation. They knew they would need Tate's computer expertise and Reynolds cooperation would be needed to release Steve Butler and Jack Tate to the operation. As far as anyone else was concerned, it was a sensitive missing person investigation for a wealthy and secretive client.

Other than MI5 being concerned that a nuclear weapons engineer was missing, there was not actually much for the bikers to discuss.

Jonah needed to set up a meeting with the Security Service handler for their contract.

"The Service want to go a bit Cold War on this Jim lad", said Jonah. He explained that MI5 were so worried about the American CIA finding out, that they were going to deal with Security Service bosses though tradecraft usually reserved for international espionage.

"Face to face meetings will be through a single handler, at neutral locations. They will provide encrypted comms for all other contact", added Jonah.

"All sounds a bit James Bond to me", replied Stone. "That's how they're treating it Nev lad", said Jonah. "We've never been close to losing nuclear secrets before. Don't underestimate the international incident that losing one of our bomb builders would cause."

Jonah went on to explain who was going to be their contact with MI5. "Our chief spook is Jonny Johnson. I've worked with him for years, so meetings will pass as personal. He's a bit old school, but a nice guy and a terrific spy catcher". Jonah had already set up the first meeting with their handler. "Jonny will be at the Ace in about half an hour. Let's keep the first meet small, myself, Nev, Skull and Jim should about do it".

Although the Ace Cafe was within walking distance of their clubhouse, the Watchers would always arrive by bike. Jonah did take the opportunity of stretching his legs, but the others went straight to the clubhouse garage to sort out their bikes.

This was the first time Nev Stone and Skull Murphy had seen the loan bikes their London bike dealership had found them. Skull had a 1700cc Triumph Thunderbird Storm, while Stone and Cuba had 900cc Triumph Bonneville Speed Masters. "Nice said Skull. The T Bird always comes a close second to my Rocket III".

The huge Joao Alva needed an equally huge motorcycle. He was given the only Japanese bike in the bunch, a Honda Goldwing. The enormous armchair on wheels was ideally suited to the giant Sergeant at Arms.

London members Jim Reynolds and Steve Butler had their own bikes. Reynolds also favoured the Triumph Thunderbird, but unlike the standard matte black model Skull was using, Reynolds's bike was a highly customised version.

Ex Royal Marine Steve Butler had more military tastes. He rode a 1200cc Triumph Tiger Explorer, the same as Stone owned in Portugal. But Butler's bike had been customised into an apocalyptic nightmare.

It was often difficult for the larger than life bikers to be unnoticed. So, when they needed to cover their intentions, they preferred to hide in plain sight. Using this tactic, the five Watchers headed for the Ace Cafe riding loud motorcycles and wearing their club vests and back patches. No one could fail to notice their arrival. But no one would suspect they had come to meet secretly with an MI5 spymaster.

The bikers arrived before Jonah, so headed for the bar. Jim Reynolds played host and started to take their orders, when Skull took over. "When in Rome, do as the Romans do. When in London, drink tea".

While their order was coming, Stone turned to Skull and asked, "spot the spook?" Stone was looking towards the dapper looking gent at the far end of the cafe. The clean cut, middle aged man looked a little out of place among the bikers, but the Ace attracted all sorts. The man wore corduroy trousers, a checked shirt, and the closest he could get to a leather jacket, a brown leather blouson.
Before long Jonah had caught up with the Watchers and walked into the cafe. Stone's suspicions were confirmed when Jonah sat with the dapper gent. The Watchers soon followed, mugs of tea in hand and sat with Jonah.
"Jonny lad, meet the Watchers", said Jonah. Moving on to make the introductions. "Jonny and I go back a long way. Cold War, Red Brigades, IRA and Bin Laden. We've been through the lot".

After the introductions Jonny Johnson started to brief the bikers. In his cut glass, perfect English accent, the spymaster told them about their missing Bomb maker. Matthew Saint was one of the rising stars at Britain's Atomic Weapons a Establishment, or AWE.
The 30 year old had sped through Bachelors and Masters Degrees in physics. He had then completed a Doctorate in nuclear weapons. AWE had snapped him up when he graduated and entered the job market.

Saint had little social life to speak of, outside of church attendance. The quiet, religious young man devoted himself to his work and was an instant hit with his bosses.

In his five years at AWE he had never taken a days sickness and rarely used all of his holiday entitlement. Then, six months ago, he had begun to take holidays and two weeks ago he disappeared from the face of the earth.

Chapter 3

Jonah had heard most of the briefing before, but he had never visited the Ace Cafe. So, his attention was distracted to the framed press cuttings from the heydays of the Rockers on the walls. "Must ask what the Ton Up Boys were", thought Jonah as he looked at articles from a time when 100 miles per hour was fast for a motorcycle.

Jonah was brought back on subject by the feel of something being pushed into his hand.

While Jonny Johnson spoke to the bikers, he had surreptitiously passed a computer memory stick and a key to Jonah, under cover of the table. Jonah knew the stick would hold encrypted secret documents about the case. The key would be for a locker at the nearest public leisure centre. The locker would hold some of the technical equipment and possibly fake documents, which Jonny could not be seen handing over. The spies called this part of their tradecraft a dead letter box.

Back in his usual professional mode, Jonah listened to Johnson explain that Matthew Saint had no family to speak of. He had been raised by a succession of foster families after the death of his parents during his early teens. Saint had bucked against the stereotype of the foster child, by focusing on his schoolwork and his family's Baptist beliefs. While studying for his doctorate,

Saint switched allegiance to the Seventh Day Adventist Church. His massive intellect had no difficulty in memorising the many bible passages his new religion took quite literally.

It was Saint's landlady who had reported him missing. Saint had lodged with an elderly couple in Aldermaston throughout his whole time at AWE. They had grown very close to their bright young lodger.
Christians themselves, they always took a keen interest in Saint's bible studies and spent many hours talking to him during what time he did spend away from work.
Saint had always been diligent in telling the couple when he would be away. He had come to view them as another set of foster parents and knew they would worry about him.
So, when he had not returned from work by their bed time, they began to worry. When his bed had not been slept in, they contacted AWE. His employers were already concerned as the previous day was Saint's first ever absence without permission. By the time he failed to arrive on his second day, they contacted his landlady, who in turn reported him as missing to the police.

The local police had started a missing person, or misper enquiry, but they only classified Saint as a very low risk case. AWE had played down Saint's work with them, as they could not admit to losing a nuclear bomb builder. Thinking him only a low level admin clerk, the police took the view that 30 year old men were entitled to disappear.

Stone had been listening intently to Jonny's briefing and his mind was now performing the analysis it had been trained for through his 20 years in the police. "Ok Jonny, where do we start?" asked Stone. "Has his house been searched? And what can you tell us about the Algarve visits Jonah mentioned?"

"In a way, we are lucky about the house search", replied Jonny. "Police misper procedures say the local officers should search the home address. But it was given lip service, they only looked for Saint. You have a free run at what's left behind. But it will need to be discrete".

"You mean a burglary?" asked Skull. "I couldn't possibly suggest how you do it", replied Jonny. "So, what about Portugal?" asked Stone. Jonny had very little to go on there either. "We have airline and passport records. He's flown out five times in the last six months. But once there he goes off the grid. No hire car, no credit card use, nothing".

"Sounds like next stop Aldermston", said Stone. "My thoughts exactly Nev lad", replied Jonah. "But I need to take a swim first". All the Watchers looked puzzled at Jonah, as it seemed an odd thing to do when they were about to leave on a mission.

"I'll explain later", said Jonah. "Just have a briefing room ready for when I get back". With that, Jonah walked off to visit Jonny's dead letter box at the local swimming pool.

As expected, Jonah found a small holdall waiting

for him in a changing room locker. He quickly completed a short workout, to maintain his cover, but was soon on his way back to the clubhouse with Jonny's bag of tricks.

Stone had figured out why Jonah suddenly needed a swim. He too had worked closely with MI5 while he was a Special Branch officer and he had used the same trick several times. So, by the time Jonah returned, Stone had set up a makeshift incident room in the London Chapter's Church.

Jonah handed the memory stick to Stone. "Here Nev lad. Have a look what's on here for us".

Stone plugged in the memory stick and connected the computer to a digital projector. The first image to fill the screen was the photograph from Matthew Saint's AWE identity card.

"Looks pretty straight laced to me", said Stone. The young, slightly built black man on the screen did indeed look well turned out. He was smartly dressed, with a neat hair cut and looked every inch the studious professional.

"What trouble can he have got into?" asked Skull. "He looks like butter wouldn't melt".

"Never judge a book by its cover Skull lad", replied Jonah. "Let's see what else is on the stick". Stone took them through the other documents on the memory stick. There were photographs of Saint's adoptive parents, and the elderly couple he now lodged with.

There was also a copy of his AWE personnel file, which gave Saint's academic background, as well as details of his current specialism in the secret world of nuclear missiles.

Most importantly for the next phase of their operation, were photographs, maps and plans of Saint's home address in Aldermaston.

"Next stop Berkshire", said Skull, anticipating Jonah's next suggestion.
"Yes Skull lad. His house has to be our best chance of a lead. Jonny has given us a base to work from". Their MI5 contact had left the keys to a safe house in the bag collected by Jonah. He found details of the house on the memory stick. Jonny had used his covert budget to rent a large detached house in Aldermaston for the Watchers to work from. There was ample space for their team of six to work and sleep. There was also a large double garage for their motorcycles.

But Berkshire would have to wait. It had already been a long day and despite the Prospects driving none stop, their van full of kit was yet to arrive from Portugal.
"Ready your bikes and personal kit, and then get some sleep", instructed Skull. Then he added "early start tomorrow, we've a lot of catching up to do".
Many of the Watchers had military backgrounds, those who hadn't were experienced security professionals. They all knew the benefit of rest and got their heads down wherever they could find a space. All except Jonah, who still had work to do. He would run their operation and needed to memorise Jonny's files and familiarise himself with the kit he had provided.

London President Jim Reynolds also had some work to do. He would not be leaving in the morning with the operation team, but he knew they would need one particular specialist.
Their first task would be a search of Saint's lodgings, so he had to find an alarm and lock specialist from the hundreds of technicians in the Watchers' employ. Reynolds had one man in mind. Phil Harris had worked for the Watchers' security business for the last five years. Other than high end bank or military security, there was no lock or alarm system that could defeat him.
Harris had also fitted in well with the bikers' social brotherhood and he was being seriously considered as a future Prospect.
Prospecting would put Harris on the fast track to becoming a company director, so Reynolds thought this an excellent opportunity to prove himself. Harris did not need asking twice and the technician was soon riding his six cylinder BMW across London to the clubhouse.

As dawn broke across North London, the Watchers woke and readied their motorcycles. The Lagos Prospects had arrived with Skull's van full of kit and Jonah would take over for the drive into Berkshire.
Before long Skull was forming up his convoy of bikes. In the MC world position in the convoy depended on pecking order within the club.
Skull and Cuba rode two abreast at the front, as President and Vice President.
Behind them came other club officers, such as Joao Alva and Steve Butler, who both held

Sergeant at Arms rank. Next would come full members, without rank and then Prospects, although there were none on this trip. Then, at the rear, would ride the none members such as Stone and Harris. Taking up the rear was usually a back up van, on this trip, just like in Morocco, it was Jonah who took this role.

Riding along the North Circular in the quiet of the early morning, the bikers' loud exhausts attracted the attention of London's early risers. But, before long even the noise of their bikes was swallowed up in the heavy traffic of London's motorway network.

The small convoy headed west from London towards Aldermaston. The small town in rural Berkshire falls mid way between the bigger towns of Reading and Newbury. It is a most unlikely location for what is probably Britain's most secure site.

The Atomic Weapons Establishment, or AWE, sits in 750 acres of former WW2 airfield. Its security is often described as being like an onion. The 4500 employees gain access deeper into the many layers of fencing as their security clearance increases. Matthew Saint was one of the most skilled and trusted employees, with access to the most secret layers of the site.

Like most military sites, a small town had grown outside of the fence to service the needs of the base. Many of Aldermaston's residents depended on AWE in some way for their livelihood.

The convoy of bikers riding into this Middle

England town would be guaranteed to cause a stir. But the Watchers had grown used to the reactions they caused. They had also learned to work it to their advantage. They called it hiding in plain sight, as no one would suspect their business was security and private investigation. So it was that the Watchers pulled onto the driveway of the large house in Aldermaston's suburbs. Jonny Johnson had personally paid cash for three month's rental of the house. The neighbours would by now be cursing the landlord for his new tenants. The Watchers thrived on these reactions to maintain their cover. Noisy and flamboyant activity at the front masked quiet and stealthy comings and goings at the rear.

Once inside, Stone and Jonah quickly reverted to their years of police work and converted one of the reception rooms in to their incident room. Powerful laptop computers, along with portable printers, scanners and projectors came out of Jonah's van and were skillfully fitted together. Rolls of instant whiteboard quickly covered the walls to allow a visual representation of their investigation to grow.
The security professionals now at work inside the house were a far cry from the image their arrival projected on the local people. But that was the point and it was precisely what the Security Service were relying on to cover their involvement.

Once happy that the incident room was to his liking, Jonah started to draw on his whiteboards.

"We have three places to start", began Jonah. "AWE needs a visit. We need a look around Saint's lodgings. Other than home and work, his church seems his only contact with anyone". The old detective turned to Miguel Cuba and asked, "could you pass as interested in the Seventh Day Adventists"? Cuba had been raised a Catholic. While his parents were away doing missionary work, Miguel and his sister Barbara had boarded at Ampleforth Monastery School in York. Barbara had gone on to become a nun, but Miguel had lost his faith and joined the MC. Jonah hoped that Miguel could pass as devout enough to interest Saint's church members.

"I should think so Jonah", replied Cuba. "Seven years with the monks, and a nun for a sister. I expect I can still act religious".

"We just need to remember how to be policemen", said Jonah, looking towards Stone. MI5 had provided Jonah and Stone with ID and checkable backgrounds with the Metropolitan Police. The former DI had been retired over a year, and it had been more than 20 years since he did anything but counter terrorism work. To get into the AWE site, he would have to pass as a senior detective on a missing person enquiry. For Stone, it had been even longer since he was forced to resign from the police.

Aldermaston is covered by Thames Valley Police, but their false identities would be better hidden by the bigger London force. Given the security risks involved, it was also believable that the government would send in the Met.

That just left Saint's lodgings to deal with. "His house is your project then Skull", said Jonah. "Miguel will need some back up, and the rest of the team are on the house".

When any of the team went undercover, they always had some back up close by to extract them if necessary. To some, it may have seemed an excessive precaution to have back up at a church. But the Watchers' took care of their own, and they had no idea what they were dealing with. "Joao, take point with Miguel please", said Skull. Between Miguel Cuba and his Chapter's huge enforcer, Skull was confident they could deal with most eventualities.

"That leaves me, Steve Butler and Phil Harris on the house", added Skull.

As soon as it got dark, Butler and Harris headed out on a recce. Their first task was to place hidden cameras near both house and church. The Watchers were expert with security and surveillance technology. By pre placing tiny remote cameras, their safety and effectiveness would be increased many fold. Jonah was particularly skilled in running investigations remotely through surveillance cameras. Once he had visited AWE, the old DI would take over coordinating their operations.

With their cameras in place outside the church, Butler and Harris turned their attention to Saint's house.

Jonny Johnson had provided aerial and drive by photographs of the house. But if the Watchers were going to risk their liberty with an illegal entry, they wanted to be sure of the lay out. Most importantly, Harris needed to assess the security he would have to breach when they went in. One mistake would have the local police on them. Aldermaston's rural location meant the houses had big gardens, with plenty of shadow to cover Butler and Harris. Carefully garden hopping, the two bikers worked their way around the house, placing hidden cameras as they went.

"Patio door", said Harris. "It's an old design and will be easy to open. I should be able to do it without leaving a trace. The alarm is a simple one too, I'll have that bypassed in seconds".

"Elderly, religious couple, who are much to trusting", added Butler. "Lucky we aren't planning to steel from them. I'll get Jonah to arrange a crime prevention visit when we move on". The Watchers thought little of breaking the law when it suited their needs. But they had their own standards and always did what they thought was right. They would burgle the old couple's home, but they would do no damage and would ensure it never happened to them again.

Chapter 4.

Butler and Harris returned to the safe house to study the couple's routine and pick the best time to enter and search their house.
With the cameras in place at the church, Miguel Cuba could safely make his move towards infiltrating the Seventh Day Adventists.
Cuba's degree was in engineering, so he had no trouble passing as an AWE employee when he introduced himself at the church. He claimed to be new to the area, with few friends and in need of some spiritual support to settle in. The congregation welcomed Miguel with open arms, settling him into their regular bible study classes. Despite having lost his catholic faith two decades earlier, Miguel was touched by the friendly supportive nature of the church group. "Seems a little like the MC", thought Miguel. "I guess everyone needs a support network". Slowly, over a period of days, Miguel gained the confidence of the Seventh Day Adventists as he listened to their bible lectures and discussed their beliefs with them.

Joao Alva was beginning to feel like a spare part. He sat outside in the Watchers' van, listening to the feed from Miguel's tiny radio. Alva was ready to go after Miguel with; battering ram, baseball bat, and if absolutely necessary, a shot gun. The Watchers' close brotherhood meant that Alva would not let his concentration wander, despite how dull the radio feed was getting.

Slowly, as Miguel got to know the other churchgoers, some started to talk about their other AWE church member. The quiet young man, Matthew Saint, had been a regular attendee at their services and bible classes. His shy nature meant that, although well liked by the other members, no one really knew him.

They were a little surprised by his disappearance, but not overly worried.

A group of three young Americans, a man and two women had joined together about a year earlier. Saint had become drawn to the group. It was out of character for the shy, socially awkward young man. But, some suggested, the girls were very pretty.

Within a few months of their arrival, Saint had begun to take holidays with them. Then, without warning, all four stopped coming to the church. The police had visited about Saint, but it appeared there was no one to miss the three Americans.

Back at the safe house, Jonah led a debrief of their operation so far. The old couple were proving to be creatures of habit, attending their church between seven and nine each evening. So Stone, Butler and Harris were on standby for the following evening.

Their immediate concern was the three Americans who had disappeared the same time as Saint.

"What do we know Miguel lad?" asked Jonah.

"Not much Jonah", he replied. "I've copied their admin computer, but they keep very few records.

Just address, phone number and a list of bible classes completed". "Other than that, everyone just thinks they were travellers in need of some spiritual support".

Then Joao Alva added his news about the vanishing Americans. "I checked out their address on the way back here. If they ever were there, they are gone now. It's empty and up for sale". "Curiouser and curiouser Joao lad", replied Jonah.

Stone and Jonah started their next day with a visit to AWE, using their fake Metropolitan Police identities. Neither man had visited Britain's nuclear weapons plant before and were surprised at the level of security.
They parked their van outside the fence in a huge visitors' car park. All their phones, cameras and technical gadgetry had to be left in the van, as they knew they would be searched.
The two bogus policemen then boarded a visitor's bus to carry them through the first levels of fenced security. Next came registration at the security reception. Here they were closely watched by CCTV as they queued to see a receptionist. Their ID was checked, copied and verified with the Metropolitan Police. "Here's where we find out how good Jonny really is", thought Stone.
Jonah had no concerns, as he and Jonny Johnson had spent the last 20 years working on far more difficult operations, and Jonny had never let him down.
With their identities confirmed, Stone and Jonah

then had to sit through the site's safety and security video.

Finally, they were met and walked through what they thought was the final security gate.

Following the uniformed guard towards the HR block, Jonah's attention was drawn towards the many people cycling around the site. "They look like Boris Bikes", commented Jonah.

The guard was quick to explain that AWE was always keen to exploit anything that gave them an eco friendly image. The 750 acre site was so vast that the staff clocked up huge mileages in their cars travelling around its many buildings. Then, they introduced a fleet of bicycles for the staff to use. The heavy duty cycles looked very like the hire bikes that London Mayor Boris Johnson had introduced to England's capitol city.

Stone could not help but be amused by Jonah commenting on anything about London's larger than life Mayor. He had always thought Jonah very similar to Boris Johnson, both in appearance and eccentricity.

Careful to stick to their missing person script, Jonah and Stone questioned the HR Officer for all they could learn about Matthew Saint. AWE was very vague about what work Saint actually did, save to confirm he did work on warhead production.

Saint's work life mirrored everything else they had learned about him. Despite being something of a loner, Saint was well liked by his colleagues. The quiet young man worked hard and, other than his church, appeared to have very little life outside the Aldermaston site fence.

Then, six months ago, he started to take some of the huge amount of leave that was owed to him. He talked of walking in Portugal's Algarve, but some colleagues thought he seemed to know very little about walking. They suspected there could be a girl involved, but no one could get him to open up.

Jonah asked if they could see Saint's workspace. It was all the HR Officer could do to avoid laughing at the suggestion. "I've never been in there", she replied. "I think you need the tour". Before long Stone and Jonah were on board one of AWE's mini busses, touring the huge site. It soon became apparent that the deeper you got onto the site, the greater was the security. Stone thought the security had been strict in getting to where they were. But as they drove around the site, their host explained that all the nuclear work took place behind yet more layers of fencing and security. Huge hanger size buildings sat behind a double skin of fencing. Then, at first sight of their mini bus, military police dogs came running along the gap between the fences. "Don't fancy any terrorist's chances there Nev lad", said Jonah. Stone did not get chance to reply before their HR host said, "that's the idea. Makes any sort of intrusion too unattractive to contemplate".

With the tour over, and all they could glean from AWE achieved, Stone and Jonah worked their way back through the complicated layers of security and returned to the safe house.

As their visit to AWE produced no new leads, Jonah was pinning his hopes on something being in Saint's room. So he busied himself preparing the radios and video feeds for their entry of the house that evening.

Jonah had backed his van close enough to the door that the team could slip into the van unseen. A couple of streets away From Saint's home, Jonah slowed the van enough for Skull, Butler and Harris to jump out of the moving van and climb quickly into gardens.
While the black clad figures moved silently through the neighbouring gardens, Jonah parked his van at the end of the street.
Jonah would monitor the cameras and radios, while Stone and Alva were ready to support Skull's team if needed.
True to his word, Harris found it child's play to bypass the alarm and unlock the patio doors. The three men were inside in no time at all.
"Definite old folk's pad", commented Skull. Saint's landlords were an elderly couple and it was clear the house had been styled much earlier in their marriage.
The rest of the house would get attention if they had time, but their priority was Saint's room and the dark figures moved up the stairs with night vision goggles lighting their way.
The Watchers would not risk turning on any lights and their sophisticated equipment made it unnecessary.
Inside Saint's room, powerful infra red lamps supplemented their goggles, bringing their own

personal daylight to the room. This was a much more modern looking room. Saint had repainted and probably bought his own curtains and carpet. The style and colours were much different to the rest of the house. Most noticeable, was the scientific nature of the bookshelves, models and posters.

But the room was not all science. Stone watched the feed from the team's body cameras and was struck by the contrast of religion and science. Stone had always considered the two to be in some way mutually exclusive. But Saint's room was filled with the journals of his trade in nuclear science, and the iconography of his devout religious beliefs.
Former Royal Marine, Steve Butler, had a reasonable understanding about the principles of nuclear weapons, so he began by looking through the scientific texts. Most of the very technical papers were way beyond the limits of Butler's knowledge. But he recognised enough to know what they would mean to an expert such as Saint. It seemed obvious to Butler that Saint could design a warhead by piecing together all the bits of information in the room. "His skills are definitely at the sharp end", said Butler. "He's not in the support trades. With the right kit, he could easily build a nuke ".
"Let's hope he doesn't have the right kit", thought Stone. "No wonder Jonah's MI5 pals are jumpy".

Harris went straight to Saint's desk. The empty docking station suggested a missing laptop. But

Harris was looking for anything that Saint might have backed up his work to. Few people completely trust computers not to crash, and Harris hoped Saint may have left something behind.

Sure enough, in the desk drawers were a selection of memory sticks. Harris excitedly plugged each of them into his own laptop for copying. But his excitement was short lived, as they all contained religious texts. Harris copied them anyway, and then went on with his search.

Steve Butler was next to shout up. "He's quite a magazine collector. There's lots of really old religious stuff here". Butler started going through the yellowing papers. "Signs of the Times. Vermont Telegraph. The Advent Message to the Daughters of Zion. The Advent Shield", listed Butler as he worked his way through the collection of old publications. "There's loads of different stuff here, and most of it dates from the 1800s in America", he added.

"Who are the Millerites?" asked Skull, as he too looked through the old papers.

Miguel Cuba was still at the safe house, so as not to risk recognition by other church goers, but he was monitoring the Watchers' radios. "They're a long dead church movement", he said in reply to Skull. "They believed in the Apocalypse. That God would destroy the sinful Earth, and then recreate it as a much better place. Reverend Miller worked out a couple of dates in the 1800s for the Apocalypse, but when they passed without incident, most of his followers became Seventh

Day Adventists."

Skull thought for a moment, then replied "likely just history of his Church then. We'll photograph them and move on".

Butler had moved on to the wardrobe when he made another discovery searching Saint's clothes. "Receipts from Villa Do Bispo", Butler exclaimed as he went through one of the jacket pockets. Villa Do Bispo, or Bishop's Town, was a semi industrialised town, a short ride from the Watchers' Algarve base in Lagos.

"Mostly junk food and stuff. But lots of supermarket visits over a few different trips. Looks like Saint spent most of his time in Bispo", said Butler.

"Sounds like some work for Pedro and Paulo", said Skull. "I'll get them making enquiries with the supermarket security".

The Watchers' security company provided guards and CCTV systems to many Algarve supermarkets. Skull was hopeful that the guards might know Saint, or the CCTV recordings might hold useful information. Jonah was quickly on this task, as soon as Skull uploaded photographs of the receipts, Jonah emailed a package to the De Costa twins. Soon all of the Watchers' Algarve employees would be looking for traces of Matthew Saint.

Butler, Harris and Skull continued to work their way through Matthew Saint's room, but found nothing else of interest to them. Except, they did take an interest in what was not missing from his room. "He thought he was coming back here", commented Skull. "There's too much stuff here for a moonlight flit".

Monitoring their cameras and radios, Jonah added his agreement. "I agree, clothing can be replaced, but all his journals and magazines can't. Especially the 19th Century religious stuff. That must have taken some collecting".

A steady move through the rest of the house produced nothing for them either. So the Watchers left as silently as they arrived, leaving no trace that they had ever been in the house. Harris expertly secured the patio doors and reset the alarms. The old couple would be none the wiser about their visitors. Although in the next few days they would be visited by the local Crime Prevention Officer on an apparently routine advisory visit. Their doors and alarm would soon be much harder to defeat.

The dark figures moved through the shadows of the gardens, working their way back to Jonah's van.

The many signs around the area suggested Aldermaston was proud of its Neighbourhood Watch, but the curtain twitching locals had never met burglars so proficient as the Watchers. Using their night vision goggles, Skull and his team reached the van undetected and without any encounter with the Neighbourhood Watch.

Chapter 5.

The De Costa twins were both at the Lagos clubhouse when Jonah called them. Pedro and Paulo had made sure at least one of them was by the phone since their club brothers left for England. The twins treated their roles as Secretary and Treasurer of the MC as being interchangeable. This mirrored most aspects of their lives, as the identical twins were very close. It helped that, with their long biker beards and John Lennon glasses, no one could tell them apart anyway.

The old DI did not have to wait for Skull and Stone to return. He already had the Portuguese supermarket receipts, thanks to the live feed from the Watchers' cameras.

CCTV recordings have a limited life span, before they are recorded over, so he knew they would need to act quickly in following up the lead.

The MC's Secretary and Treasurer wasted no time in calling their senior uniform security employees.

The Watchers MC was structured that the full members of the MC were also directors in their security and surveillance businesses. All their employees knew, that as they climbed the ranks of the business, the brotherhood and financial reward of full membership came closer. The twins knew they could command absolute loyalty from their senior employees, who would immediately prioritise the search for Matthew Saint.

Jonah knew he needed to update Jonny Johnson about the new development. The Security Service was paying for the operation and their MI5 handler needed to be kept in the loop.

Now that Jonah had the kit bag left for him at the swimming pool, there was no need for clandestine meetings in a biker cafe. Jonah now had one of the latest generation of encrypted cell phones, with which to contact Jonny. As Jonah made the call, he suspected Jonny may already know his news. There was a good chance that Jonny could operate the phone remotely and listen in to the Watchers.

If Jonny had been listening, he was not letting on. The spymaster listened intently to Jonah's briefing, interrupting only when he needed clarification. "It's the best lead we have so far, Jonny lad", said Jonah. "Luckily the Watchers are at their strongest on the Algarve, so I already have some good people on it".

Jonny was worried about bringing more people into the operation. "I hope you aren't risking security Jonah", asked the MI5 handler. "Mums the word on this one remember".

But Jonah had this covered. "Other than the De Costa twins, the staff think it's a missing person hunt. With a fat pay check from wealthy parents". The De Costa twins wasted no time getting amongst the security guards of Villa Do Bispo. Many of the town's bigger establishments were under contract to the Watchers. So the twins had no difficulty in getting CCTV searched and staff questioned.

Those businesses who did not employ the

Watchers, still had a deep respect for the bikers. It had taken the Watchers many years to begin countering fear of the protection rackets run by O Lobo.

Carlos Lobo was now in his 80s, but he was still as feared as his namesake, the wolf.
He began his ruthless career working for the Dictator Salazar's PIDE intelligence service. When the Dictator fell from power, O Lobo had salted away enough money to assume command of Salazar's network of spies, turning it into a criminal empire to rival the Mafia.
O Lobo had begun to lose his grip on the Algarve when he chose to take on Nev Stone and the Watchers.
Most 1% MC's would not entertain working with the police. But the Watchers were different. When it suited their own moral compass, they would feed information to the authorities. O Lobo's drug trafficking network would never be popular with the Watchers' anti drugs stance. But putting a contract on Stone really got them fired up.
Stone and Jonah's Interpol contacts were eager recipients of evidence the bikers brought back from their Moroccan adventure. Coordinated police raids across Portugal and North Africa badly damaged O Lobo's grip on the Algarve. The Watchers filled the void by offering security to prevent the gangsters returning. It was this void that Pedro and Paulo exploited. While their employees were checking hours of supermarket CCTV, the twins were visiting the town's many small bars and cafes.

Their persistence paid off, as many people remembered Saint and his friends. In truth, they were an odd group among the area's bohemian surfer community.

The neatly turned out black man, with his polite English accent was different enough to be memorable on his own. Add in the Americans, with two very attractive girls, and the group easily stood out from the norm. The four young people had been regulars among the town's shops and restaurants, on and off for the past year.

It was always the most extrovert of the group, a blond woman called Ellen White, who booked the tables. But the nice, black, Englishman was the one most people remembered fondly. However, no one had seen them for several days.

Despite so many sightings of Saint's group, no one was quite sure where they stayed when they were in the area. They talked of being on a bible retreat. But, other than small churches and chapels, there was nothing local that fitted their rather enthusiastic brand of Christianity.

Reaching a dead end with the restaurants, Pedro and Paulo turned their attention back to the supermarkets. "We must find something there", said Pedro. "Those receipts show he spent a small fortune on crisps and pop. So he should be on camera somewhere".

"Got him!" shouted the CCTV operator. Black faces were rare at the South Western tip of Portugal, making the operator's task easier. He had found Saint queuing for the tills with an attractive blond woman, a few years younger than him. "She's a looker", added Paulo. "Covered up more than the young foreigners though". The woman was too pale and blond to be a native of Portugal. Paulo had noticed that, although attractively dressed in a long sleeved blouse and long linen trousers, she was not baring as much skin as the tourists usually did. With the operator expertly manipulating the controls, the bikers followed Saint and his friend through the tills and out to the car park.

"Find me that car!" said Pedro to his security manager. The couple had loaded their provisions into a battered blue Peugeot and driven off, leaving excellent footage of their car.

The Peugeot became the De Costa's top priority. All of their local employees, and everyone who aspired to work for the Watchers, were out looking for the old car. Rural Portugal is sparsely populated, giving them huge wild areas around the town to cover.

Villa Do Bispo itself had spread with industrialisation. The central town was as interesting and beautiful as any old Algarve town. But it had spread around the edges. The supermarket where the twins caught Saint on CCTV was in a small retail development to the west of the town. To the north and east, mixed among the agriculture, were small industrial developments. The small units were spread thinly among the fields of crops and animals. Tarmac was rare, with dirt tracks linking together the small clusters of workshops and warehouses. All this made the Watchers' task of finding a single car a very difficult proposition.

But find it they did. Such was the respect for the MC in this tip of Europe, that their employees and supporters would have turned heaven and earth to achieve favour with the bikers.

The battered Peugeot was sitting in a small parking area, full of equally trail weary vehicles. The twins wasted no time in checking it out, although they decided to take one of the Watchers' supply of nondescript cars for the recce. The De Costa twins usually rode a pair of customised Triumph Thunderbird motorcycles, as identical to each other as their owners. Such a spectacle would have drawn too much attention in the small industrial enclave, so they reluctantly chose the anonymity of an ordinary looking car. Driving slowly along the unmade road, the twins stopped only long enough to place a hidden camera in view of the Peugeot. But as they drove, they were taking notice of everything there.

Of the four industrial units surrounding the cars, three were owned by established businesses known to the watchers. The fourth building was lacking in maintenance and had regularly changed hands through a variety of engineering and car repair businesses.

The twins regrouped to their Lagos clubhouse for a video conference with the Watchers in England. In a little over 24 hours, Pedro and Paulo had achieved a lot. They had images of the American girl, a, (possibly false), name and a building which had possibly been used by them. But they felt no further forward. No one had seen the group for several days and the hidden cameras had captured nothing of interest to them.

Across the video connection, Skull and Jonah we're delighted with the twins' progress. But the De Costas, like most of the Watchers, drove themselves hard. They would not settle for anything less than a firm lead.

"You've done great in a short time", said Skull. "Keep surveillance on. We're heading home for a search". Jonah had already checked in with his MI5 handler. Jonny had agreed the unit needed searching, but only wanted Jonah's tight group to do the job. There was no telling how damaging the contents of Saint's hiding place could be to Britain's interests.

Things were moving too quickly for Jonny to put the Watchers on scheduled airlines. He had to be careful about leakage of the threat to Britain's nuclear secrets. But Jonny knew there was a section of the British Armed Forces, who spent their lives in the shadows and could be trusted not to ask questions. Most people have heard of Britain's famous Special Air Service Regiment. But less widely known, and based alongside the SAS at Hereford, is the Special Reconnaissance Regiment, or SRR.

This shadowy unit is young in comparison with the more famous Special Forces Regiments. It was formed in 2005 to relieve the fighting units of surveillance tasks.

Jonny had no plans to mobilise the SRR. But he knew how to exploit the diversity of the Regiment's 500 soldiers. Such was the variety of surveillance roles the SRR undertook, that they could look nothing like soldiers. Jonny knew the bikers could pass easily as SRR Troopers.

The Royal Airforce crew who landed their Merlin helicopter at RAF Welford were on a strict need to know briefing and needed to know very little. The Berkshire airbase, 50 miles west of London, was not a usual destination for them. With instructions to prepare for a long flight, but no destination, the aircrew assumed it was a Special Forces mission. So the disparate group who raced from van to helicopter was not a surprise. The stereotype Special Forces soldier is a rough, tough young man. But the experienced aircrew knew the SRR drew its men and women from a wide range of backgrounds. They automatically thought that this odd bunch, with either long hair, or shaved heads, must be a SRR surveillance team.

Minutes before takeoff, Jonah handed the pilot his sealed orders and the crew prepared for their flight to southern Portugal. The three Rolls Royce engines easily lifted the big helicopter from the airfield and started its flight south. Designed for up to 24 fully equipped soldiers, the seven Watchers were quite comfortable in the Merlin's passenger compartment.

Of the Watchers aboard, only ex Marine Steve Butler had previous military experience. He had spent many hours in Royal Navy Sea King helicopters. But the modern Merlin was a much improved aircraft, with a relatively silent passenger area. The silence allowed Jonah to properly brief the team on Pedro and Paulo's discoveries. The Watchers had been busy with their own tasks, and only Stone, Skull and Jonah knew the full extent of what they were heading back for.

"Don't forget, we are a secretive military unit", warned Jonah. The MC was in their blood and the bikers needed reminding not to talk about their club.

"The twins will pick us up north of Lagos, in the Sierra Monchique hills". There was no diplomatic permission for the Watchers' mission, so the RAF could not use a Portuguese military airfield. But the Merlin was designed to operate in tough terrain, so would have no trouble setting down in the foothills of the mountain range.

Nev Stone was strangely quiet during the flight. He had worked on Jonah's team for close to 10 years before leaving the police. Despite their two rank difference, Jonah had always leaned heavily on his young protégé. Stone's natural ability to see all the pieces of an investigation as a single whole, had provided the key to many terrorist investigations.

But this job felt different. Stone was still playing catch up, as the case had started without him. He could not shake the feeling that he was missing something.

Their flight seemed over much sooner than a commercial flight. Stone thought it was probably due to the lack of airport red tape. The Watchers would need no passports where the RAF pilot was about to drop them.

Stone was snapped out of his thoughts, as the

copilot came back to brief the Watchers.

"We're on a NATO sanctioned training flight", said the RAF officer. "We don't have clearance to land, so it will be a very short stop, out of radar cover, in one of these valleys. You need to be ready in five minutes".

In exactly five minutes, the military helicopter touched down on the dusty valley floor. The rotor blades were kept spinning, sending clouds of dust into the tree lined valley walls.

The dust storm gave the Watchers extra cover for their arrival. With long practiced teamwork, they threw out their kit bags, then ducking clear of the rotors, ran for the cover of the nearby Cork Oak forest. Barely had their feet touched the ground, than the helicopter took off and resumed its scheduled mountain training flight.

Already hidden within the Cork Oak, were two large 4x4 vehicles, driven by the De Costa twins. The needs of the job had prevented them choosing identical vehicles, as was their usual preference. Today they had brought a nine seat Landrover for the team and a pick up truck for the kit. The two vehicles set off along the network of unpaved roads.

This mountainous part of Portugal is served by a network of wind farms, which sit on top of the highest hills. The turbines need regular maintenance, and while the access tracks are well maintained, they are far from smooth.

Jonah had chosen to ride with Pedro in the kit truck. As they bounced along the track, Jonah heard first hand what the twins had discovered.

Chapter 6.

"I guess we need to get in that unit Pedro lad",
said Jonah. Pedro thought the statement was
unnecessary. He was certain that Jonah would
not have risked blowing their cover by using an
RAF flight if the decision had not already been
made.
Pedro was only partially right. It was a big risk
using a military asset. So Jonah and Jonny were
confident in their decision. But, both of the old
campaigners would change plans if it no longer
seemed right. Pedro's briefing was far more
valuable to Jonah than the twin imagined. The
Watchers were going to commit a crime by
entering the industrial unit, Jonah would not
sanction such an action lightly.

With the Watchers all back inside the Lagos
clubhouse, Jonah led them through a thorough
briefing of what had been learned in both England
and Portugal.
The De Costa twins had been busy while they
awaited the helicopter. The MC's conference
room, or church, as the bikers called it, was now
covered in maps and photographs. The Watchers'
security business subscribed to much better
mapping systems than is freely available on the
Internet. In addition, the twins had used a small
helicopter drone to overfly the site. They now had
excellent aerial photographs to complement the
maps and satellite imagery.
"O Lobo!" exclaimed Stone. He had been closely

examining the twins' photographs and spotted a wolf's paw logo carved into the door. Carlos Lobo had, for years, used a stylised paw print as his logo. It's similarity to the Jack Wolfskin outdoor company logo helped cover its real meaning. The logo's presence meant the building was owned by, or under the protection of, O Lobo's gangster organisation. "How can he be involved?" asked Stone.

"No way of knowing yet Nev lad", replied Jonah. "But whatever his involvement, it won't be good".

Stone and Butler got straight to work planning how to access the industrial unit. Their combined skills learned in the police and Royal Marines had produced many successes in their Moroccan adventure. Stone's covert surveillance experience and Butler's Commando training had proven a match for everything O Lobo could throw at them. Now they turned their attention to what, should be a fairly straightforward operation.

"Night time Nev", advised Butler. "The area is so remote, there will be no one to see us once the neighbouring units pack up for the day".

Stone could see the sense in Butlers plan. There were several small groupings of units off the main access track. But no one lived there and there was no street lighting. "Agreed", replied Stone. "We can walk in across these hills. No one should be around to see us and there is no security".

With practiced ease, they split the preparation tasks. Stone worked on the surveillance, slipping into the area with extra cameras. Butler prepared the night vision equipment and entry tools they would need.

As soon as darkness set in, the Watchers were ready to move. Jonah had set up his control centre in the Watchers' 'church'. He would expertly watch the cameras and heat sensors placed earlier by Stone. The former Detective Inspector slipped easily into a role he had performed for several decades. It was only the technology that had changed, removing the need for him to run an operation from a nearby vantage point.

Stone and Butler would lead the entry team, assisted by Miguel Cuba and their technician Phil Harris. Skull would take care of back up. Together with his huge enforcer, Joao Alva and the De Costa twins, he would be close by in a van to evacuate Stone's team if necessary.

Just as planned, Stone's team walked across the small hill from a neighbouring farm. The low, shrubby vegetation provided little cover, but they were unlikely to meet anyone out here. The clear night made their night vision goggles redundant until they got inside the unit.

"Better security than I expected", said Harris, as he examined the unit's doors and locks. "This has been upgraded recently, with excellent locks and a decent alarm system. Nothing I can't handle though".

With the security upgrades, Jonah was now sure there was something more interesting than car parts inside.

It took Harris a little over 20 minutes to breach the unit's security and Former Commando Butler led the team into the unit.

"Quite a set up", said Stone, as he put on night vision goggles and looked around.

Two caravans had been brought inside to provide sleeping accommodation. A lounge area had been set up with sofas and a TV. But most of the unit was taken up with a spotlessly clean technical work area.

The Watchers split into two search teams. Butler and Harris took the workspace, while Stone and Cuba concentrated on the living areas.

The whole unit was the same odd combination of science and religion they had found in Matthew Saint's bedroom. Technical equipment and diagrams, mixed with religious posters and icons.

"This is too weird", thought Stone, as he moved towards the lounge area. A cheap coffee table held a selection of Seventh Day Adventist magazines, along with a note pad full of bible quotations. But alongside the religious material, were copies of Nuclear Futures magazine. Stone went straight to the nuclear magazine, but found it was just the journal of Britain's Nuclear Institute, containing nothing sensitive.

Butler was having no more success in the workspace. There were leftover wiring looms and computer chips. There were also shaped metal panels and containers, but it was all beyond his soldier's level knowledge of nuclear technology.

"It could be a bomb", said Butler. "But it could equally be a prototype car, for all I recognise".

Despite their frustration, Butler and Harris continued their search of the workspace, while Stone and Cuba moved onto the caravans. Many would have split their resources, by taking a caravan each. But Stone's long police experience taught him that it was far more efficient for one searcher to watch the other. That way, nothing got missed.

It was with this slow, meticulous method that they worked their way through the first caravan. It was immediately clear that this was the caravan used by Matthew Saint. But it seemed, the caravan had also been used by a woman. "Looks like he's been less than a saint", said Cuba, as he looked through the female toiletries.

"Naughty, naughty", replied Stone. But he soon snapped back from his joking, to the task in hand.

"Hey Miguel!" exclaimed Stone. "There's your name all over the place here". There was indeed a collection of items relating to The Caribbean Island of Cuba. Everything from maps and guide books, through to Che Guevara t-shirts and caps. "Some of this stuff was bought in Cuba", added Stone. "So it looks like they have been there. Can you think of a church reason?"

Despite losing his faith, Miguel kept some ties with religion through his sister, the nun. But the Caribbean was well outside his area of knowledge. "It will have to be Professor Wikipedia, I'm afraid", said Cuba as he pulled his smartphone from his pocket. "Mostly Catholic", read Cuba. "With a bit of native African religion and some Protestantism. Oh! and about 30,000 Seventh Day Adventists!"

"That sounds like a link to me", replied Stone. "I think we have some more research to do".

While Stone was working his way through the caravan, Butler had moved to the wet side of the workspace. Butler had been suspicious of a smell coming from the wet area, but he followed protocol and searched the dry side first, avoiding contamination.

Through the Watchers' security work, they had access to all manner of explosive detectors. It was these that Butler used to confirm his suspicions.

"They've been working with explosives", said Butler, as he checked the display on his detector. "It looks like they've been working on shaped charges", added Butler, examining the equipment around the workplace. Both the ex Marine, and ex cop Stone had plenty of experience with shaped explosive charges. Often, explosives were crafted into shapes to focus their explosive power. Both the police and the military used them to blow open doors for rapid entry.

Stone was trying to figure out why Saint and his friends might need method of entry devices, when Butler made a sinister discovery. "I hope I'm wrong Nev, but this looks like a concave lens", said Butler.

This meant nothing to Stone, but he could see his friend was worried and made his way over to the workspace. Butler showed him a mold, which might have been designed to cast part of a football. But Stone was sure it meant more than football to Butler.

"You need 32 of these", added Butler. "They direct the explosive force inwards, causing a plutonium sphere to implode".

Stone was barely keeping up with the implications of Butler's find, when the ex Marine added, "we're basically looking at a version of Fat Man, the Nagasaki Bomb".

Jonah had been following the live feed from the Watchers' body cams. So too, had their MI5 handler Jonny Johnson, in London. Both men were now getting very worried.

Matthew Saint had the ability to build a nuclear weapon, and now, it seemed, he had been trying to do just that. Key to an implosion device would be a carefully machined plutonium sphere. Jonny knew that was way beyond the kitchen laboratory he had seen in the unit. The next urgent action was to see if there was any trace of radiation at the unit.

"Have the Watchers got anyone in Lisbon?" asked Jonny. The spymaster knew that MI6 would have radiation detectors at the British Embassy in Portugal's capital city. But he also knew that he had to maintain the British Government's distance from the growing security risk.

Jonah had soon arranged for a member of the Watchers' Lisbon Chapter to pick up a diplomatic pouch from the Embassy. The biker had no idea why his delivery was so important, but when the MC's International President, Skull Murphy, said quickly, things happened quickly. It was a hard ride for the Lisbon Watcher, but he got his package to Stone well before dawn.

Before his resignation, Stone had been trained in police Chemical, Biological, Radiological and

Nuclear, or CBRN, tactics. So he was able to move through the unit with the alpha radiation detector. "All clear", said Stone with a sound of relief, as the detector indicated no trace of plutonium.

Back at the clubhouse, the Watchers debriefed the night's work with Jonah. "I don't know if it's good or bad, Nev lad", said Jonah. "He can't build a nuke without fissile material, and there's been none at the unit. But what's the point of everything else, if he can't make it go bang?"
Stone turned to Pedro and Paulo. "I don't like putting you in a spot. But would you see your godfather?" The twins relationship with their godfather was a strange one. Hugo Franco had doted on the twins throughout their lives, but there were parts of their lives which caused them all conflict.
Hugo was a commercial printer and black market art forger. The twins' parents had been insistent on Hugo becoming their godfather. He tried to turn them down, but could not do so without revealing his links to organised crime.
For most of his adult life, the forger had worked for O Lobo. First in the intelligence service, then directly for the gangster. Hugo was very much against the drug trade, but you did not refuse Carlos Lobo.
Even after they learned of his criminal connections, the twins still loved their godfather. They just had to be careful about where their two worlds touched.
Hugo had risked helping the twins in their search

for Lucy Varley. Now, they hoped he would think a nuclear bomb was equally important.

The twins often visited their godfather at his art studio, so the sight of their customised Triumph Thunderbirds pulling up was not unusual. Despite his advancing years, Hugo was considered something of a bohemian, so his friends and neighbours had become used to his biker visitors. There was a risk in seeking Hugo's confidence. But the old forger had been part of O Lobo's organisation for so long, that little escaped his notice. The twins gambled right that their godfather would not willingly have anything to do with a bomb.

As they sat among the part finished old masters, Hugo told the twins of the documents he had forged for entry into Cuba. "The papers were for four young people", said Hugo. "Two young black men and two white women". "I just thought it was to do with sex or drugs".

Hugo went onto explain that he had forged the first set of documents about six months ago. Four passports, with supporting ID, and four entry visas for Cuba. He had produced more visas over the ongoing months, with the last set four days ago. The twins thanked their godfather and hurried away from his studio. With so many trips to Cuba, there had to be some connection to what had been found in the industrial unit. But neither twin could think what the connection might be.

"Cuban Missile Crisis", said Jonah. Even the old Detective could only just remember the Kennedy

Administration's 1962 stand off with Russia. The 13 day US crisis was just a blip in history to the younger Watchers. But Jonah could remember his parents' deep concern about a war with Russia.

He explained that, as the Cold War arms race developed, the Russians were losing ground to the Americans, who were testing Intercontinental Ballistic Missiles. Nikita Khrushchev desperately needed a launch base for his shorter range missiles, which could reach the heart of the United States. Khrushchev found a partner in post revolution Cuba.

Frightened of a communist state so close to his southern coast, President Kennedy had allowed an ill fated invasion of Cuba. A group of CIA trained Cuban refugees launched an unsuccessful invasion at the Bay of Pigs. The invasion was unsuccessful, but it pushed Cuba's new President, Fidel Castro, straight into the arms of the Soviet Union.

An elaborate deception passed off the Soviet technicians as; machine operators, irrigation and agricultural specialists. But the 42 missiles, Ilyushin bombers and 40,000 troops could not be hidden from American U2 spy planes.

Within two weeks of the U2 photographs, a combination of diplomatic negotiations and a naval blockade removed the missiles from Cuba. 'But", asked Jonah, "what if they weren't all removed?"

Chapter 7.

"We might have a head start in Cuba", said Skull. "Prince and Simms are out there".

John Prince and Kenton Simms were technically members of the Watchers' London chapter, but they spent most of their lives working overseas. The two bikers were both Former Parachute Regiment soldiers, who left after the second Gulf war, to chase bigger earnings in the private sector.

During the Moroccan adventure, Prince and Simms worked as body guards for European businessmen, who had set up in competition with O Lobo's factories. The violent end to Stone's time in Morocco led to the paratroopers also needing new employment. They had found new clients needing protection in Cuba's growing oil industry.

Butler jumped in, as he was also from the London chapter. "They are really good guys. If anything is happening in Cuba, they will have the contacts." Butler added that Prince and Simms had recently started selling motorcycle tours, so they would have cover for a visit.

Jonny Johnson soon approved the Watchers' team to go to Cuba. But there would be no RAF assistance this time. "You will have to fly commercial", he said. "Cuba is much too sensitive to risk any official assistance".

Stone had heard many horror stories about the way Castro's regime treated political prisoners. He hoped the stories were wrong, or at least that he could stay out of harm's way.

The Caribbean heat hit Stone like a wall as he

stepped onto Havana Airport's runway. The Watchers had stopped briefly to refuel in the Dutch Antilles, but it had been night time and much cooler. His first sight of Cuba gave Stone a very mixed reaction. All around the airport were the palm trees he had been expecting, but everything looked much more modern than the stereotype. "Where are the old American cars and historic buildings?" he asked.

Jonah, as usual, had an answer. "They are out there Nev lad. But mostly in the heritage areas, preserved for the tourists. A lot of Cuba is quite modern these days". Jonah would later learn that he was only partially right. Business trips had only ever taken Jonah to the cities. What he had not seen, was the gap between the haves and the have nots, in rural Cuba.

Miguel Cuba had much more to occupy his mind than Cuba's heat, or its history. His sister Barbara would be waiting in the terminal building. Barbara had been a great help to the Watchers in Morocco, with the attractive nun achieving many things the male bikers could not. But, as there seemed to be a religious undercurrent to Saint's disappearance, the help of a nun could be very useful here.

Like her brother Miguel, Barbara had attended a catholic boarding school in England. Unlike Miguel, Barbara had grown more devout in her faith and taken holy orders.

But it was no ordinary convent that attracted Barbara. She joined The Good Shepherd Sisters, an order of nuns devoted to fighting prostitution and sex trafficking.

The order had grown into a United Nations funded NGO, whose work took Barbara throughout the world.

Mostly though, her office was in New York. The recent relaxation in hostilities meant that Barbara could take one of the new, direct flights from Miami to Havana.

Then, Miguel saw his sister. The beautiful, shapely woman did not fit anyone's stereotype of a nun. With her Latin looks and long dark hair, Barbara looked more actress than nun.

The siblings ran for each other with an embrace fuelled by months apart. Then, after their emotional reunion, they joined the other Watchers, who were also pleased to see Barbara.

Leaving the Airport Terminal, the Watchers were on the look out for Prince and Simms. All the team had met them before in Morocco. But even if they had not, the two former Paratroopers still fit the ex soldier image. The big, powerful men still looked every inch the soldier. They maintained the short hair, sunglasses and slightly military style of dress which suited their profession. Their only real concession to Cuba were the Che Guevara t-shirts, which Stone thought was probably more irony than sympathy for the revolutionary's beliefs. The bigger giveaway though, was the Che Moto Tours sign that Prince held up. The Watchers had agreed that their best cover was as tourists, so they were getting full treatment to Prince and Simms tour schedule. They left the airport in a smart looking coach, hired for the trip. It was soon obvious that the Watchers would have to play their roles, as the driver and courier did not know their true purpose. As they drove, Prince used the microphone to explain they would spend their first night in central Havana, then have another coach trip in the morning, to collect their motorcycles.

While Prince was giving his tourist commentary, Simms sat at the back, bringing Stone and Jonah up to speed on Cuban protocol. "In some ways, it's still a bit totalitarian", said Simms. "We can't operate without the Cuban Tourist Authorities. We'll have more freedom once we ditch the coach, but we're stuck with Freddie the courier. Thankfully, he can't ride, so will be following in the van".

Stepping off the coach was like stepping back in time. The modern buildings of the suburbs had given way to historic central Havana. Little appeared to have changed since the 1930s, when Hemingway spent time in Cuba. Beautiful old buildings and hotels lined the many squares, all dating from before the revolution, when American Mob money fuelled Havana's casino trade.

The bikers had time on their hands. They would not collect their bikes until the following morning, and Jonny was tapping the resources of British Intelligence for a lead. So, true to their biker nature, they made the most of Havana's tourist spots.

Their official shadow was not a constant fixture, as Freddie had returned home to his family. So the Watchers were able to talk freely.

John Prince had left to put his own contacts into play, so Kenton Simms took over as tour guide. Walking into a park near their hotel, Stone spotted a familiar statue. "Is that John Lennon?" he asked. Stone did not need a reply, as he walked closer the distinctive Beatle became clearer, sitting on a park bench. "Lennon visited here once and the statue is a good tourist draw", replied Simms. "It's also an example of how good job prospects are out here. That old guy's job is to look after the specs and put them on the statue for photos". The bikers could not help but stop for a photograph with the English rock legend, tipping the old man appropriately.

If anything so far had seemed a culture shock, it was nothing to what they would encounter in the main square. It was a riot of colour, with street entertainers of all descriptions. But above everything else, the brightly dressed black women stood out. These old women wore the brightest clothing Stone had seen in a long while and all smoked huge Cuban cigars. The bikers could not resist another photo opportunity, tipping the women for their trouble.

As darkness started to fall, Simms took them to a restaurant on a rooftop terrace. Looking out over the lights of the city and Havana's old port, all the bikers stood silently at the terrace edge, taking it all in. Simms broke the silence by offering Cuban cocktails. "Mojito and Piña Colada are the most popular. But watch the quantities, rum is cheep and they give generous measures. Don't forget we are riding tomorrow". The warning was not really necessary. The Watchers could party like any bikers, but they were always professional when working.

Most of the men chose Ernest Hemingway's favourite, the Mojito. The mix of white rum, sugar, lime juice, sparkling water, and mint, was refreshing in the high humidity.

Barbara traveled widely through her UN role and ordered "Piña Colada sin ron", or without rum. The mix of pineapple juice, crushed ice and coconut milk suited Sister Barbara better without the rum.

Jonah was pulled away from the party to take a call from Jonny Johnson. "It's getting complicated finding much out", said Jonny. "Cuba is a bit of a gap for us, and most of what I'm interested in happened in the 60s, when it was very much the Cousins' show"

The CIA, or the Cousins, as British Intelligence called them, had played the Cuban Missile Crisis close to their chests. The British had little involvement in the removal of nuclear weapons from Cuba, or setting up the hotline between Moscow and Washington which resulted from it. "We do know that Castro was not happy at the withdrawal, so if he had chance to keep any, chances are he will have done." Jonny continued that, there were a few double agents on the Soviet side. Wherever you have defectors, there is usually some divided loyalty. "I just need to locate the right handler, assuming they are still alive".

So, until either Jonny, or Prince came through

with some intelligence, Jonah and Stone would
have to do some basic police work.

"I think we should head north in the morning",
said Jonah. "Of the nine missile sites the Soviets
started to build, four were operational at San
Cristobal. It would be useful to talk with the
locals". San Cristobal was north west of Havana,
in the sparsely populated north of the island. With
a light population and only 90 miles from Miami, it
made perfect sense as a location for the missile
sites. Jonah hoped there would be some older
people about who remembered the whole
episode.
"It will fit with the bike tour cover", said Simms.
"We can head north, then follow the west coast
road. We'll have Freddie along, but we work well
with him and he won't be under our feet". The
tourist regulations meant that for an organised
group, they needed an official courier. But small
independent groups were permitted. The
Watchers' plan was for Jonah and Stone and to
tour independently, while the others covered their
tracks with an official tour.

Morning came and the Watchers again boarded
the coach to collect their motorcycles.
The courier, Freddie, was already on the coach.
The young man was typically Cuban. Many of the
world's big cities describe themselves as melting
pots. But in Cuba, this really seems to have
happened. Such is the ethnic variety on the
island, with French and Spanish settlers, African
slaves and American businessmen, that cross

ethnic relationships were inevitable. Most Cubans, like Freddie, had predominantly Latin features, but usually with a darkness suggesting a few African genes.

Prince and Simms kept their motorcycles at one of the oil compounds they helped protect. As the coach left Havana and headed into more rural areas, Stone was struck by the contrast. Havana had a colonial splendour about it. But out in the country, tiny one or two room concrete shacks became the norm.
Crossing a bridge over a large river, Stone saw how traditional rural life could be. A solitary black man, dressed only in shorts, stood in the river fishing. But a rod and line were not for him. The man was expertly casting a huge net into the river's flow. This was commercial fishing, but on a cottage industry scale.
Soon Stone spotted the drilling rigs and nodding donkeys that signified oil country.
Here, the contrast between rich and poor became most stark. Driving towards the oil compound, Stone watched villagers ploughing their fields with oxen. Then, on the other side of a chain link fence, sat the brand new Japanese vehicles of the oil company.

"Great to see Scramblers again", said Stone, looking at the line of identical Triumph Bonneville Scrambler motorcycles, which were lined up waiting for them. They remembered the model fondly, as they were the type loaned to them for the Moroccan trip.

Simms had to quickly stop Stone. "Shh. Freddie thinks you aren't riding remember."
Already waiting at the compound with John Prince was Freddie's driver Albert. The two would travel loosely with the tour group, meeting occasionally with water and snacks. Stone was sure they would also check the Watchers didn't go too much off plan.

Stone thought it odd that the larger group warranted open surveillance, but his group of two could travel unsupervised. While Simms showed his group their Scramblers, Prince took Jonah and Stone away to show them the motor home hired for them. Also prepared for them, but out of Freddie's sight, was a closed trailer containing an 800cc Triumph Tiger adventure bike. This was a lighter and more maneuverable bike than the more retro styled Scrambler, which would serve Stone well in the days to come.

Simms led his convoy out of the compound. He too rode a Triumph Tiger, allowing himself to stand out as tour leader. Behind him on their identical Scramblers rode Skull, Butler, Alva, Miguel, Barbara and Harris. Only Alva and Barbara were easily identifiable within the group's matching bikes and riding gear. Barbara was too shapely not to be noticed among a group of men, while the huge Joao Alva could never blend in. Light dust rose from the motorcycle wheels. Among the oilfields, this was one of Cuba's better rural roads, but it was poor by European standards, and would become much worse.

"OK Nev lad, let's roll", said Jonah, as soon as Freddie and Albert drove out of sight.

Stone would not unload his Tiger until he was well away from the oil compound. So he enjoyed a rare opportunity to ride up front with his old mentor.

Prince had collected the diplomatic pouch sent by Jonny to the British Embassy. Safely hidden away in the camper was a selection of surveillance and communication devices, along with the vital radiation detectors they would need. Also well hidden was a selection of weapons sourced by the Embassies MI6 resident. The Watchers were accustomed to using shotguns, in order to stay loosely within the law. With the support of British Intelligence, Stone now had access to the self loading pistols and carbine rifles he had used during his police career.

Both groups of Watchers were headed for San Cristobal. Simms would lead his bike tour an indirect, but scenic route. Stone and Jonah wanted to get there ahead of them, to set up out of Freddie's way.

Chapter 8.

Stone had enjoyed the drive north. It was rare for him to forsake a motorcycle, and travel on four wheels. But he had few opportunities to spend time with his old boss. They had caught up on each other's news. But, more importantly, they had thoroughly analysed the information gathered so far.

Despite their thoroughness, neither of the experienced detectives could make the pieces fit. It seemed certain that Matthew Saint was trying to build an improvised nuclear device, or IND. There appeared a religious angle, but the Seventh Day Adventists were peaceful people. Then, O Lobo's involvement made no sense. He was a Catholic, but even if it involved religion, O Lobo would do nothing without a profit.

None of the pieces seemed to fit. For now, all they could do was try to prevent Saint obtaining Plutonium. The why, would have to wait for later.

Jonah had reached a quiet area outside of San Cristobal and was busy setting up their motor home for the night. The other Watchers would sleep at a hotel in the town, but Stone and Jonah intended to keep a low profile.

While Jonah set up their communications equipment, Stone prepared his Triumph Tiger. He had been on four wheels all day and longed for the exhilaration of a motorcycle.

"Ride carefully Nev lad", said Jonah, as Stone sped off along the dusty back road.

Stone wanted to see which of the villages and hamlets would have been best placed to witness the Soviet withdrawal. The Watchers were always good at getting people talking, as the motorcycles acted as a great icebreaker.

There were police everywhere. Never outside of London, or New York, had Stone seen so many uniforms out and about. Some of the major roads had permanent check points, where identity and travel documents were checked. Often though, the checks were more informal. A couple of local cops would sit in their battered Lada, randomly stopping drivers. Stone noted that it was not the aggressive tactics he had expected of a totalitarian state. But rather, each interaction was friendly, beginning and ending with a handshake and a smile.

No matter how friendly the police seemed, Stone wanted to avoid them. The other Watchers were hiding in plain sight, Stone wanted to remain more covert. His adventure bike was ideal for this, allowing him to bypass checkpoints across open country.

On the official tour, the Watchers were making slower progress. They too were heading towards San Cristobal, but they were taking more time about it. Simms was leading them on a scenic, coastal ride. At pre arranged points, their Cuban escorts, Freddie and Albert would be waiting for them. They always came supplied with local fruits and a much needed top up of water.

At one such stop, the Watchers learned why there

were so many uniforms about, as not all were strictly police. "It's National Service", explained Freddie. "Our government still likes National Service, as it's good for discipline and employment. But there isn't room in the army for them all, so the conscripts are used as: security guards, park keepers and the like. All uniformed and all armed".

Skull was, as always taking everything in and asked, "what's happening at the junctions?"
He had noticed that at every major junction, there were more uniformed officers carrying clip boards. Groups of people were gathered around the junctions and seemed to be getting into random vehicles.

"They're Transport Marshals", replied Freddie. He explained that public and private transport had been in short supply since the collapse of Cuba's benefactor, the Soviet Union. Cuba had adapted by requiring all public and commercial vehicles to carry passengers, for a state regulated fare. The Marshals ensured the vehicles stopped, and then allocated passengers according to destination. Skull thought it sounded an excellent idea, except that it provided yet another group of state employees who could be watching them.

While Skull was learning what he could about Cuban security, Barbara had spotted a group of old men, gathered around, playing guitars and singing.
Even without her nun's regalia, Barbara was always able to integrate into any group. Her good looks and easy manner opened many doors.

Here, in Cuba, her fluency in Spanish was another asset. Barbara started by joining in with the men's songs. Her soft female voice in stark contrast to the gritty salsa of the local men. Eventually, she managed to steer the conversation around to history. The men talked eagerly about growing up in Cuba, the schools, the music, the dancing and the bringing down of the dictator, Batista, in the revolution. But no one seemed willing to talk about the missiles. Although the heat of the crisis was only 13 days, Barbara was sure it would have been a memorable period in their lives.

As the afternoon drew on, the Watchers rode into San Cristobal. It was a strange arrival for them, as the flamboyant bikers had been upstaged. Back home, with their customised bikes, loud exhausts and three piece back patches, the Watchers always attracted attention. But here, their identical Scramblers and borrowed motorcycle suits were less outlandish. Even so, a large group of bikers might have drawn attention. Except that the Harlistas were already in town. Cuba is famous for the way that its people have lovingly kept classic 1950s cars running, since trade with the USA ended after the revolution. What is less well known is that there is a smaller, but equally passionate group of Cubans, who have hung onto classic Harley Davidsons. Among the Cuban bikers, it was not just Barbara who found it easy to integrate. There is a sense of brotherhood among bikers the world over, and all of the Watchers dropped easily into the Harlistas' party atmosphere.

"These guys are fanatics", said Butler towards Skull. "They all started out as Panheads and Knuckleheads from the 30s, 40s and 50s. They would be bike show classics back home, but these are ridden every day".

The Harlistas were indeed fabulously inventive mechanics. Since US relations ended in 1959, no spares could be officially imported from the States. But these passionate owners kept their Harley's running with all manner of made and adapted parts.

The more rum that was drunk, the more talkative the Harlistas became. Where Barbara had been unable to get the old men talking about the missiles, their sons were happy to tell the stories. Few of the Harlistas were old enough to remember the period vividly, but their parents had often talked about the crisis.

The 13 day period had become known to the Cubans as the October Crisis, from the month it occurred. It was the closest they had come to fearing war, and the old people remembered it well.

Thousands of Russian troops dismantled the missile infrastructure. While more and more of Castro's troops flooded into the area to watch over them. Add to that, the regular over flights of American airplanes, and the U.S. Navy blockade off the coast, and they described a scene of near chaos.

Jonah and Stone were in the motor home,

watching live feed from the Watchers hidden body cameras. "Well Nev lad. That sounds the sort of chaos where someone could have mislaid a part or two", said Jonah.

"Yes", replied Stone. "If Castro wanted a nuclear deterrent badly enough, I'm sure something could have been spirited away".

"The big question is, where to?" added Jonah. It was an easy question to ask, but it was not going to prove an easy one to answer.

The next big lead came from Jonny Johnson. "Our hackers have been busy Jonah", came the voice over the encrypted telephone. MI5 computer experts had been working on some of Cuba's less secure computer systems.

The forger, Hugo Franco, had given his godsons the identities on the fake documents he had prepared. The hackers had been searching for these in the Cuban Tourist Authority database. "Trinidad de Cuba", said Jonny. "All four of them spent a couple of nights there. The database is a few days behind, but they were certainly there".

Jonah passed the information to Skull and Simms, for them to meet in Trinidad, the following day.

"We'll have to take in Playa Giron, just to look good for Freddie", replied Simms. "But I'll get the group there as early as I can".

Girón village and its beach were named after a 17th century French pirate Gilberto Giron. But it was more recent seaborne adventurers who had made the beach and its surrounding bay notorious.

Playa Giron sits at one end of Bahia de Cochinos, or Bay of Pigs. This is the bay where 1500 armed Cuban exiles landed in the 1961 CIA-sponsored attempt to overthrow Fidel Castro's new government. After 72 hours of fighting, Playa Girón was the last stand for the invaders. The Museo Girón, a small museum dedicated to the conflict, had to be on the tour which acted as a cover for the Watchers.

Simms led his convoy of Triumphs into Girón, and to a holiday camp, which looked straight out into the Bay of Pigs. Freddie and Albert had arrived ahead of them to organise lunch at the camp restaurant.

After their lunch, the Watchers casually fell into their preplanned tasks. Most of the group kept their Cuban shadows occupied with the type of light hearted conversation bikers are so good at. Barbara and Butler slipped quietly away.

Barbara did what the young nun excelled at. She made the local people feel relaxed and able to open up to her.

Butler headed for the museum. The ex Marine had an almost encyclopedic knowledge of international warfare. He was sure that he could have a meaningful conversation with the museum curators about their country's military history. Butler came away disappointed, the museum staff were very knowledgeable about the failed invasion, but were too young for first hand experience. They knew very little of the missile crisis and its aftermath.

Barbara fared slightly better. The ageing domestic staff knew little about the missiles. But they did have something to interest the young nun who had spent her life battling the sex trade.
Despite Cuba's closed policy to foreign influence, the Good Shepherd Sisters had done some work in Cuba. Barbara's involvement had been with Cuban adults and children trafficked abroad. She knew that Cuba had its own internal sexual black market, comprising the Jineteras and the lower ranking Chupachupas, but she was not aware of any foreign control of the trade. For decades, organised crime in Cuba had sat with the gang Sangre por Dolo, or Blood for Pain. Now, Barbara was hearing about Russians being seen in control of the sex workers. Barbara recognised the significance of this, particularly as, for Russian, they could probably substitute any former Soviet nationality. She quietly slipped away to telephone Jonah.

"If O Lobo is working in Cuba, then Russian probably means Georgi Dimov", suggested Jonah on hearing Barbara's news. Dimov was a former Bulgarian Intelligence Officer, who, like many redundant KGB operatives, had turned to crime after the collapse of the Soviet Union. These newly mercenary spies had found kindred spirits in the Portuguese spymaster's criminal organisation. Dimov had trafficked Eastern European women from their home countries, to be sold into sex slavery in Africa and Western Europe by O Lobo.
"It will give Jonny something to look at legitimately

too", added Jonah. "British Intelligence can investigate Dimov's travels, without it linking back to Matthew Saint".

Stone had bypassed Giron, and rode directly to Trinidad de Cuba. The surrounding area was full of tobacco plantations, and Stone was enjoying powering his adventure bike along the type of dirt road it was intended for.

The centre of Trinidad is a UNESCO World Heritage Site, with some of Cuba's oldest colonial buildings. Stone knew it was the tobacco which had funded the town's growth and provided a tangible link with the island's past.

Much as Stone was enjoying the plantation roads, he knew it was the tourist areas in the town centre which had most likely attracted Saint and his friends. So, Saint began his ride into town, in search of the hotel in which Saint had stayed.

It was obvious to Stone that the entire town's renovation budget had been spent in the centre. As he rode though the surrounding barrios, Stone saw that many of the old houses were falling into disrepair. Then, riding into the cobbled streets of the Plaza Mayor area, he saw why the guidebooks describe the town centre as, "an open-air museum of Spanish Colonial architecture." The historic area has cobblestone streets, houses painted in pastel colours with wrought-iron grilles, and ornate, colonial-era buildings like the Santísima Trinidad Cathedral. But Stone could not linger in the Plaza. The hotel he needed to check out was a modern building, high on the opposite hillside, overlooking the town. Stone wanted to avoid presenting his documents at reception, so headed straight for the hotel restaurant, making sure he could see reception.

After two days of he and Jonah cooking in the motor home, the prospect of a steak was making his mouth water. As Stone ate, his attention was torn between the reception and the view from the huge picture windows. The hotel had been cleverly designed to take advantage of its position overlooking old Trinidad. But, much as Stone was drawn to the view, he had a duty to their mission and did a lot of people watching.

The bar and reception were much as he had expected. The tourists were mostly European. Hovering around the male tourists were small groups of Jinteras. These elegantly dressed and very attractive women were towards the upper end of Cuba's sex trade. While they did accept payment for sex, most aimed to marry a tourist and escape Cuba's hardships. Several approached Stone, who would have been quite a catch. But he politely put them off. Stone knew the Jinteras usually worked without pimps, but he still listened out for Eastern European voices.

After his steak, Stone moved to the bar area, where he took time over coffee, then even longer over a Mojito. All the time Stone's senses were on full alert for anything that could cause the bigger group of Watchers any problems. Satisfied, Stone quietly updated Jonah, who called in Simms and his tour group.

With the Watchers on their way, Stone made

tracks, so as not to be seen with them.

By now he was used to the constant presence of uniforms. But there seemed something suspicious about the officers in the ageing Lada which was parked near his motorcycle. They seemed to be taking more interest than usual in his bike.

Chapter 9.

"Maybe they just like the bike", thought Stone. He put on his helmet and jacket, started the motorcycle and pulled away gently, trying to attract as little attention as possible.

The road down the hillside twisted and turned in wide loops, giving Stone a panoramic view of the whole valley side. Tucked away in side roads and hotel driveways, were yet more police Ladas and motorcycles. "Too much of a coincidence", thought Stone. "But goodness knows what I've done".

Never one to panic, Stone held his nerve and rode steadily towards the valley floor. He was still unsure if they were interested in him, or there for some other reason. Then, through his mirrors, Stone saw that two cars and a small motorcycle were now following him. Stone speeded up slightly, to open a gap, but his followers matched his speed.

Suddenly, it was clear to Stone that he was the target of the police attention. A police Lada rolled out of a hotel driveway, blocking the road ahead of Stone. Stone reacted instantly. The narrow road was completely blocked by the small police car, so Stone aimed his bike into the hotel garden.

Stone was accustomed to riding his 1200cc adventure bike around the rough Algarve roads. So the much lighter 800cc version was putty in the expert rider's hands. The carefully manicured hotel garden suffered badly as Stone powered his motorcycle through flower beds and well kept lawns. Then, with his back tyre throwing soil all over the police car, Stone rejoined the road and sped towards the town.

Two more police motorcycles joined the fray from a side road, pulling out behind him. Stone saw them long enough to see they were 250cc bikes. Like most Cuban police motorcycles, they were Chinese copies of old Honda models. They were nothing like a match for Stone's Triumph Tiger, but the riders would know the area much better than Stone.

New infrastructure turned rapidly to old as Stone reached the valley floor. The open spaces of the modern hotel gardens rapidly narrowed into tight colonial streets, and Tarmac turned to cobble stones. Descending the road, Stone had been opening space between him and the police. But, in the town, his bigger, more powerful motorcycle was less of an advantage. As his wheels slipped on the cobbles, Stone could see the smaller bikes gaining ground. Turning a corner, Stone found himself in a market square. Rows of stalls held; clothing, crafts and musical instruments. By necessity he slowed his pace to work through the crowds, but with use of his horn and frantic shouting, the crowds jumped aside to let him pass.

Then, one large organised tour group did not react quickly enough to his approach. Stone quickly assessed his options, which were few in number. He could not risk injuring the tourists, so took his only other option. Pulling his bike sharply to the left, Stone crashed through a souvenir stall. Luckily for Stone, the stall was of flimsy construction, and splintered at the impact of his heavy adventure bike. As he rode through, the stall holder's wares were sent flying. Sets of maracas, necklaces made of coffee beans and other local crafts showered the now panicking tour group as they ran in all directions.

The sudden activity surprised the two pursuing police motorcyclists, breaking sharply, both slid off their machines. Stone immediately took advantage and powered his motorcycle towards the market's exit and into one of the many cobbled side streets.

The much lighter 250cc machines were quickly upright again, and the officers regained the chase.

The pursuit twisted and turned through the narrow streets of the heritage area. The pastel coloured houses were punctuated by simple shops, with wrought iron grills open to display textiles and souvenirs. The shop keepers were one minute shouting their wares in the street, and the next diving for cover as the three speeding motorcycles approached.

Suddenly and without warning, Stone found himself at the top of a long flight of stairs. The stone staircase dated from colonial times, when the builders did not have to consider speeding motor vehicles. With no time to react, Stone was suddenly airborne. Ten steps down, the motorcycle tyres landed heavily, with the adventure bike's suspension compressing its full travel from the impact. It took all of Stone's skill to keep the bike upright. Then a little dazed from the landing, Stone rode down the remaining half of the steps.

The police were not so lucky, or skilful. Their motorcycles were intended for the road and could not handle the impact that the Triumph Tiger had just survived. Both officers flew from the top of the stairs, in the same way Stone had just done. But both landings went very badly indeed. The bikes' short travel suspension could not take the punishment the Tiger had just taken, and the two officers were both thrown from their bikes. Policemen and motorcycles all tumbled down the remaining stairs. By the time they reached the bottom, neither bikes nor riders were in condition to resume the chase.

Until now, the local police had been of no interest to Jonah. But as the chase progressed, Jonah tuned his sophisticated scanners to their frequency. Jonah feared that O Lobo had bought the local officers. But the reason for their interest in Stone was much simpler.
Throughout the ride from San Christobal, Stone had been using tracks and fields to avoid the many police checkpoints. He had underestimated the Cuban officers, judging their competence on

their outdated equipment. But, despite their lack of modern vehicles, these were experienced police officers. Each sighting had been passed to the next area, and Stone's distinctive motorcycle was easy to spot.

Despite his years as a surveillance motorcyclist, Stone had made a schoolboy error. It was one which he would not make again in a hurry.

Outside of town, Stone hid his motorcycle away in the trailer and joined Jonah in their motor home. Stone had placed hidden cameras while he lunched in Trinidad. He and Jonah sat down to watch the camera feed. They were just in time to watch Simms lead the tour group into their hotel. The Watchers had one night to find out anything they could about Saint's time in Trinidad. They would have to do it all under the cover of their motorcycle tour.

Their official guide, Freddie, had to put on a foot tour of the old town. No tourist visit to the historic unesco site would appear legitimate without it. In truth, many of the Watchers were interested in Cuba's culture, so, they had no difficulty sending some of their number out with Freddie.

Barbara and Miguel led a small group out with their tour guide. Barbara especially enjoyed the culture of countries unlike her own. Her group walked through all the sites which Stone had earlier ridden through. Barbara smiled to herself as she realised she would take in much more than she would have done aboard her motorcycle. Along the way, Barbara and Miguel were able to ask locals about the town's many churches.

Although under cover of a tour, they were using their own identities, which in Barbara's case, was as a nun.

While the others toured the old town, Skull, Butler and Alva played the role of boys on holiday. The three bikers sunbathed, swam and exercised around the pool. To all observers, they were relaxing on a Caribbean holiday. The muscled bikers attracted plenty of attention, especially the giant Joao Alva. But, despite appearances, all three were alert, and taking in all of the hotel staff routines.

Skull knew they would need access to the hotel office, so paid particular attention to activity behind the reception desk. The hotel had a lot of domestic and service staff, as labour was cheep in Cuba. But there seemed relatively few who had cause to go behind reception, or into the office beyond. "Shouldn't be too difficult", said Skull, talking through the options with Butler and Alva. "When the others return, we should have more than enough to distract the staff".

With a small number of simultaneous incidents around the bar and lobby, the Watchers would be able to access the information held in the hotel office.

That evening, the Watchers appeared to relax around the pool and bar, while Stone and Jonah watched their every move through hidden cameras.

At the pool, two muscled and heavily tattooed men were fooling about. Each man took turns in throwing the other across the pool, with each throw getting higher and further.

Then, after a particularly high throw, Simms landed heavily on the water and stopped moving. Butler began screaming for help, and hotel staff came running to their aid.

Meanwhile, two very large men began a very vocal argument in the bar. The big, bald man was dwarfed by the even bigger hairy man. But still he seemed to antagonise him. Then, without warning, the giant Joao Alva rose to his feet and pushed Skull from his stool. Staff ran to the bar, but stood off, reluctant to tackle the big angry men. Their shouting and pushing was to keep staff distracted for some time yet.

Then, in the lobby, all male eyes were on a beautiful young woman as she walked past the reception desk. Barbara Cuba was wearing high healed shoes that she had bought that afternoon in Trinidad. In her room, she had cut part way through one of the heals. Now, with staff attention already on her, she stepped heavily, breaking her heal. Barbara had barely hit the floor before the two reception staff left their posts, to run to her aid.

Miguel and Harris lost no time slipping behind the desk and into the office beyond.

Harris was the technician, so went straight to the computer. Within seconds he had hooked up a hard drive, and began to download in its contents. Miguel had taken his camera to the manual record cards. Cuban hotels were not yet fully computerised. All registrations were done manually, then, over a period of days, copied onto the computer.

"Bingo", said Miguel, as he leafed through the registration cards. "I've found Saint and his friends". The card showed that Saint and his three American friends had checked out the previous morning. They had given their next destination as Santiago De Cuba.

"I'll photograph a couple of days each side, we might spot someone else of interest staying here too", said Miguel.

"Nearly done here", replied Harris, as the last of the data was copying to his hard drive.

As soon as Jonah saw Miguel and Harris slip out of the office, he let the other Watchers know via their ear pieces. "They're clear, you can wrap up the entertainment".

While the Watchers were calming down their incidents, Jonah and Stone were packing away for the drive south to Santiago.

The tour group would have to spend the night, as planned, in Trinidad. But Stone could get a head start in the motor home, with his motorcycle tucked out of sight in the trailer.

While Stone drove the van, Jonah busied himself with research. Santiago De Cuba is Cuba's second city. It has a much more modern feel than the capital, Havana, and is more of a holiday destination. It was also the seat of Fidel Castro's revolution against the regime of Fulgencio Batista. "Thriving sex trade there, Nev lad", said Jonah. "If O Lobo has a power base anywhere in Cuba, it will be here".

Stone and Jonah drove through part of the night, to reach the outskirts of Santiago. Before he could settle to sleep, Stone had work to do. With the police looking for his bike, it needed to change appearance. So Stone got busy with fiberglass filler and spray paint. By morning, the mouldings and new colour scheme would be dry. With a change of number plate, Stone's Tiger would look different enough to enter Santiago.

As Stone tried to relax into sleep, he looked through the research Jonah had done about the southern tip of Cuba. Santiago's close proximity to Guantanamo Bay surprised Stone. If Batista's regime was supported by U.S. money, he would not have expected Castro's resistance movement to grow so close to the US Naval Base. "Perhaps the Cactus Curtain is more of a barrier than it sounds", thought Stone.

Guantanamo Bay had been in American hands since 1898, when it was of strategic importance in their war against Spain. The Bay's uses changed often over the years, but never grew less important. When the US Navy relied on coal, the base was vital as a refuelling point in their dominance of the Caribbean.

During WW2, the base protected merchant convoys heading up the US East Coast.

After Castro's revolution, the base took the use which Stone envisaged, as a focus for the U.S. backed resistance to Castro's Communism. It would have been around this time that physical security was increased to prevent Cubans fleeing to the U.S. Where "Iron Curtain", had been coined as a metaphorical term for the border between East and West, the Cactus Curtain was more tangible. A hedge of cactus formed the main barrier between Cuba and the U.S. territory to the south.

Now, with terrorist prisoners held at Guantanamo Bay, the base was unlikely to have any significance to Stone's mission. But that did not stop him dreaming about breaching the Cactus Curtain.

Stone and Jonah were awake with the dawn and started their preparations for the Watchers' arrival later in the day. They both had tasks to complete. Jonah needed to check in with their MI5 contact, to see what Jonny could find about O Lobo's interests in Santiago.

Stone headed out on his motorcycle to familiarise himself with the area. If they were going head to head with the wolf, they would need every advantage they could get. This time, Stone would not underestimate the local police. He would either submit to their checkpoints, or take greater care in circumventing them.

Kenton Simms had woken early to prepare Skull's group for the ride south. There were many historic revolution sites which his tour group would be expected to visit. But he had convinced their Cuban shadow Freddie that the bikers were desperate to party and would visit the tourist spots on the way back north.

Heading straight to Santiago meant a good day's ride. But "we could be in worse places than the

Caribbean", thought Skull as their convoy of Triumphs rode through rural Cuba.

The hotel which Matthew Saint had used in Santiago was a surprise to Skull. They had used a range of hotels from colonial buildings, through to the modern hotel at Trinidad. But this was something different. Their Trinidad hotel boasted a bar and swimming pool. This resort hotel was something else entirely. It was a large modern hotel, with extensive grounds, and a huge, intricately shaped swimming pool. "I could get used to this", said Skull, playing up his tourist routine in front of the hotel staff.

Chapter 10.

The Watchers sat in the hotel's plush lounge.
Having reached their destination, they had again
lost Freddie for the evening, as he would sample
the entertainment away from the tourist trail.
Miguel and Barbara Cuba sat together, people
watching. "There's a lot of white guys with black
and mixed race girls", commented Miguel, certain
that it was something connected to the sex trade.
There were a lot of women who looked out of
place with their companions. Brightly dressed and
considerably younger than their male escorts,
none looked like genuine couples.
Barbara had been researching Cuba's sex
workers, through her connections in the UN and
the Good Shepherd Sisters. "Cubans don't say
mixed race", replied Barbara. "They call
themselves "Mulato". Cuba has been colonised so
many times, that many of them have lost track of
their ancestry. Most consider themselves the
islands future, with all the races mixed, how could
there be any racism".
"What about the women?" asked Skull. "Where
will O Lobo fit into all this?"
Barbara carried on briefing the Watchers on what
was happening around their hotel.
She explained the women at the hotel were most
likely Jineteras , Spanish for Horse Rider, or
Street Jockey. Some were professional women,
teachers or office workers, selling their bodies to
top up meager salaries. With an average wage of
$25 per month, the prostitutes could easy double

that every night. "Exploitation thrives where poverty exists", said Barbara. "In a way, it's no different here than Thailand". She went on to explain that most of the girls were self employed. But, when the authorities had a clamp down on prostitution, it could mean two years in jail for the girls. So many of them pay gangsters, who in turn, buy off the police.

"There is zero tolerance on drugs here", said Barbara. "So if O Lobo and Dimov are making money in Cuba, then it must be from the sex trade".

This was a world in which Barbara was comfortable. She had spent most of her adult life as a Good Shepherd Sister, helping the world's vulnerable and exploited. With so many jineteras plying their trade around the resort hotel, Barbara was certain she could get one to open up.

So, while the men worked out how to access the hotel computer, Barbara started breaking the ice with any of the women who were not occupied with men. It never took Barbara long. Her beautiful, but friendly face and pleasant nature complemented her years of experience. The women would almost always talk to her.

Twenty three year old Hermita told Barbara that she gave up working as a hairdresser and started sleeping with tourists two years ago. She said she came close to striking it rich when an older Italian tourist had offered to pay for an apartment for her. But they quarrelled on a subsequent visit, and she is now on the hunt again. "I can collect $40 to $70 a night from any tourist I lure back to their room", said Hermita. "But the Russians always take a cut for protection".

Jonah was listening to the feed from Barbara's microphone. Instantly, at the mention of Russians, Jonah suspected Georgi Dimov's men. Dimov was Bulgarian, but after many years of Soviet influence, the Cubans would automatically class anywhere in the former Soviet Union as Russia. Jonah soon got confirmation from the cameras worn or placed by the Watchers. His practiced eye quickly picked out the men who didn't fit in. "Soviets", thought Jonah. He had spent so much time in Special Branch, that despite the collapse of the Iron Curtain, they were all still Soviets to him.

"Nev lad", began Jonah over the radio. "I think we have Dimov's men at the hotel. You had better stay close by".
Stone had parked his motorcycle in the shadows surrounding the resort. He had crept in close, using his years of police surveillance training. But now, with Dimov's gangsters inside, Stone crept back to the bike to retrieve the pistol MI5 had provided in the Diplomatic Bag. Then, feeling much safer, he slipped back into the bushes surrounding the swimming pool and familiarised himself with the lay out.
Through their battles with Dimov's men, the Watchers had become adept at spotting the distinctive features of the Eastern Europeans. Stone was easily picking out the gangsters.
"Looks about five of them Jonah", said Stone. "All

wearing jackets in this heat, so they're probably packing ".

Skull had already made the same observation about Dimov's thugs and sent the two Sergeants at Arms out for their pistols. Joao Alva held the position of Sergeant at Arms with the Lagos Chapter. Steve Butler filled the role for the entire International Organisation. Mostly, they were just enforcers of discipline, but they were also expected to be proficient with weapons, when the need arose.

Wary of the potential threat from the gangsters, the Watchers still needed information.

Barbara was striking up quite a rapport with Hermita. As always, when his sister was involved in a mission, Miguel was keeping a close eye on her.

Skull and Harris moved over to the reception desk, where a single receptionist was on duty. They had been watching the desk, where the staff seemed much more relaxed than the previous hotel. Skull was able to engage the receptionist in conversation, over a map of Santiago. They were used to tourist questions and thought nothing of Skull's approach.

While Skull kept the receptionist distracted, Harris leaned casually over the counter. He slipped a flash drive into the computer terminal and left behind a Trojan Virus. The virus was another gift from MI5. It would transmit everything on the computer to Jonah's machines in the motor home. But more importantly, it would continue to send anything new that was saved on the computer.

Barbara was about to run out of luck with Hermita. She had done incredibly well in getting the young Jinetera talking. But their apparent friendliness was drawing the attention of the East Europeans, and one of the men started to close in. The muscled young man, with cropped hair and tightly fitting suit, looked military in appearance. "Spetsnaz", said Butler. The former Royal Marine had led adventure holidays in Bulgaria, after leaving the forces. He instantly recognised the look and bearing of the Soviet Special Forces.

The Spetsnaz worked mostly under the direction of the Soviet Union's GRU, Military Intelligence Service. The best of their operatives were the equal of Britain's Marines and SAS.

"Dimov is going up in the world if he's hiring Spetsnaz", thought Butler. He quietly hoped that they would not go head to head with such well trained soldiers, but thought it inevitable if Dimov and O Lobo were hiring such serious muscle.

Under instruction from the Spetsnaz, Hermita moved away from Barbara to concentrate on the resort's available men. But he kept a close eye on Barbara, and the group she had arrived with. Miguel moved to sit with his sister, and said "we won't get to her again very soon. Did you get anything from her?"

"More than I expected", replied Barbara. "The East Europeans have a small resort in the mountains. Sort of a collection of log cabins, where they can take the sex tourists. She said it was less than an hours drive".

"Interesting", said Miguel. "I'll pass it to Jonah to see what he can come up with".

As soon as Skull moved away from the desk, Butler approached him. "Whatever we do in here will attract the attention of the Spetsnaz", said Butler. "Can we keep them entertained while Stone busies himself outside?"

"Like it", replied Skull. "They don't know about Stone, so he should have a free run".

While the Watchers behaved like noisy tourists, Stone moved methodically through the resort's shadows. Every open window and every parked car got his attention. One car in particular drew Stone's attention, as it pulled out of the car park. At first, the mix of two white faces and two black faces seemed typical of the resort's clientele. But then, the difference registered with him. The genders were reversed. It was two black men, with two white women.

Now they had Stone's attention, he looked more intently at their faces. Sitting in the back seat were Matthew Saint and Ellen White. Stone had watched and re-watched the Portuguese CCTV and would recognise them anywhere.

All four occupants of the car were laughing and talking amongst themselves.

Stone reacted quickly, running through the gardens surrounding the hotel, to where he had hidden his motorcycle. Saint's car already had a head start on him, but there were only two options of direction. Stone gambled, turning inland, towards the mountains. He gambled correctly and was soon behind the car. But, with so little traffic on the road, Stone could not follow for long, without being spotted.

Reaching into his pocket, Stone pulled out a small magnetic device. The tiny tracker would allow Jonah to follow the car's progress from his computer screen. Stone accelerated his motorcycle and overtook the car. As he passed, Stone expertly flicked the tracker onto the car roof, where its powerful magnet held it secure.

Stone kept the power on, until he was out of sight of the car's occupants. He then pulled off the road and into the cover of the surrounding trees, allowing Saint's car to drive past.

"Signal strong, Nev lad", said Jonah, as the tracker's signal blinked on his screen.

Stone pulled out of the trees and rode after Saint. Jonah kept a steady commentary going through Stone's earpiece, advising of each junction's turns.

"You were right about this being the revolution's heartland Jonah", said Stone. As he rode steadily uphill towards the mountains, the roadside was decorated with bill boards commemorating the revolution. "Viva Revolucion", "Viva Fidel", "Viva Che", proclaimed the signs.

"Back off a little, Nev lad", advised Jonah. "It looks like end of the road, at a small settlement. I'm trying to get satellite images from Jonny".

Stone knew that if he rode into a dead end, there was a good chance that he would be spotted. By holding back for details of the area, Stone could plan a covert way into the settlement.

Jonah was soon back on the radio. "No live feed, Nev lad. Satellite is in the wrong position. But we've got some recent pictures". Jonah described a collection of log cabins, around a waterfall and pool.

"That's what the girl was describing to Barbara", replied Stone. "It must be Dimov's sex resort".

"Aye Nev lad. It certainly sounds like it. We had better find a way of getting you close".

Talked in by Jonah, Stone hid his motorcycle and crept through the forest, to a vantage point above the settlement. It was a small mountain resort, just as Hermita had described. A large, thatched canopy sat at the centre, with a view of the waterfall. This was the communal dining and bar area. In a semi circle around the canopy, were individual huts for guests to sleep in. Stone imagined this was all built for much more innocent recreation than Georgi Dimov's clients now enjoyed.

While he was a police officer, Stone had years of training and experience in what the police call CROP, or Covert Rural Observation Post, tactics. Often he had lain undetected, for days at a time, watching criminal targets. So, he had no difficulty in observing this small collection of buildings.

It was humid, high on a Caribbean mountain, surrounded by vegetation and close to a waterfall. But Stone was a professional and disciplined himself not to find discomfort in the dampness surrounding him.

Night drew in and Stone resigned himself to a sleepless night, maintaining surveillance on the settlement.

It was a different story for Skull and the Watchers, back at the resort. Somehow they had avoided antagonising the ex Spetsnaz gangsters, and their guns had proved unnecessary. They turned in for some sleep, taking shifts with two of them keeping a watch on the resort. With Saint and his friends away in the mountains, little was expected to happen in Santiago.

The Watchers' sleep was to be short lived, not for anything in Santiago, but for something Stone saw in the mountains. A short distance from the sleeping cabins, was a more industrial looking building. Stone had assumed it to be some sort of maintenance unit for the small resort. In the early hours of the morning, just as dawn was starting to break, the unit's double doors were opened from inside.

A small van drove out of the unit and quickly began its decent of the mountain. Stone could not see the occupants of the van, and he was in no position to follow, particularly as his primary target was Matthew Saint. He was a little worried in case Saint was inside the van. But his concern did not last long, as Saint and Ellen White walked out of the unit and crossed to their cabin.

Now, Stone was torn between two targets. He had the van, with a clear connection to Saint, leaving the settlement in quite suspicious circumstances. But he also had his primary targets, Saint and White, still there, along with the maintenance building which needed to be searched.

His decision was an easy one, stay with Saint, and hope the Watchers could pick up the van. A rapid radio message alerted Jonah, who just as quickly contacted the Watchers at Santiago. Skull and Butler were on the current watch, so they were the first to react. Within minutes, their Scramblers were tearing out of the car park and heading towards the Sierra Maestra Mountains. Hermita had told Barbara that the settlement was an hour away. Skull and Butler would cover the distance much faster on their motorcycles, but they both feared they would not be fast enough. Roads in Cuba are not that plentiful, but there were still opportunities for the van to pull off between the settlement and Santiago. As Skull coaxed every scrap of power from his motorcycle, he hoped they could get close enough to see where the van was going.

But, it was not to be, and Skull and Butler were soon as close to the settlement as they dare ride their bikes. With their bikes hidden from the road, Skull checked in with Jonah and Stone to agree their next actions.

"The three of us should be able to do a search", suggested Stone.

"Not with the Spetznaz about", replied Butler. The ex Royal Marine had experienced the Soviet Union's elite troops before, and did not underestimate them. "I'd be happier with back up close by", he added. The Watchers knew when to value each other's expertise, and they readily agreed to call in reinforcements from Santiago.

Some would need to remain on the official tour, to placate their escort, Freddie. But Miguel and Alva were able to slip away before Freddie arrived for breakfast.

Freddie was not happy when only Simms, Harris and Barbara walked into the dining room. Simms knew Freddie would have to report the four missing tourists to the Cuban authorities. But Simms hoped they would accept that the bikers had just gone off to party, and would rejoin them at their next stop.

Chapter 11.

Miguel and Alva sped along the winding mountain roads. Like Skull and Butler before them, they were riding too hard to take in the revolutionary placards lining the route. Their brothers were facing trouble and they needed to be there for them. Daylight had well and truly broken through by the time the five bikers met under cover of the forest. "It's risky, going in during the day time", said Miguel.

"I know", replied Stone. "But Saint has been doing something in that shed, and something went out in that van. If it's a nuke, we don't have the luxury of time".

"I agree", added Skull. "Can you and Butler come up with a plan?" Skull knew that the combined police and Royal Marines experience of Stone and Butler was their best chance of pulling off the search safely. It did not take long for the two covert specialists to come up with a plan.

"Joao, take the eyrie please", said Stone. He knew that the huge man's weapons skills would be more help than his ability to break heads. The eyrie, or eagle's nest, was the term used for a high surveillance, or sniper's vantage point.

"If Skull and I take the Shed, Miguel and Steve can do close support".

The MC always worked as a democracy, so all the others were open to challenge Stone and Butler's plan. But they respected their brother's expertise and set about preparing weapons and equipment.

Joao Alva had removed a folding carbine rifle from his pannier, together with a powerful telescope, and was working his way through the trees to a cliff top ledge. Miguel Cuba and Steve Butler also selected short carbine rifles. But Stone and Skull chose pistols, for greater manoeuvrability inside the shed.

As the four of them moved stealthily through the settlement, they placed tiny cameras. These would send images back to Jonah, who could give early warning of anyone approaching.

At the shed door, Stone took out a tiny black box. It was a sensitive listening device, which linked wirelessly to his earpiece and would warn him of any noise inside the shed.

"Clear inside", said Stone. "How are the cameras Jonah?"

"All clear Nev lad", replied Jonah. "Looks like lunch time, they are all under the canopy. Including Saint and White, I've seen 10". With that, Stone picked the lock and he and Skull slipped inside.

The inside of the large shed was much as they expected. Its main purpose was obviously for maintenance of the small resort. Tools, lawnmowers and other handyman materials were stored inside. But one workbench looked tidier than the rest. "I'd say that's had an engineer's attention", observed Stone, as he walked towards the bench. Rather than the oil, dirt and grass cuttings around the other benches, this one was swept clean and the work surface was organised. That made Stone's task of searching the bench easier, as he quickly looked through the boxes of technical engineer's tools, stacked neatly at the side of the bench.

Stone had found nothing definitive, when he turned his attention to a large metal chest, at the side of the bench. The chest was padlocked, but it soon opened to Stone's lock picking skills. Their worst fears were realised, as Stone and Skull looked at the two containers within. Neither of them could read the Russian, Cyrillic script. But they both clearly understood the international radiation symbol. "Oh shit", said Skull. "Looks like our theory about the Cuban connection was right".

Stone did not reply, as he was busy unpacking his radiation detector. "Very faint trace of alpha", said Stone. "Consistent with Plutonium having been handled here". Pulling on thick gloves, Stone lifted one of the containers. "It's far too light", said Stone. "There can't be anything in it".

"its evidence", replied Skull. "Pack them, and then we'll finish with the untidy side".

Stone slipped the containers into his rucksack, and then joined Skull, who was already searching through the clutter of the maintenance men.

"Stand by, stand by", came Jonah's urgent voice over the radio. "Looks like lunch is over. You have two heading your way."

Stone and Skull quickly slipped out of the shed, while Butler and Miguel got into position to head off the gangsters. They all hoped vainly, that the men would turn away. But they were heading directly towards them, and at a pace too.

Butler knew his brothers would not be clear of the shed, before the men were on them. So he coughed to distract them. His fears about the former Spetznaz troops' skills were well founded, and they instantly located the source of Butler's cough. "Contact", shouted Butler into his radio, as the first bullets flew towards them.

The shots alerted the gangsters remaining under the canopy, who all started moving in their direction.

Alva was quick to react. The huge enforcer did not have military training, but he spent many hours practicing on the range. His short carbine rifle was not the ideal sniper weapon, but it was good enough at the relatively short range. The first shooter fell to the ground, seconds after Alva's bullet hit him in the chest.

Butler and Miguel started to send covering fire towards the approaching gangsters, to allow Stone and Skull to join them. They would always avoid killing if they could. One man had died already; they hoped their shots would keep the others back.

Once the four Watchers were back together, they started moving in pairs. Two providing covering fire, while the others made ground towards their motorcycles.

Butler was keeping a sharp watch, as he knew not to underestimate the Spetsnaz training. Sure enough, they were not all coming at them from the front. Butler's trained eye caught the slightest movement off to their flank. "Movement, two o'clock", said Butler.

Alva turned his attention to this new threat, laying down fire into the area indicated by Butler. The Spetsnaz were quick to return fire, but Alva was well shielded by the rocky ledge.

The extra gunfire provided enough confusion for the four Watchers to make fast progress towards their bikes. Once at their bikes, the Watchers fanned out into a curve, with four guns giving Alva the cover he needed to leave his eyrie.

The huge enforcer looked anything but an athlete. But despite his height and enormous build, Alva maintained a good level of fitness. He zig zagged through the trees at tremendous speed towards the bikes. Then, strapping guns over their shoulders, the five bikers rode down the winding mountain road at speeds which would terrify the average rider.

Once out of the steepest part of the mountains, the area became open enough for the Scramblers' off road capabilities to be used. The Watchers picked their way carefully through networks of farm tracks, to a point where they could safely meet Jonah.

Jonah trundled the motor home along one of the better quality tracks. He was following a GPS signal, to meet up with Stone and his group. Stone needed to hand over the radioactive material cases, which he had carried down the mountain. But they all needed to lie low to see if the gunfire had attracted the Cuban authorities.

Freddie was far from happy that some of his tour group had given him the slip. It was clear that he would be in trouble with his bosses. Independent travel is allowed in Cuba, but organised groups needed an official representative, who was expected to watch the tourists. With five of his group off piste, Freddie would have some explaining to do.

"What can I say?", asked Kenton Simms. "They are bikers, they love to party, and won't follow rules. They'll meet us in Camaguey". Camaguey is another of Cuba's UNESCO World Heritage Sites. It is a must see on the tourist trail, and allowed Simms to keep up the Watchers' pretence of being a tour group.

Jonny Johnson, the Watchers' MI5 handler had been busy behind the scenes. Under the guise of tracking O Lobo and Dimov's interests, Security Service analysts had been watching for Saint and his group.

Jonah's encrypted phone rang in the motor home. He knew instantly that it was Jonny calling.

"We've got them booked on a flight from Havana tomorrow", said Jonny. "It's our worst nightmare though. All four of them are going to the States". Jonah knew what this meant to his friend. The Watchers' involvement was all about keeping Saint's behaviour away from the Americans.

"Well, Jonny lad. That puts us in a bit of a spot. Missing bomb builder, U.S. technology, traces of plutonium, and now he's going to the last place we want him". Jonah's comment did not need a reply, British interests were very much on the line and it was starting to get out of even Jonny's comfort zone.

"Regroup and hold tight Jonah", replied Jonny. "We've more analysis to do, and then I need to get your guys over there".

While the Watchers were holding tight, a Portuguese merchant ship was sailing past Bermuda. Its Captain was being very cautious to steer a course towards northern Florida. The superstitious seaman knew that he must turn south soon, but he would put it off as long as possible. The ship needed to pass south of Florida, to enter the Gulf of Mexico. But in order to do so, the Captain would have to enter one of the world's most feared ocean areas. The area, demarcated by The Florida Keys, Bermuda and Puerto Rico, was reputed to have cost countless sailors and airmen their lives.

The Captain observed every maritime superstition he knew of. But, of all his superstitions, the one he feared most was the Bermuda Triangle. The only thing that took him into this fabled area was that he feared O Lobo more.

Carlos Lobo was a master at turning fear to his advantage. Usually it was his ruthless willingness to use extreme violence. But often he would use religious or superstitious observance to make people do his bidding.

Eventually, the Captain could not put off sailing into the Triangle. He had to pass into the Gulf of Mexico, but first, he had a rendezvous off the coast of the Bahamas. The string of Caribbean Islands sat inside the Bermuda Triangle, but they were also within easy reach of Cuba's north coast.

Usually, the Captain would be delivering a package to the luxury cruiser he soon expected to see. He asked no questions, but assumed his deliveries were to service the recreational needs of Bahamian playboys. This time it was different, he was collecting a package. One that he was being paid a great deal of money to deliver safely.

The cargo ship's radar had spotted the fast moving cruiser, long before it came into sight. Despite the Captain's fear of the Triangle, O Lobo had taught him to use its legend to cover his tracks. The Triangle has many mysteries, from disappearing aircraft, to malfunctioning compasses. But most regular of its dangers is its unpredictable weather and quickly forming fog banks. This was what the Captain exploited, when he met O Lobo's cruiser.

As soon as the ships radar operator spotted the approaching boat, other crew members rushed to a very unusual piece of ship's equipment.

Minute by minute the fast moving cruiser closed the gap towards the cargo ship. Then suddenly, the larger ship was gone, hidden in a thick cloud of fog. The cruiser reduced speed and continued on dead reckoning, using the boat's compass to stay on course towards the cargo ship.

Any unexpected craft would avoid the strange fog bank, fearing it to be a manifestation of the Bermuda Triangle's legendary power. But the crews in both of O Lobo's boats knew differently. The equipment being operated on the cargo ship was a military grade version of the fog machines used by the entertainment industry. The fog is created by vaporising water and glycol-based fluids. The fluid, or fog juice, vaporises inside the machine, then, mixing with cooler outside air the vapour condenses, causing a thick visible fog. Navies had used their engines to create fog screens since the days of steam ships. O Lobo's technicians had adapted the latest military technology to mask his smuggling operations around the Bahamas. The rouse had worked perfectly for some time now. But the Captain worried constantly that they would somehow upset the dark forces inside the Triangle.

This time, as the hook descended from the cargo ship deck, it carried no package of drugs. O Lobo would not risk such a profitable mission being thwarted by a drug bust.
The hook was empty as it descended, but was soon connected to a cargo net and rising back towards the deck.
No sooner had its deadly cargo left them, than the cruiser's crew was speeding back to Cuba.
The cargo ship crew soon had their boxes buried deep within the ship's secret compartments. With the fog machine turned off, they continued into the Gulf of Mexico, leaving the Bermuda Triangle as quickly as they could.

Chapter 12.

Skull had been busy making calls while they waited to hear from Jonny. He knew they would have to leave Cuba quickly, if they were to head off Saint's group in America.

The Watchers had members in all manner of security related business. One of their most unusual fields of work was in oil rig disaster. Years ago a long standing member of their London Chapter, had gone to work for a fledgling company offering to clean up the oil companies spills and fires. Chris Andrews, known as Red, after the legendary oilfield troubleshooter, was now a senior executive with the successful operation.

Skull knew that Red could provide a fast way into the U.S. with a minimum of red tape. Now all they needed was a legitimate reason to be there.

Knowing they would soon be leaving Cuba, the rest of Simms' tour group had given Freddie the slip. Their official Cuban escort would have a long and fruitless wait in Camaguey.

Simms, Harris and Barbara had pulled off the main road north, in answer to Jonah's call. Soon their motorcycles were rolling along the farm tracks to meet the other Watchers.

As they waited, Jonny had come through with his intelligence contacts. Matthew Saint and his friends were booked from Havana to Florida on their false documents. But Jonny's analysts had found them, switched to their real names, booked

on an internal flight to New Orleans.
They still had 24 hours before Saint left Cuba. But they had to be in New Orleans before them, to have any chance of surveillance. They also had to be there without US Intelligence having any idea why they were there.

Barbara Cuba came up with the perfect cover for the Watchers being in the Southern States. "Nun Run", said Barbara, rather cryptically. She waited to see who would be first to ask what she meant. It was Stone who gave in first to curiosity. "Ok Barbara, what's a Nun Run".
With her dark beauty and motorcycle clothing, it was easy to forget that Barbara had been a Nun for all of her adult life. But she was very serious about her calling, and about her NGO work with the Good Shepherd Sisters. "It's a biker fundraiser for a convent clinic in Texas", replied Barbara. "The Sisters of Charity of the Incarnate Word ride with about 250 bikers, raising funds for their clinic. There's lots of law enforcement and military back patch clubs attend, so why not the Watchers?"
Skull was soon on the phone to their Texas Chapter, to arrange their attendance. Now all they needed to do was get out of Cuba.

The big Lockheed L-100 Hercules transport plane circled for approach to Antonio Maceo Airport at Santiago. The pilot was a little nervous, as he had never landed on this runway before, and he knew that most of the airport's traffic was short haul. Some international flights connected with

Santiago, but most of its trade was in turbo prop aircraft. However, the pilot knew that, on occasions, the enormous Russian Antonov cargo aircraft had landed there during the Soviet era. He was also safe in the knowledge that the Hercules still holds the record, attained in 1963, for the heaviest plane to land on an aircraft carrier. It takes many years for pilots to graduate to aircraft the size of a Hercules, and the pilot executed a flawless landing.

The huge aircraft, with its courier company livery, taxied towards the airport's freight terminal. The enormous mural of Che Guevara on the main terminal, reminded the pilot of the airport's role as a revolutionary base. With his aircraft parked, the pilot presented his paperwork, which, thanks to the intervention of Jonny Johnson, was all in order.

His cargo, amounting to the personnel and equipment of a motorcycle display team, would soon arrive.

With airport security already expecting their arrival, the Watchers' convoy was waved straight through the cargo terminal gates. Everyone loves a bit of celebrity, and Jonny had provided a wealth of fake publicity material for the pilot to show the Cubans.

Skull led his small convoy of bikes onto the airfield. Following close behind was Jonah in the motor home, its specialist equipment now hidden away.

Kenton Simms had waved off his brothers on the outskirts of Santiago. His business was with John Prince in the Cuban oilfields. Texan Watchers would replace him when they landed and Simms would soon be compensated for the loss of his tour company's motorcycles.

The Watchers' convoy rolled steadily across the taxiway, and straight up the waiting cargo ramp of the Hercules. Steve Butler had done this many times before, as a Royal Marine, driving onto the military versions of the Hercules. But for the others, it was a new and exiting experience.

"I feel like an extra in Apocalypse Now", thought Stone as he remembered the Vietnam War movie. He would later learn how prophetic his thoughts of apocalypse would be.

It did not take long for the efficient Hercules crew to raise the rear ramp and start the aircraft's four huge turbo prop engines. As soon as they were airborne and the engine noise reduced to a cruising level, Stone turned to skull. "Ok, how did you pull this one off?" he asked.

"It's Red Andrews' oil spill company", replied Skull. "The plane is owned by Red's company, but on long term lease to the courier firm. Their contract gets the Herc back at short notice, when there is an oil emergency. Then they use it like Thunderbird Two, to get their kit to the disaster zone".

"But there isn't a disaster", said Stone. Skull explained that Prince and Simms had used their positions in the Cuban oil company, to fake the necessary alerts. As far as the couriers were concerned, there was an oil spill in Cuba, and their parcels would have to be late.

The flight deck door opened, and even Skull got a surprise, as a man in Watchers' colours walked out. His bright ginger hair and bushy beard made him instantly recognisable.

"Red!" exclaimed Skull. "What are you doing here?"

"All the cloak and dagger sounded too exciting", replied Red. "I qualified to fly the Herc last year, so I decided to co-pilot".

Red Andrews knew that, with the speed and efficiency that the paperwork had been produced for their flight to Cuba, that it was no ordinary client. He also knew that, if they were leaving Cuba under cover of being a display team, there was a covert nature to their mission.

Skull knew that Red's contacts in the Texan oilfields could be useful to them inside the USA. So he briefed Red on their mission and arranged for another co-pilot to return with the plane to England.

It was a relatively short flight for the Watchers. When Red told them they would be landing at Houston's George Bush Intercontinental Airport they were pleased to learn it was named for the first President Bush, not the more comical son. Again Jonny had come through with the paperwork, and the Watchers passed smoothly through US Immigration. Some of the Watchers, particularly Stone, with a manslaughter conviction, should have had difficulty with US visas. But Jonny, and his contact in the British Embassy in Washington, had made any problems disappear.

With their paperwork checked, the Watchers rode off the airport, into the Texan sunshine. Red now travelled with Jonah in the motor home, as he would need a motorcycle from their Texas Chapter.

Outside of the airport's fence, a welcoming committee awaited them. They expected the two senior Texas members, who most of the group had already met.

With them was a stunning blond woman, riding an American Buell Lightening street fighter motorcycle. All of the men wondered who this woman could be, and why the Texans had brought her on such a secretive assignment.

Stone was concerned by the absence of one key person they were expecting. Jonny Johnson had promised them a trusted contact from Britain's US Embassy. In order to operate in the States, without government sanction, they would need some official top cover. So the Embassy contact would be vital.

The bikers pulled to a halt in the parking lot, alongside the three waiting motorcycles. As Jonah walked from the motor home, Stone asked, "hey Jonah, where's our man in Washington?"

"Well Nev lad", replied Jonah. "He's already here". Then, turning towards the blond, he added "meet Amber Swift. Military Attaché to the British Embassy in Washington and Jonny Johnson's favourite niece".

Stone knew that for Military Attaché, you could read the Secret Intelligence Service, or MI6. He also knew that if Jonny put his trust in her, then he could too. Putting his hand out to Amber, Stone said "you're not quite what I was expecting."I rarely am", answered Amber with a smile.

While Stone and Jonah were greeting Amber
Swift, the other Watchers were being welcomed
by their Texan brothers. The biker greetings were
as enthusiastic as always, with ritual hugs and
back slaps.
With the rituals completed, Skull introduced Stone
and Jonah to the two American Watchers. First to
be introduced was Texas Chapter President,
Brandon Knox. Formerly a police officer, Knox
had resigned from the force, disenchanted with
how politicised policing had become. He soon
found kindred spirits in the Watchers, who made
good use of his detective skills. As a detective,
Knox looked so much like the TV cop Kojak, that
he adopted his trademark lollipop. There was a
certain comedy to it while a policeman, but a lolly
pop sucking biker seemed somehow wrong.
Alongside Knox, was a large, silently brooding
man, with buzz cut hair and five o'clock
shadow. This was the Texan Sergeant at Arms,
Randy Salt. The ex U.S. Navy Seal had served in
Iraq and Afghanistan along with many covert ops
in South America.
Stone thought that he looked every inch the
stereotypical U.S. Marine.
Both Texans rode Triumph Rocket III
motorcycles. They had to stick to the Watchers'
European bike rule, but in a country where
everything is big, they needed to outgun the
local's Harley Davidsons.

With introductions complete, the bikers started the

23 mile ride from George Bush Airport to the Watchers' clubhouse in downtown Houston. Partying would always be on the agenda with a visiting chapter. But they first had work to do. Knox, Salt, Andrews and Amber needed to be briefed on the mission so far, and they needed to prepare for the following day's Nun Run.
Setting up their Incident Room, Stone and Jonah were pleased to see that Knox was as much an old school detective as they were. Not for him, the computer screens of the young hot-shots. The older detectives favoured filling the walls with photographs, connection lines and lots of Post It Notes.

With slightly sore heads from last night's party, the whole Texas Chapter, and their visitors, prepared for the charity Nun Run.
Jonah would miss the day's festivities, as he left for Louisiana, with a small team of the Watchers' surveillance employees. The contractors thought that Saint was cheating on a wealthy wife, and that they would be tailing two adulterous men on a weekend in New Orleans.
With a plan in place to pick up Saint at the airport, the other Watchers could maintain their cover on the charity ride.
They followed their usual formality when the MC rode together, following a strict hierarchy for position in the convoy. As International President, Skull rode up front, with local President Brandon Knox at his side. Then followed the other international and local officers, followed by members without specific rank. At the back came

those accepted by the club, but who had not been awarded the Watchers' coveted three part back patch.

Despite his trusted position within the Watchers' businesses, Stone was not a full member of the MC, so took his usual position at the rear.

The Nun Run was an unusual spectacle. Barbara had already briefed the Watchers about the event. Started in 2012, the 50 mile ride from Houston to Galveston was started by another Harley Davidson riding nun, Sister Rosanne Popp. The 63 year old nun knew that bikers raised huge amounts for charity and hoped their generosity would extend to her order's Christus Foundation for Healthcare.

Despite having been around Sister Barbara Cuba for so long, Stone was still taken aback by the scene at the rally's start. The Christus Foundation's Houston Centre had been taken over by 250 bikers, from a whole range of backgrounds.

Rock bands played and bikers queued for the tattoo stall to commemorate their visit.

Health was also on the agenda, with the Christus Foundation offering flu shots to the assembled bikers.

Nuns of all ages moved among the bikers. But far from being intimidated by their black clad visitors, the nuns seemed excited by the whole occasion. Nuns jostled for spare pillion seats, where the riders had brought spare helmets for their passengers. Age was no bar, as 90 year old Sister Mary climbed into a sidecar, a black Harley

Davidson bandana fastened over her veil.

"This is too weird", thought Stone, as the 250 bike convoy formed up to leave.

Barbara had found kindred spirits in the few nuns who also rode motorcycles. "I wondered if I was the only one", she said to the nuns leading the pack.

Before long, the 250 motorcycles roared out of the hospital grounds, followed by a coach, carrying the rest of the nuns.

It took two hours for the bikers to cover their 50 miles to the Lone Star Flight Museum, in Galveston.

The Watchers moved though the historic aircraft exhibits with the other bikers. Above all they made sure that they featured prominently on the TV news coverage. That would help maintain their fiction of being on holiday in the States.

The whole Watchers convoy left Galveston together, for the ride back to Houston. Although, once out of sight of the rally festivities, Texas Sergeant at Arms, Randy Salt would lead Stone's group away from the main convoy. The plan was for Texas President Brandon Knox, to lead his Chapter back to Houston. While Salt would lead the visitors on the 300 mile ride into Louisiana.

Aside from Randy Salt, the two women were the only ones who had ridden through Louisiana before. Barbara and Amber rode side by side, shouting over the roar of their exhausts. Although Stone's gaze occasionally strayed to Amber, he was too taken by the scenery to engage in conversation. All the old songs of the south ran through his head, as they neared New Orleans.

Chapter 13.

While the Watchers were at the Nun Run, Jonah
and the Texas surveillance operatives had been
covering Saint's arrival at New Orleans' Louis
Armstrong Airport. Airport arrival halls are a
surveillance operative's dream. Crowds of people
to hide amongst, and your targets funnelled
through immigration towards you. So it was with
the arrival of Saint and his three friends. The team
picked them up easily as they cleared
immigration.
One of the team casually bumped into Saint,
placing a tiny tracking device in his pocket.
Jonah had hoped they would collect a hire car, so
a more powerful tracker could be placed. But a
car and driver were waiting outside for them, and
quickly left the terminal.
With their subject mobile, the team had to
scramble quickly for vehicles. The signal from the
small tracker would not carry far.
Two cars were already mobile, but those on foot
in the terminal had to race through the car park.
They would be too late to join the chase.
Saint's driver clearly knew the area, as the car
weaved in and out of traffic, always in the right
lane for an efficient manoeuvre. Despite their skill,
the driver's local knowledge defeated them and
Saint's car was lost. Now, the Watchers had to
hope the car could be found, or the weak tracker
signal could be picked up.

Early in the evening, the Watchers' motorcycles reached New Orleans. They chose to stay in the old French Quarter, mostly because of its beauty, but also to maintain their tourism cover story. The Americans could not know why they were there. Before Saint's plane came in, Jonah had identified an ideal base for them. It was a large hotel on the edge of the French Quarter, built in the traditional way, around a central courtyard, with a fountain. Its best feature for the Watchers was that the rooms were actually small apartments, with bedroom, lounge and kitchen. This would allow them the space to be inconspicuous and to run their operations. The ten Watchers were spread between five apartments in the hotel. The old and narrow corridors were like a maze, but the team soon gathered in Stone and Jonah's apartment. They had taken the biggest of the apartments, as this would double as their incident room. As always, the old school detectives quickly transformed their lounge into an incident room. The notes and photographs, which had already covered several previous walls, now featured on another one.

Amber had used her embassy contacts to put an APB on the car which had collected Saint. The car was registered to a fictitious address. Amber had claimed the driver was involved in Visa irregularities, so the terrorism conscious Americans would be on the look out. With no sign of the car, or signal from Saint's tracker, the Watchers headed into the old town. No one would visit New Orleans without seeing Bourbon Street. Stone hoped Saint and his friends would be tempted too.

Bourbon Street had just closed to cars as the Watchers arrived. New Orleans' most famous street took on a carnival atmosphere after dark. Much to the Watchers' delight, the street was not completely pedestrianised, as motorcycles were allowed access.

The motorcycles were far from ordinary, as they were some of the most highly chromed and shiny Harley Davidsons that Stone had ever seen. Most were adorned with a mass of additional lighting, reflecting from the polished chrome. "I'm not a Harley man", said Skull. "But even I'm impressed".

There had just been one of Louisiana's frequent downpours, and every one of the Harley riders had started to polish their bikes, the second the rain stopped.

The 80% humidity was stifling for the Portuguese Watchers, but for the English, it was close to unbearable.

Stone had taken the opportunity to chat with Amber. Despite his many years with Special Branch, Britain's overseas intelligence assets had never been his area. "In a way, it's a bit of a joke", explained Amber. "I'm here under Diplomatic Immunity, and everyone knows that Attaché equals Spook. But the real spying is done by agents here under fake identities. I'm more of a liaison with US Intelligence".

"So", asked Stone. "If you're so tight with the Cousins, why does Jonny Johnson trust you to keep quiet about us?"

Amber's smile led into a reply which Stone was not expecting. "Uncle Jonny has always trusted me". Despite trying not to mix business with pleasure, Stone was attracted to Amber. But with her Uncle being one of Britain's most respected spymasters, he knew he had to back off.

Ancient street cars trundled along their tracks through the French Quarter. Most had no glass in the windows, to allow some breeze to flow inside. All had peeling paint, as the humidity stripped them faster than the painters could keep up.

The Watchers marveled at scenes they had only seen before in old films. As they walked, they saw many of the bars and restaurants had verandas, overlooking Bourbon Street. Men sat on the verandas, tossing a steady hail of beads down to passing women.

Many of the women lifted their tops to catch the beads, sometimes exposing their bodies as they did so. Amber got in on the act, as the lovely blond was certainly noticed by the men above. She was not completely indiscreet though, as a vest worn under her blouse hid her modesty.

Barbara too was singled out for attention with the beads. But the nun would not lift her top. She politely acknowledged the attention with a smile, then walked on with her brother.

Stone was finding the culture shock intense. Jazz buskers, with trumpets and saxophone, played on every corner. More jazz flowed from the many bars. Voodoo shops advertised their strange wares.

Sex was openly sold, with women sat in open windows, and walking into the street to entice men inside. "I wonder if any of this involves Dimov, or O Lobo", thought Stone.

Barbara must have been having the same thought, as Stone watched her walk over to one of the women. Oddly, she was not at all phased at being approached by another woman. The hooker was enthusiastic about Barbara bringing all her friends into the house.

Stone watched as Barbara talked. He saw no leakage of fear or repression, as he had seen in most sex workers he encountered. The woman seemed to blend seamlessly with the Quarter's carnival atmosphere. Barbara realised she was getting nowhere and resolved to return earlier in the day, when the street was quieter.

The Watchers walked on, partially to take in the culture, but with an eye always open for Saint.

Jonah had stayed at the hotel, as he needed to coordinate their employees efforts in tracking Saint. The four surveillance operatives were now cris crossing the area in separate cars. The tiny tracker they had planted on Saint would only transmit for about 100 yards. So they were driving a pre-planned grid pattern in the hope of picking up a signal. All of the operatives thought it a lot of effort for an unfaithful husband. But they were being well paid and would try their hardest to please the Watchers.

While the operatives drove their grids, Jonah took a call from Jonny Johnson. With evidence that Dimov was involved with the Cuban connection, Jonny had been able to use MI5 resources. Dimov and O Lobo were both responsible for many of the women trafficked into Britain, so Jonny could investigate them, without showing his nuclear cards.

"I think we can be pretty sure they have plutonium Jonah", said Jonny. "The empty cases Stone found are the right type for the R-12 missile, and Dimov is certainly connected".

Jonny went on to explain that he had been tracking down some of the retired agent handlers from the Cold War years. Although the Cuban Missile Crisis was only in the public eye for 13 days, it actually played out behind the scenes for much longer.

One of the most sensitive of sources within Soviet Intelligence was Oleg Penkovsky, a double agent in the GRU working for CIA and MI6, who reported the Soviet plans and even provided details of the missile placements, which were eventually verified by U-2 flights.

"I've found Penkovsky's MI6 handler", said Jonny. "It was mention of Dimov that got him interested. Not Georgi, but his father, Vasil Dimov". The ageing spy had told Jonny about an officer within the Soviet Intourist organisation, who was well respected by Penkovsky.

Intourist was the branch of Soviet Intelligence which spied on visitors to the Soviet Union. Dimov Senior had a particular specialism, he organised elaborately baited honey traps, to compromise visitors.

"Penkovsky's handler told me the GRU used Vasil in Cuba, to get leverage amongst Castro's advisors". Fidel Castro initially objected to the missiles deployment, for fear he would look like a Soviet puppet, but was persuaded that missiles in Cuba would be an irritant to the US and help the interests of the entire socialist camp.

"So, Jonny Lad", replied Jonah. "At least one of Castro's team was caught in flagrante and persuaded Castro to get into bed with Khrushchev".

"It certainly looks that way Jonah", replied Jonny. "And if Dimov's father was so involved in the Missile Crisis, it's safe to bet junior has made use of daddy's contacts".

There was still no update from the surveillance team, and the Watchers had seen no sign of Saint. Stone also had a receiver capable of detecting Saint's tracker, so they continued on the tourist trail.

Their next stop was an old haunt of Louis Armstrong, the Preservation Hall. Less grand than its name suggests, it is an old, run down front room, which is entered from an alley. An old man sat at the door counting people in and out for occupancy limits.

The crowd was squeezed in with, cushions on floor, benches behind, then standing room at the back. The whole room was lit by a single central light. Stone had to squint to read the notice board near the stage "$2 traditional, $5 other, $10

Saints". "What's that?" he asked Amber, pointing at the sign.

"It's the Request Board", she replied. "The musicians are so sick of playing 'When the saints go marching on' that they charge extra for it".

They had not been settled long, when the band came on. A bunch of ageing men playing: trumpet, piano, sax, drums and euphonium. It was the closest Stone had come to feeling on holiday since they left Portugal. He was relaxing in Amber's company, he had his brothers around him, and "who doesn't like jazz"?

While Stone, Amber, Barbara and Miguel were enjoying the Preservation Hall, Skull had taken the rest of the team down to the Mississippi. The riverside was the second favourite tourist draw, behind Bourbon Street, so Skull hoped Saint may show up at one of the river's many restaurants. But Skull also needed to see the river itself. The Mississippi delta starts in Gulf of Mexico, where Float planes are the main form of transport. Then, the delta turns into river, heading towards the modern high rise metropolis of New Orleans. The route into Louisiana for Saint's plutonium could be by sea, or air. The Watchers desperately needed to know which.

Skull sat with his brothers, drinking weak American beer and looking out across the biggest river he had ever seen. The huge river was also winding, up and round, then up and round again. Close by, the river busy with small boats, further out, he could see cargo ships in the distance.

Refineries dominated the skyline further down river, with ugly industrial buildings on the quay. As Skull watched a huge container ship, with multi coloured containers stacked on its deck, sail by, Jonah spoke into his earpiece. The old detective had been watching the feed from skull's tiny body cam, and started to give him some river information. "Well, Skull lad, the river sees about 6000 ships every year. There is so much river trade, that the port of New Orleans is 15 miles long. The currents are so strong; they can sink a small boat in about 30 seconds. There's less than 5% chance for a man over board."

"So, old man", replied Skull. "I'm sure you've got a big revelation to follow all that interesting information".

Jonah did, as usual, have a theory. "Float plane is a possibility, Skull lad. But it would still need putting on a small boat to come up river. With the danger to small craft, I favour one of the bigger cargo ships".

Skull thought for a moment, then replied, "6000 ships a year, equals about 16 every day. Which ones do we watch?"

"That, Skull lad, is something for Amber to help us with". Jonah would use Amber's contacts to access shipping manifests for the port. From them, they could narrow down the likely ships.

Jonah left the radio to phone Amber for help with the manifests. Skull and his crew were getting hungry, so went off in search of food. The bikers were spoiled for choice. Cafes and restaurants lined the riverside. The food all looked delicious, a mix of Cajun and Creole.

Oddly for a biker, Skull had an old Carpenters song going through his head. "Jambalaya, Crawfish pie, Filet gumbo. Cause tonight I'm gonna see my ma cher amio. Pick guitar, fill fruit jar and be gay-o. Son of a gun, we'll have big fun on the bayou." Skull spotted the Bubba Gump restaurant and said, "come on, let's see if Forest Gump can get Karen Carpenter out of my head". The themed Restaurant was based on the shrimp business from the Tom Hanks movie and the bikers all ordered mud bugs, or crayfish as they are better known outside Louisiana.

Amber needed to leave the Preservation Hall to get her office busy accessing shipping manifests, for cargoes heading in from the Gulf. Stone left with her. Amber was beautiful and easy company. But Stone was also intrigued to learn something of how the Secret Intelligence Service worked within America.

Amber continued the cover story begun by her uncle. She maintained that Britain had an interest in Carlos Lobo and Georgi Dimov's drug network. "The manifests will be e-mailed before morning", said Amber. "Fancy walking me home? We've a lot to do tomorrow".

It was not long before the other Watchers followed Stone and Amber back through the French Quarter, to their hotel. The Watchers would party hard when they could, but they had important work to do.

Chapter 14.

Amber's team at the Embassy were true to their word. Before the Watchers had woken, the shipping manifests were in her e-mail box. "That's a job for Uncle Jonny", thought Amber. His senior position in the Security Service had the clout to task skilled analysts with making sense of the manifests.

Amber, along with the Watchers, was needed for a job on the ground. Their operatives were still tasked with searching for Saint's tracking device, and had been sleeping in their vehicles. That left 15 miles of port area that needed covering. This was today's job for the Watchers.

The 11 Watchers could not thoroughly cover 15 miles of river. So, Stone and Jonah had to come up with a plan.

Analysis of the shipping manifests, when it arrived, would help. But, until then they needed eyes on the port. The Watchers' default tactic is to place remote cameras, but they had not brought enough to cover such a huge area. Which was where oilfield troubleshooter, Red Andrews, started to prove his worth. Remote cameras are routinely used in the oil industry, both for security and to watch critical parts of the drilling process. Red knew there would be plenty of cameras in stock with his contacts throughout the Southern States. These would be on their way to New Orleans, by fast courier service.

With Jonah running their improvised control room,

10 bikers headed towards the Mississippi. The bikers had split into pairs, to cover more ground. Miguel would not let his sister ride without him. So, with no other women to ride with, Amber chose to pair up with Stone.

After a night in the historic French Quarter, Stone was surprised at how modern and industrialised the rest of New Orleans was. Although the scenery was less pretty, Stone was still enjoying the feel of his motorcycle. In Louisiana's high humidity, the cooling breeze created by the ride, was especially welcome.

Stone had always been impressed with the way Barbara handled a motorcycle. He saw that Amber was handling her Buell Lightening just as expertly, showing herself to be a very experienced rider. Her street fighter motorcycle was based around a 1200cc Harley Davidson, but it was in a much higher state of tune, and with more agile running gear.

Stone had to work hard to stay with her. His Scrambler had only a 900cc engine, and was a much less sporty bike. But his advanced police training put him beyond the ability of most civilian riders, so he was not working so hard that he could not admire Amber's figure hugging motorcycle leathers.

"Concentrate on the bridges", advised Jonah over the radios. He was watching the camera feeds from five pairs of helmet cameras.

The miles of concrete river walls and industrialised docklands looked to busy for the few cameras they had with them. But the many bridges, like huge Mechano sets with their framework of girders overhead, provided ideal sites to cover large stretches of river.

Stone and Amber were approaching one of the bridges as they recovered Jonah's message. Vehicles were not allowed to stop on the bridges, so they pulled up on the dockside to prepare a camera and plan how to fit it.
"High in the framework will give us the best view", said Amber.
Stone was surprised at the suggestion, as he had envisaged a quick installation, close to the bridge's guard rail. "How will we get it up there quickly", he asked.
Stone knew little of Amber's background, and it turned out that she had some very useful skills to offer. "I was a REME Captain before Uncle Jonny recruited me into the Service, and I've always been good with heights".
Stone knew that time spent in the British Army's, Royal Electrical and Mechanical Engineers made Amber the ideal person to fit the camera. With this revelation, their plan soon came together. Amber would ride on Stone's pillion, with the camera ready in her jacket. While Stone kept the bike running, Amber would scale the girders, fit the camera and descend quickly to the waiting motorcycle.
Even knowing Amber's history, Stone was still surprised at how quickly the lithe, former soldier scaled the girders. Her controlled slide down was even faster and they were soon riding back to where she had parked her Buell. "Oh oh", said

Amber, looking over her shoulder.

Just as they left the bridge and hit the port road, a Harbour Police scooter turned after them. "Looks like I was spotted on the bridge", added Amber.

"Hold on", replied Stone, as he opened up the Triumph. Stone stopped momentarily, as Amber jumped onto her own machine. Then with a roar of her high performance exhaust, she powered after Stone.

Thankful for his foresight in covering their number plates with dirt, Stone and Amber quickly lost the smaller engined Police scooter.

"Let's hope they don't spot the camera", said Stone.

Amber's reply was a confident one. "They will have to climb up to find it. I've hidden it well". Stone hoped that the cop would not see beyond the motorcycles and daredevil climbing.

With 6000 ships per year and all their Homeland Security considerations to worry about, the Harbour Police's 62 officers would easily write off the incident as adrenalin seeking bikers.

The other Watchers had also placed their cameras. None had been as athletic as Amber, but they all provided views, either from bridges, or the apex of bends in the river.

Jonah looked at the camera feeds with satisfaction. Together, the five cameras gave reasonable coverage of everything coming up the Mississippi. "Looking good from here lads", said Jonah, over the radios. "Can you regroup and head north. The guys got a faint signal on Saint's tracker, close to the Evergreen Plantation".

At their peak, there were close to 400 plantations In Louisiana. Most grew sugar, or white gold, as it was called at the time. Today, the Evergreen plantation is one of few still working, and doubles as a tourist attraction.

By the time they left the city limits, all 10 bikes were together and riding in convoy. As always, the MC had organised itself into rank order. Skull and Randy led, with Butler and Alva behind. Then came the more junior members, followed by Stone and the two women.

Stone was highly thought of by the MC, and indispensable to their business interests. But he was not a patch holder, so had to fall into place when they rode together.

It did not matter how important their mission, the Watchers always enjoyed riding as a group. As soon as they left the city and headed into rural Louisiana, all the bikers relaxed into the ride. They had to move quickly, before Saint had chance to leave the area. But there is nothing more soothing to a biker, than riding through beautiful countryside with your brothers.

The surveillance team had been told to maintain a perimeter, in case Saint's signal moved. The Watchers wanted to go in themselves, as their employees still thought this was a missing person investigation.

After checking with the team, the Watchers rode onto the plantation. Without any official sanction, they still had to maintain their tourist cover. Which, with the plantation open to visitors, seemed an easy thing to do.

The 10 motorcycles rode into the visitors' car park, which, to help with the estate's aesthetics was quite a distance from the main house. The Watchers headed out on foot, again split into the same pairs they had earlier worked in.

Working their way in from the car park, the first thing Stone came across were the Slave Cabins. "Nicely out of sight from the house", commented Stone. The tracker signal was still very weak, so he and Amber paused to read the tourist information at the cabins.

They were built by the slaves, from Cyprus trees harvested from the swamp. Their work made harder by the lack of power tools. They read that, at the abolition of slavery, four million slaves were technically free, but had nowhere to go. Many carried on living in this type of cabin until the 1940s with no power or running water. Stone and Amber satisfied themselves there was nothing but tourist interest in the cabins, then moved on, following the signal.

The Watchers all reached the great house at much the same time, having found nothing of interest in the grounds. The weak tracker signal was strongest here, but was still much weaker than they would expect.

The house was more stately than Stone had come to expect in the US. The Southern States seemed to have a history all their own. Outside the house, grand curved staircases flowed to the ground, almost giving the house wings. Its high position gave the house a fabulous view of the great river. But it was also built high to avoid flood and to allow breeze from the river to cool the house.

Despite being able to wander, almost at will, around the grounds, the house was obviously not open to the public. The chain link fence around the house was ornamental and did not detract from its grandeur. But the guns which Stone occasionally saw carried by the guards were not in keeping with the plantation being a tourist attraction. "They don't look very Cajun", said Stone.

"No", replied Skull. "More Eastern Europe, I would say". Stone and Skull had caught passing glimpses of the guards, as they walked across windows. They did not have the black skin of the Creoles, or the tanned faces of the Cajuns. Their Slavic appearance suggested that Dimov and O Lobo might have significant influence here.

There was nothing the Watchers could do in daylight, with so many guards on patrol. So they decided to withdraw, leaving their surveillance operatives in place. If Saint was in the big house, he would have to leave at some point, to be picked up by the team. They would need to be vigilant though, as the tracker was in Saint's jacket pocket. His linen jacket was fine in the air conditioned airport, but in the heat and humidity of New Orleans, he was unlikely to wear it.

There was nothing more the Watchers could do, until either Saint was spotted, or Jonny came through with some intelligence, so the 10 bikers mounted up and started the ride back to New Orleans. It was time for another session with Jonah's incident boards, in the hope of making a new connection.

As they neared the French Quarter, their ride was interrupted by a surprising and colourful sight. Black men dressed in white jackets, black hats and black ties, led a horse drawn hearse. Behind them followed a brass band playing lively jazz and brightly dressed women, dancing excitedly to the music. This was a Jazz Funeral, a tradition from a time when death was a welcome release from slavery.

The early Creole's believed that dancing cut the body loose from its earthly bonds.

With nowhere they could go in a hurry, the Watchers put down their motorcycle stands and danced along side the bikes. The bikers always love a party, and with Barbara and Amber looking so good in their leathers, they were getting almost as much attention as the funeral parade. Many of the bystanders joined in the Watchers' impromptu dance. It made an unusual spectacle, local Creole people, dancing side by side with an outlaw MC.

In its own time, the funeral passed and the Watchers were able to get to their debrief with Jonah.

Riding into the French Quarter was like riding into a different country. The colonial architecture was very different to the more modern city. Greenery hung from the balconies, reminding Stone of the Hanging Gardens of Babylon. But beyond even the buildings, the old town had its own, unique feel.

The walls of Jonah's improvised briefing room now had much more information covering them. He had maps of the port area, and of the plantation. Jonny's analysis of the shipping had arrived, and Jonah had added the best possibilities to the wall.

"Nothing birthed in Cuba", began Jonah. "But we have nine which passed close enough, in the right time frame". Jonah had added details and photographs of the nine ships to his incident wall. He had also ordered them into where he thought their priorities should lie.

"Ok Jonah", began Stone. "Rationalise your thinking for us".

"Well Nev lad", replied Jonah. "We don't think O Lobo has any links with the Orient. So I've discounted China, Japan, Taiwan and Korea. That leaves; Britain, Germany, Portugal and two returning American ships." Jonah rationalised that with America being the likely target, he thought the European ships demanded their first attention. The Portuguese ship was the obvious, if not too obvious, choice.

Between Amber's Embassy contacts and Jonny's MI6 Analysts, they knew which births the three European ships would birth at. All were due within the next few hours, so the Watchers hurried to prepare the cameras which Red Andrews had obtained for them.

When the cameras were ready, the Watchers divided into three teams, to cover the three dock areas. It was getting into early evening, so they were unsure whether the ships would unload tonight, or in the morning. Either way, their cameras needed to be in place before the first of the ships docked.

After Stone and Amber had been chased from the docks, the Watchers had to be more discrete this time. Motorcycles were parked away from the areas they needed to work. They would use less athletic methods of fitting the cameras than Amber had employed.

This type of work was an easy bread and butter task for the Watchers. They had all spent many years in security, either in service to their governments, or in private enterprise. Casually placing tiny cameras was something they could easily achieve without being noticed. Their cameras would capture anything coming off the three suspect ships, but they could not tell if Plutonium was present, by use of cameras alone. Stone, Skull and Butler were all equipped with sensitive radiation detectors. When Jonah spotted anything of interest being unloaded, one of them would have to get in close with a detector.

The British vessel was the first into dock, in plenty of time for the Stevedores to begin unloading its cargo. Like any large cargo ship, this one contained a variety of different goods. Some of the containers were marked with warnings of chemical content. Others held confectionary items, including the products of Britain's famed chocolatiers. Ironically for the Watchers, the final containers to be unloaded were from England's Triumph motorcycle factory. "We could have had some new bikes shipped in", said Stone over his radio. He did not expect, or get a reply, as he had to move quickly, but stealthily through the unloaded containers.

Stone's radiation detector picked up nothing to suggest Plutonium was hidden within the cargo. The German and Portuguese ships came in soon behind the British one. But they were both too late for that day's shift to unload them. They would sit in port, awaiting the next day's Stevedores.

Chapter 15.

After a good night's sleep, the Watchers headed back to the docks to cover the next two ships unloading.

Red Andrews and Randy Salt, however, took off alone. Elements of local knowledge and some studying of Google Earth were playing on their minds. It had taken a lot of work to single out these three ships for attention, but Andrews and Salt had nagging doubts that they had missed something.

All the Watchers' assumptions had been based on transfer to a smaller boat inside the Mississippi delta would be dangerous. Suggesting the smugglers would unload in the Port of New Orleans. But Salt knew the Louisiana swamps had been used to hide contraband for centuries. If it was feasible to offload the Plutonium early, then it could now be in the swamps. The dangers of a small boat in the Mississippi's fast flowing water might be preferable to being caught with nuclear material.

Randy Salt had exercised in the swamps several times in the U.S. marines and the Navy Seals and knew how difficult it could be to track smugglers. Red Andrews was also acquainted with the swamps, as he had conducted surveys for the oil companies. In the event of a major spill, Red needed to know how to move his heavy equipment around quickly.

Since 1960, oil and gas exploration had increased dramatically In the Louisiana swamps.

Nowhere was this more noticeable than the Atchafalaya Basin, where large access and pipeline canals were dredged through deep swamp and bayou. No other swamp, anywhere in the world, has as many oil and gas access canals as the Atchafalaya River Basin. This gave Red a huge head start in understanding the Atchafalaya Swamp, but he had studied it for large scale access. Small smugglers vessels would be a different matter entirely.

Andrews and Salt had been studying charts provided by one of the oil companies, along with some that Amber had managed to get from US law enforcement. Together, these charts gave a good overview of the area, but they still wanted more detail. So the two bikers had gone out with Jonah's motor home, loaded with two of the Watchers' most sophisticated aerial drones. The tiny, four rotor helicopters, could cover vast areas, allowing them to cover ground much faster than by road or boat.

The sparsely inhabited Basin is about 20 miles across, from east to west and 150 miles north to south. The Watchers knew they did not need to cover the whole 150 miles, but even reducing it to the stretch south of Baton Rouge, there was a vast expanse.

The drones were their best tool, as few roads crossed the basin, and those that do, rely on levees and bridges.

Andrews and Salt were using Interstate 10 as their northern boundary. Interstate 10 crosses the basin on an 18 mile bridge of elevated pillars, from Grosse Tete to Henderson. Driving along this long bridge, allowed them a platform to fly the drones across the full width of the swamp. The southern end of the Basin has far fewer roads, but Red Andrews was working on a solution to that problem.

As they flew their drones from the Interstate 10 Bridge, Andrews talked through his thoughts about the Basin. The Atchafalaya River is formed near Simmesport, about 80 miles north of Baton Rouge, where the Red River joins the Mississippi. The Mississippi connects to the Red River by a 7-mile canal, called the Old River. Through the Old River Control Structure It takes roughly 30% of the water of the lower Mississippi. Although in times of extreme flooding the Morganza Spillway further downstream puts more Mississippi water into the Atchafalaya. It is only the system of levees, banks and locks, which stops the Mississippi and the Atchafalaya merging into one.

"All very interesting Red", said Randy Salt. "But how does that make it worth our attention".

"The river is navigable", replied Andrews. "We've been putting all our eggs in the Mississippi, but the Atchafalaya is navigable, and has easy access to the swamps".

As Salt watched the video feed from his drone, he started to realise the point his friend was making. "That's a lot of area to cover Red".

Both men knew they would need the planning skills of Stone and Jonah to decide where to go next.

While Andrews and Salt were flying their drones, the other Watchers' attention was on the remaining two ships at the port. The German ship was a car transporter, loaded with Mercedes and BMW cars, destined for affluent southerners. Stone passed closely among the rows of parked cars, with not a murmur from his radiation monitor. "It's no surprise really", thought Stone. "O Lobo has powerful friends, but not to the level of multi national car companies".

He then turned his attention to the Portuguese ship. "This one makes more sense, Nev lad", said Jonah, over Stone's earpiece. "It's a more downmarket boat, and from the right country". Stone agreed with Jonah's assessment. The ship was not quite a tramp boat, but neglect was taking it down that route. It was just the thing to be part of O Lobo's narcotics business.

It did not take long for the stevedores to unload the Portuguese cargo. "Is that it?" asked Skull, as the pile of timber grew on the dockside.

With no major manufacturing industry, it was to be expected that agricultural products would be the cargo. But there was not enough for the voyage to have been profitable.

"We've got to be onto something here", said Stone, as he and Skull moved forward with their detectors. "There's something more than that timber paying for that ship".

"Not a sniff", said Skull, when they had finished their sweep. "What are we missing Nev?"

Everything was pointing to this being the transport for the Plutonium. But their advanced radiation detectors had found nothing.

Despite their skill and care, the Watchers had been spotted checking out the cargo.

The superstitious Captain had been on high alert since his dalliance with the Bermuda Triangle. Just sailing through the Triangle made him nervous. But, using the fog machine frightened him. The Captain believed that such things would anger the mysterious forces inside the Triangle. Fearing bad luck bringing disaster on his ship and crew, the Captain watched constantly for anything out of place. This was how he noticed Stone and Skull carrying pieces of equipment he had never seen before. Realising they were not New Orleans stevedores, the Captain photographed them. O Lobo would be interested in anyone showing interest in his ship.

The Portuguese ship was soon unloaded, refuelled and sailing south towards the Mississippi Delta. For all their attention to detail, the Watchers had not seen the two plutonium spheres come ashore.

They had considered the Delta and lower reaches of the Mississippi too dangerous for smaller craft. So, they thought it much more likely the smugglers would use the port.

But, O Lobo could be much more frightening than the river. Particularly when he used voodoo superstition against the local Creoles. It had not been difficult to find a boat crew willing to take the risk. A small boat had met the ship, long before it came onto the Watchers' radar. The Captain had reversed the procedure he used off the coast of the Bahamas. With an artificial cloud masking his ship, the valuable cargo had been lowered over the side, to the Creole smugglers. Then, the fast RIB had shot away, out of the Mississippi Delta, and along the coast towards the Atchafalaya Delta. The Watchers would have to work much harder to find the Captain's deadly cargo.

All the Watchers regrouped back at their hotel in the French Quarter. The incident room wall in Jonah's apartment now contained even more content. For all their efforts, they were not much further towards locating the bombs or the plutonium.
Jonah began his briefing by summing up their three key objectives. Find Matthew Saint, find the bombs and find the plutonium. He then added to that the side issues of identifying the money behind the plot, and any potential target. "So", he said. "We still have our hands full. I suggest the plute should be our priority. Without that, Saint's bomb don't go bang".
Everyone agreed and they ran through the options they already had.
Skull briefed them on the Evergreen Plantation. Saint's tracking device had been detected deep inside the Plantation's grand house. The house also had far more security than it warranted, and the men appeared to be Dimov's. "It's possible that Saint, the bomb and the plute are already there", concluded Skull.

Stone spoke about the European ships he had covered at the Port. None of the European ships had set of their radiation detectors and all but the

152

Portuguese ship appeared legitimate.
Stone was still suspicious that such a small cargo
had warranted a transatlantic journey.
"Either we missed it at the Port", concluded
Stone. "Or, it was unloaded earlier, or they got
spooked and it's still on board.

Red Andrews summarised his and Randy's
excursion to the Atchafalaya Basin.
"We've found nothing concrete", said Andrews.
"But if I had anything to hide, that would be the
place. You can get a decent sized boat up from
the Delta, and then there are miles of swamp to
hide in".

"So", said Stone. Our best shots are the
Plantation, the Mississippi, or the Atchafalaya.
Each one alone is a massive area, with 10 of us
to cover them. What do you suggest?, a game of
rock, paper, scissors?"
"Oh Nev lad", replied Jonah. "It's more serious
than that. What about Stone, paper, bomb?"
Most of the group chuckled, as they usually did at
Jonah's humour. But Stone was glad to see a
sign that his mentor was still relaxed enough to
joke.

True to form, the veteran detective did have a
plan. "We have containment on the Plantation",
began Jonah. "We can place some radiation
monitors as sentries on the access roads. Those,
added to your surveillance teams, should keep
that on ice for us".
Then, Jonah moved on to the Portuguese ship.

"There is nothing there to embarrass Her Majesty. It's a Portuguese ship, the plute is from Cuba, and Dimov has his hands dirty. So there is no British connection to worry about ". Jonah asked Amber to arrange for drugs, and people tracking intelligence to be passed to US authorities. With O Lobo suspected to be involved in drugs, or Cuban refugees, there was a reasonable expectation for law enforcement interest. Amber's intervention would ensure a coastguard or DEA boarding.

That left the whole team to concentrate on the Atchafalaya Basin.

The Watchers divided to start the next phase of their search. Red Andrews was to play a key part in two of the next actions. Andrews' phone rang, just in time to brief the team that his latest surprise had arrived. Since he and Randy Salt had been flying drones across the Basin, he knew they would need a better way to cover the vast wilderness.

Right on cue, one of his oil company contacts had come through, and a helicopter was waiting for them, just outside New Orleans. Andrews had also been using his role as an oil troubleshooter towards searching the swamps. He had engaged one of the air boat tour companies, to assist him with a new survey. Now they had a helicopter for the Atchafalaya delta, and southern section of the river. Then, for the northern swamps, they had airboats and local guides.

They were now well prepared to continue the

search for plutonium. But they were no further towards finding Matthew Saint, or figuring out what it all meant. Barbara had been giving this part of the dilemma some thought.

"The church angle just doesn't sit right", said Barbara. "I've no doubt that Saint is genuinely devout in his beliefs, but he is not from a faith known for extremism. Then, add in the Americans' involvement with the Seventh Day Adventists in Aldermaston, and I have a real puzzle". Barbara had spent her entire life around religion. Her parents were missionaries, she and Miguel attended a monastery school, and she had been a nun though all her adult years. She knew religion fitted somewhere, but she could not join the dots. "I think it's time Miguel and I went under cover again", she suggested.

Jonah readily agreed. He too had been doing some internet research and could not make sense of how a peaceful church could be involved with nuclear weapons.

While Barbara, Miguel and Jonah discussed how best to investigate the church angle, the others headed for the Atchafalaya Basin. Randy Salt was a helicopter pilot, and had some knowledge of the area, so he led the helicopter team.

Skull went with Salt to the helicopter. He had excellent eyesight, which would aid their aerial search. But, as President of the MC, the overhead position was ideal for him to keep an overview of all the operation.

Red Andrews led his bogus survey team, of; Stone, Amber and Harris.

The two Sergeants at Arms had been held back as a contingency. The Watchers had their employees staking out the Evergreen Plantation for Saint, and a quick response could be needed. Also, they had Miguel and Barbara going undercover, and they could need extracting. Former Royal Marine Steve Butler and the giant Joao Alva were ideal for this role. Both were weapons experts and neither of them ever showed outward signs of fear.

Andrews' team was soon in play, when they reached the tour company at Mcgees Landing. They had to brief the air boat pilots on the needs of their survey. Andrews had to work under the guise of preparing for an oil clean up, but they needed to cover as much of the swamp as they could.

To fit with their cover story, Amber was to play an environmental specialist. Her need to collect soil, plant and water samples would provide a reason to get away from the oil pipelines and infrastructure. "I hope I can remember enough to satisfy the bayou men", said Amber. She had studied environmental factors as an Army Engineer. The exceptionally bright young woman had also spent the previous evening bringing her self up to date. But the guides they would be working with had grown up in the swamps. Amber was also looking forward to seeing the swamp's wildlife. Snakes, turtles, raccoons, rabbits, opossums, armadillos, squirrels, foxes, coyotes and deer could be found in the Atchafalaya Basin. The furry creatures were at the top of Amber's must see list.

Chapter 16.

Sister Barbara Cuba and her brother Miguel had left the hotel to begin their work with the Louisiana church groups. The beautiful young nun was able to put anyone with faith at ease.

European colonisation of Louisiana began with Spanish and French settlers. They brought their Catholic faith with them, accounting for the 28% of the population still being Catholic.

Matthew Saint and his friends did not fit within the 28%, but the infrastructure of her own religion gave Barbara a good place to start.

Barbara and Miguel began their enquiries at The Cathedral-Basilica of Saint Louis, King of France, more commonly called, St. Louis Cathedral. St Louis' is the seat of the Archdiocese of New Orleans and among the oldest cathedrals in the United States.

The first church on the site was built in 1718, with the cathedral expanded and largely rebuilt in 1850.

When Barbara's enquiries moved beyond the Catholic Church, she would consider wearing her nun's clothing. But the motorcycle riding nun, with an influential role at the United Nations, was well known within her own church. She and Miguel felt free to visit St Louis' on their motorcycles. Miguel had left behind his leather vest, with the Watchers MC patches. As a none member, Barbara could not wear the MC colours, so as always, rode in her figure hugging leather suit.

Saint Louis Cathedral is in the French Quarter, in an area obvious by its street names, as a place of religious significance. The cathedral is on Place John Paul II, a promenaded street that stretches between Rue Saint-Pierre and Rue Sainte-Anne. Barbara and Miguel we're glad to be back on their bikes. The intense humidity made New Orleans unpleasant for the Europeans, and the breeze from the ride was very pleasant.

Their ride through the French Quarter towards the Mississippi and the cathedral was especially pleasant for the historic buildings they passed. St Louis' faces the river, next to Jackson Square. It is one of the few Roman Catholic churches in the United States that fronts a major public square. All around are colonial era buildings, such as the Cabildo and the Presbytère.

Parking was difficult around the cathedral, but not for Barbara and Miguel's motorcycles.

As she climbed off her bike, she looked around in wonder at the beauty of her religion's history. Even Miguel, who had lost his faith while still a schoolboy, could not help but be impressed at the magnificence of the whole area. "They really don't build anything like this anymore, do they sis?" asked Miguel.

"No", replied Barbara. "There was a time when a building meant more to the developers than just a profit".

The Archbishop himself walked out of Saint Louis' to meet Barbara and Miguel. Through Barbara's work with the UN, combating sex trafficking,

Barbara had met most of the world's senior clergy. With Bourbon Street's thriving sex trade, she had been a regular visitor to New Orleans. "Sister Barbara, it's so good of you to visit", began the Archbishop. "What brings you back to New Orleans?"

"Thank you for making time to see us, your grace", replied Barbara, as she bowed to kiss the Archbishop's sacred ring.

Miguel also bowed slightly, in reverence to the Archbishop's position, but he politely stepped away as the ring was offered.

Barbara had rehearsed her cover story. The Archbishop was well acquainted with the Good Shepherd Sisters' work against O Lobo and Georgi Dimov. She could legitimately report that Dimov's men had been seen in the area. Where Barbara's story strayed from the truth, was the possible involvement of other church groups. Barbara explained her interest by telling the Archbishop about O Lobo's propensity for turning inter-faith suspicion into a cover for his criminal activities.

Carlos Lobo had learned how to turn religion to his advantage when he was a spymaster for the Portuguese Dictator Salazar. The rural Portuguese were always quick to follow any instruction they thought had come from Catholic clergy. Then, when he teamed up with Georgi Dimov's Bulgarian criminals, O Lobo used the countries shared Christianity to draw in the women who he trafficked to Western Europe. With the Archbishop's help, Barbara could gain the confidence of the Baptist's, Adventist's and numerous other religious groups in the State. She could then hope to get closer to Matthew Saint and his friends.

They followed the Archbishop through the magnificent cathedral, to his office. Despite the historic nature of his religious dress and the public face of his role, the Archbishop was a very modern church leader. As befits the regional head of a huge international organisation, his office was a very modern workspace.

Throughout two centuries of conquest, persecution and peace, the Catholic Church had developed an intelligence structure to rival many sovereign states. Which is in fact what the Vatican is, a small, but fiercely independent city state in Italy, with its ambassadors spread throughout the world. It was into this extensive intelligence system, that the Archbishop's powerful computers began to delve, searching for anything that could help Barbara in her work.

Every religious organisation in Louisiana appeared on his screens, from the mainstream, to the down right loopy.

The Archbishop's extensive knowledge of his area helped Barbara and Miguel make sense of the States many congregations.

New Orleans' colonial history of French and Spanish settlement resulted in a strong Catholic tradition. Catholic missions administered to slaves and free people of colour, establishing schools for them. Then, in the late 19th and early 20th century European immigrants, such as the Irish,

Germans, and Italians arrived in Louisiana. Some of these were Catholic, but many followed a Protestant form of Christianity. Although 60% of the State's population declared themselves Protestant, they were far from being a single congregation.

Unlike Catholicism, which has largely remained a unified church, Protestants fragmented into a multitude of smaller churches. Some of these churches arrived with the European immigrants. But many grew out of a fledgling American population exploring its own identity. Many of these new churches were born in America's North East in the early 19th Century. Upstate New York was a hotbed of revival, which ignited movements such as the Shakers, Mormons, Jehovah's Witnesses, the Millerites and a host of eccentric offshoots. So great was the growth of evangelical movements, that the area was dubbed the "burned-over district," because evangelists had exhausted the supply of unconverted people.

Listening to the Archbishop lecture on America's religious history, Miguel remembered some of the old magazines and pamphlets they had found in Matthew Saint's room.

"What can you tell us about the Millerites, your grace", asked Miguel.

The Archbishop was in his element, having an audience so interested in his country's rich Christian history. "They are Adventists", replied the Archbishop, explaining that they believed in a second coming of Jesus Christ. William Miller was a prosperous New York farmer, and Baptist lay preacher. His teachings of a second advent

gained favour in the early 19th century, developing a sizeable following.
Reverend Miller interpreted the bible and calculated when the second coming of the Lord would happen. He taught that Jesus would come again, cleanse, purify, and take possession of the earth, with all the saints, sometime between March 21st, 1843 and March 21st 1844. Miller spread his teachings though the prolific publication of articles and magazines, many of which Miguel had seen in Saint's collection.
"But", continued the Archbishop, "he fell out of favour when 1854 passed without a second coming. It became known as the Great Disappointment".

"So, you are saying the Millerites are long gone?" asked Barbara.
"Everyone thought so", replied the Archbishop. "Over time, the issue of a precise date got watered down, and the Millerites became the Seventh Day Adventists.
But, the Archbishop's intelligence network had been watching the activities of a group of young Seventh Day Adventists. "We think they are on the rise again", said the Archbishop. He explained that the Seventh Day Adventists were very much a young people's movement when they formed in 1860. Key to the growth of the Adventists were husband and wife James and Ellen White. Who at 23 and 16 were very young to have influence in a society which placed little value on youth and marginalized women and ethnic minorities.

The White's pioneering group was all in their teens, or twenties. Many of them were women, or blacks. Ellen White was largely responsible for her church's move away from white, middle aged men. Known for her visions, Ellen was recognised as a prophet, inspired by God.

"But what has that got to do with modern New Orleans, your Grace?" asked Barbara.
"There is a new Ellen White, Sister Barbara", replied the Archbishop. Her followers believe she is a reincarnation of the original, and a growing number of Adventists and Baptists are moving over to her church. Like their predecessors, they call themselves Millerites".
The mention of Ellen White, with whom Saint was travelling, got their attention. But it was the Archbishop's next revelation which made the hair stand up on both of the Cuba's necks. "Her teachings centre on the book of Revelation", said the Archbishop. "Particularly around the idea of the Millennium".
Barbara and Miguel both recognised the significance of what they had just been told. They needed to get as much information as they could from the Archbishop, but both were desperate to get back to the Watchers with their news.
Barbara and Miguel both knew about the book of Revelation, and it's teaching about the Millennium, but they were both interested in the Archbishop's take on it, and what he knew of Ellen White's interpretation. The Archbishop explained that White's teachings mixed the book of Revelation, with parts of other books, such as:

Thessalonians, John and Hebrews.

"She speaks of Christ and his army riding out of heaven on white horses at the start of the millennium", said the Archbishop. "Then, with the trumpet call of God, the righteous will be resurrected, and together with resurrected Saints, will rise to meet the Lord in the air."

He continued to explain that in Thessalonians, Paul said that at Christ's second coming the wicked "will be punished with everlasting destruction", and In Revelation, that the birds of the air will "eat the flesh" of the wicked.

The part of Revelation which frightened Barbara and Miguel the most was that at Christ's second coming "the entire world will be shaken by an earthquake that is so powerful that it will cause the mountains to flatten out and the islands in the sea to disappear". "Could this be what the bombs are for", thought Miguel.

The Archbishop continued that Ellen White taught that for the 1000 years of the Millennium Satan would be alone on the Earth, contemplating the terrible mess he had made of things. The bodies of the wicked will be strewn all over the earth, and the righteous will be in heaven. With the righteous in heaven and the wicked dead, there will be no one left for Satan to tempt.

Then, White draws on both Revelation and John, to teach that at the end of the Millennium, God would resurrect everyone to stand before his great white throne. He will open the books and judge them according to what they have done as recorded in the books. Then, the wicked can be judged for their evil deeds and condemned once and for all.

Then, for a second time Barbara and Miguel listened to the Archbishop tell of bible passages which White could have corrupted for her own purposes. She uses parts of Paul, to describe Hell as being "the destruction of the entire planet by fire at the end of the millennium".
Then, from Revelation, that the lake of fire is followed immediately by the re-creation of the Earth into "a new heaven and a new earth", as a home of righteousness, where God's people will enjoy fellowship with God, Jesus and the angels throughout all eternity.
With so much destruction drawn from so many bible passages, it was easy to see how White might have corrupted the teachings as a need to destroy the Earth. But, thought Miguel, "how could she achieve that, with so few bombs?"

As the Archbishop came to the end of his lecture, he realised how far he had strayed from Sister Barbara's work against prostitution and sex trafficking. "But", began the Archbishop, "how can this help you in your work?"
"I'm really not sure", replied Barbara. "We do know that O Lobo has used religious fear in the past. So, maybe he is somehow using Ellen White's brand of evangelism to oil the wheels of his sex trade". Barbara hoped she had said enough to convince the Archbishop that she was only working within her United Nations remit. An

entire order of Catholic nuns turning into crime fighters against the sex trade was one thing. But a nun teaming up with MI6 to track down nuclear weapons was another thing entirely. She hoped that her church's hierarchy would approve, but with so much at stake, it was not something she wanted to test.

The Cubas learned what they could about Ellen White's new church, then bid their goodbyes to the Archbishop. This time Miguel also bent to kiss his ring, he was so pleased to feel that some of the pieces were fitting together. But somewhere, deep inside, his family's devout Christianity left him hoping for any help the world could get. Their ride back to the hotel became an adrenalin fuelled rush, to give the rest of the team their news. Both missed their own bikes, but by now were becoming used to the Triumph Scramblers that the Watchers used as loan bikes. The French Quarter almost rattled with the twin cylinder engines growling through their high level exhausts. In no time at all, they had crossed the old town and reached their hotel. The other Watchers had been recalled by Jonah to discuss the new developments, but it would be some time yet, before they could get away from their own tasks. So, for now they brought Jonah up to speed with what they had learned from the Archbishop.
"Well, Barbara lass", said Jonah as Barbara finished her briefing. "I think we know where the two of you need to focus your attention". Barbara and Miguel would soon be trying to find some way

of infiltrating Ellen White's Millerite group.

Chapter 17.

While Barbara and Miguel were with the Archbishop, Red Andrews had been leading his bogus survey group deep into the Atchafalaya Swamp. Working under the guise of surveying for a potential oil clean up, Andrews, Stone, Skull, Harris and Amber had engaged a bayou tour company to act as their guides.

Andrews had more than enough oil field experience to convince the bayou men of their purpose. But the subterfuge was added to by Amber playing the role of an environmental specialist. Her need to collect soil, plant and water samples had taken them far beyond the oil companies canals.

Their airboat had left Mcgees Landing that morning, loaded with impressive looking peli cases of equipment. Some of it was genuine surveying and sampling kit that Andrews scrounged from his oil contacts. But much of the boxes held weapons or surveillance equipment. Amber had flirted with the airboat pilot, to get the seat high up alongside the driver. With the huge fan spinning behind them, both Amber and the pilot wore ear defenders. Amber was pleased there was little opportunity to talk while the boat was under way. She had studied some environmental science as an Army Engineer, but she doubted that she could maintain a convincing conversation for the whole day. The guides they would be working with had grown up in the swamps and had already told Amber about the swamp's wildlife. Amber was looking forward to seeing the turtles, raccoons, rabbits, opossums, armadillos, squirrels, foxes, coyotes and deer that could be found in the Atchafalaya Basin. The furry creatures were at the top of Amber's must see list.

Despite the serious nature of the mission, the whole team was looking forward to heading out on the airboat.

The tour company's base was among a lot of other tourist infrastructure. So, as they left the dock, they passed the other tour companies boats on the river.

Steadily the airboat's big aeroplane propeller began to work faster, driving the Boat at a steady pace across smooth waters of the river. Soon the buildings began to disappear, as the banks became much wilder and greener. It was a perfect boating day, blue skies were punctuated with fluffy white clouds and the sun glistened from ripples in the river.

Before long they left the main channel, heading into the low hanging trees of the swamp lands. The clear shimmering water was now gone and they were sailing through a thick brown soup.

The guide stopped the boat, so they could watch an alligator sunning itself on a floating log. With the propeller still spinning slowly, the alligator slipped into the water as they passed, its head barely showing above the brown soup. The guide was throwing marshmallows to keep the alligator interested and close to the boat. As the alligator chased the marshmallows, the guide explained a little about these prehistoric throwbacks.

As the water cools down the alligators digest food more slowly and become much slower moving. They are capable of hibernating for up to 3 months under the water, slowing their heart rate to 1 or 2 beats per minute. Their very small brain needing very little oxygen.

"I can think of a few people like that", joked Skull. Skull regretted cracking the first joke, as their guide followed suite. "What is the difference between a Yankee and a Damn Yankee?" asked the guide.

Amber had spent enough time in the States to have heard that one before. She replied "Yankees come to visit, Damn Yankees stay". Their guide seemed to revel in the pretty girl knowing his punchline and began to shout, "go home damn Yankees!"

Having spent enough time with the alligator, their boat moved off again. The agile boat skimmed the top of the water straight over patches of weed. The guide even took the boat over short sections of the bank, just like a hovercraft.

Soon it was time to stop and collect some samples. While Amber collected her samples and kept the guide occupied, Stone acted on the real reason for the stop.

Some craw fish fisherman were working from another airboat using bell shaped nets, to catch the small lobster like delicacy. Stone wanted their local knowledge about anyone other than the tourists and fishermen on the river. The former policeman had not lost the skills needed to get local people talking. Few tourists bothered speaking to the fishermen, so they were pleased that Stone paid them attention.

Their boat guide's joke about Damn Yankees was only partly in jest. The Cajuns were very territorial about their Southern States. So, if they were resentful of their northern neighbours, they were really suspicious of Ruskies.

Friendly as the fishermen were, Stone was struggling with their accents. They spoke with one of the strongest varieties of the New Orleans accent, called the Yat dialect, from the greeting "Where y'at?" This distinctive accent is dying out generation by generation in the city itself, but remains very strong in the surrounding parishes. But even through the broad Yat accent, Stone could understand the resentment of the East Europeans who had been disturbing their fishing grounds. Small groups of four or five East Europeans had been passing through regularly on a very powerful airboat.

The fishermen thought they were just rich tourists, hooning about on their expensive toy. But Stone was sure it was evidence of Georgi Dimov's former Spetsnaz fighters.

Stone got the rough direction they travelled, but got little more from the fishermen than "damn Ruskies", and "reds under the bed".

Red Andrews was using a 1980 oilfield disaster as the main cover for their survey, a repeat of which would be the biggest disaster his company had ever dealt with.

The Louisiana swamps are rich with two valuable minerals; oil and salt. Where large domes of salt form underground, they are often pushed upwards by geological forces. This provides ideal conditions for oil to accumulate in the voids created. Occasionally, the extraction methods for the two minerals come into conflict. It was this potential for disaster which genuinely interested Red Andrews. Although they were there to search for plutonium and a nuclear bomb, the data gathered would be useful to Andrews' oilfield troubleshooting business.

While Amber was collecting her samples, Andrews explained the problem to others in the group.

Although the guide was more than familiar with the Jefferson Island Disaster, he did not fully understand what caused the 400 meter sinkhole. Andrews explained that salt had been mined under the Louisiana swamps for decades. One of the deepest salt mines was under Jefferson Island and its surrounding lake. The 1500 meter deep mine had one of the biggest man made caverns in Louisiana. The oil company knew of the Jefferson Island cavern when they began their exploratory drilling. But they were confident that their surveys would keep them clear of the mine workings.

Then, on November 20 1980, disaster happened, when at 500 feet, the drill punctured the top of the salt cavern much earlier than expected. The waters of the lake began to drain into the small bore hole. But, as the lake water flowed through, it dissolved the salt in the rock, rapidly enlarging the hole.

Within 90 minutes the drill rig and all the mining equipment disappeared under water. Still the hole and its whirlpool continued to grow as more and more water and mud was sucked into the confined space. Heavy barges were pulled towards the vortex as their crews jumped to safety. Eleven huge barges were sunk by the vortex. Then as even more salt was dissolved by the lake water, a huge section of the lake bed collapsed into the cavern. By its end, 65 acres of Jefferson island had been sucked into the vortex. Then, when the mine had sucked in all that it could hold, the water's forces changed direction. A 150 foot waterfall formed as the river changed direction to flow into the nearly empty lake bed. Then, a 400 foot geyser began to shoot out of the top of the mine shaft.

What had been a very shallow lake was now one of the deepest in the area. Some of the fishermen were happy, as it increased the variety of fish able to live in the lake. But the owners of the 65 missing acres of Jefferson Island were far from happy.

It was about preventing a similar disaster, that Andrews was explaining his team's activities in the swamp lands.

With the information Stone got from the fishermen, the Watchers started to place surveillance devices. The tiny devices were placed in both directions from where the fisherman had seen the Ruskies". Any boat passing the devices would trip a beam, alert

Jonah, and transmit video of the passing boat. In that way, they hoped to identify Dimov's men, and find out where they were going.

The more that Stone looked at the swamp lands, the more perfect it looked as a smuggler's hide out. "I've got a good feeling about this", said Skull, reading the look on Stone's face.

"We'll see what the sensors show", replied Stone. "Until then, all options are open".

The airboat had a limited ability to act as a hovercraft. But the Watchers needed to look deeper into an area away from the river. This was an area with both oil and salt workings, so it fit their cover story. But there were also many abandoned buildings, which was the real reason for the Watchers' interest.

Earlier in the day, one of the guide company's bigger boats had pre placed some cargo for them. Six specially adapted quad bikes sat waiting in the mud as the Watchers' airboat arrived. "That's what I'm talking about!" said Skull looking at the four wheel mud bikes.

Each of the quads had been adapted with raised exhausts and air intakes, to avoid the engines drowning. But they also had the most aggressive looking mud tyres any of them had ever seen. "These should cut through all that swamp", thought Stone as he looked at the bikes.

The five bikers could barely wait, while their guide prepared the quads. They might have four wheels, but they were the closest the Watchers were going to get to bikes today.

"They look like something from a Lara Croft film", said Skull.

"Just don't expect me to wear her shorts", replied Amber, as she jumped aboard her quad.

The guide tried his best to keep the Watchers in convoy, but the bikers were having fun. All of them were competitive adrenalin junkies, who could not resist a race. Even Amber, who had only recently met the Watchers, was caught up in their excitement.

As the trail through the bayou narrowed and widened, the quads jockeyed for position. Each move towards a softer surface threw up a wave of liquid mud. All five now looked like extras from a horror film, but still they pushed hard along the trail to the abandoned workings.

Suddenly, their race came to an end, as Skull's lead quad became stuck in the thick, sticky mud. The harder Skull tried to free himself, the deeper his tyres dug into the mud.

"It's like treacle", he shouted, as he wrestled with the machine.

Eventually and reluctantly, the alpha male MC President had to hand over the quad bike to their guide. The swamp man had been born and raised in New Orleans, swamps and bayous. He had also designed and adapted the quad bikes. But even he was struggling with how deep Skull's machine had dug itself in. Left and right he threw his weight, rocking the bike from side to side. The aggressive tyres alternated between gaining a little traction, and throwing the thick brown soup into the air. Gradually, as the quad slid about in the mud, the tyres found some purchase. Then,

with an even thicker cascade of mud, the quad
lurched forward onto the trail.

With all six bikes back on the trail, they moved off
along slightly firmer ground. The track was still
very wet, and the trees hung low with moss. The
Watchers' earlier exuberance had been tamed by
Skull's mishap. This time they rode in a much
more orderly convoy.
Before long, they reached their destination. The
collection of temporary cabins were falling into
disrepair. This had only been an exploratory drill
site, so the more permanent buildings had never
followed. But most still appeared habitable.
Amber, Andrews and Harris again went through
the motions of surveying and sampling.
While they made things look good for the guide,
Stone and Skull looked around the buildings.
People had been there. The remains of camp
fires and empty beer cans were scattered around
the site. But none of it looked recent.
It was not the easiest place to reach. The oil
companies had helicopter lifted their equipment.
Without the quads, it would have been a two hour
hike through the swamp. But its very
inaccessibility was why Stone suspected it for a
smugglers hide.
Stone's trained policeman's eyes were first to spot
the signs. The wet mud of the trail to the site had
obliterated any tracks. But the drill site was on
slightly higher ground and was consequently a
little dryer. Here it was easier to discern recent
tracks from the older ones. "Look Skull", said
Stone, pointing at some foot prints near one of the

better cabins. "They look much newer than the other tracks. They are deep too, as if they were carrying something heavy".

The cabin did show signs of more recent occupation than the camp area. There was nothing permanent, but Stone could read the subtle signs. Attempts had been made to brush out some of the dust, coffee stains on the table looked recent and four sleeping mats had left their impression on the dirty floor.

Stone's keen eye spotted even more subtle traces, which he thought even more worrying. "Look here", he said to Skull, indicating towards where the men had slept. "There's not much of an outline, but I think there's been automatic weapons here". Stone pointed to feint lines in the dirt. Looking carefully, Skull could also see what Stone had spotted. Vague marks indicated the stock, magazine and foresight of a small automatic carbine.

"The bayou boys are not usually that well armed", said Stone. Guns are part of the culture in the Southern States, but they usually favour hunting rifles. Modern military weapons are more expensive and difficult to obtain. "Certainly smells of Dimov's Spetsnaz boys", observed Skull.

The more Stone and Skull looked, the more signs they found. Dimov's men had removed all the tangible signs of their presence. Stone found no food remains, or wrappings. They had certainly left no equipment or conclusive evidence.

Moving outside the cabin, Stone and Skull continued their tracking. All the time they maintained their cover story of examining evidence left by the oil drillers.

"Here", said Stone, waving Skull over to a clearing alongside the cabins. Embedded in the mud was a series of small, regular squares. "I'm thinking cargo net", observed Stone.

"A chopper would be the fastest way to get anything in or out of here", replied Skull. "And, since there's nothing here, out seems the most likely direction", he added.

"Military grade weapons and access to a helicopter. It looks like O Lobo's paw prints are on this", said Stone.

Chapter 18.

Stone and Skull fitted more hidden camera traps around the site, before preparing to leave. If Dimov's men had been using these huts, the Watchers needed to know if they returned. Andrews, Harris and Amber had just about exhausted their repertoire of fake sampling too, so they were pleased to start loading up the quad bikes. Amidst the stress and danger, they were also keen to get back on the exciting toys. The small convoy set off again along the waterlogged trail. This time, the Watchers had learned the signs of deep mud, and were avoiding getting stuck. Skull especially wanted to avoid needing assistance for a second time. Huge smiles again crossed their faces, as they rode the unique machines through the swamp mud. Just like their last ride, the aggressive tyres threw mud in all directions, as the quads cut their way along the trail.

Without the delay of freeing Skull's quad from the mud, they completed the return journey much quicker, and were soon back at the airboat. They had enjoyed riding in the airboat, but somehow, they all thought it would be an anticlimax to their quad bike ride. They would be very wrong about that thought.

The bigger boat would return later to collect the quad bikes. For now, the Watchers left their machines and sailed off, blown by the huge propeller. Amber was again seated next to the guide. Ear defenders held her hat in place, and she had wrapped a thin scarf around her face.

The airboat cruised at 40 mph, but even at such a relatively slow speed, the bugs hurt.

They had not been going long before Stone's radio earpiece buzzed. "Heads up Nev lad", came Jonah's familiar voice. "Your camera traps on the river have just gone live, and the sailors don't look Cajun". The cameras were placed where the fishermen had warned Stone about "Ruskies". An airboat had broken the infra red beem, activating the cameras. Jonah had been alerted, and told Stone that its occupants looked Slavic. He could also see, all too clearly, that they were heavily armed.

Leaning across to Skull, Stone warned him "the cameras have just picked up Dimov's Spetznaz goons, and they are heading our way".

While Amber kept the guide's attention by pointing and smiling, the three men started to surreptitiously prepare their weapons. All the Watchers had pistols hidden under their clothes. But they had also packed carbine rifles among their survey equipment.

The airboat used by Dimov's men was smaller and faster than the tourist boat the Watchers rode in. Jonah could tell from the camera timings, that the distance between them would soon close. "Nev lad", began Jonah, over the radio. "It's a fast boat, and it's gaining on you quickly".

Steve Butler and Randy Salt were still overflying the Atchafalaya Delta in their borrowed helicopter when they heard Jonah's warning about the Spetsnaz. The delta area was pretty, but they had not seen anything of note to their investigation. But, even if they had been tracking a lead, they could not ignore their brothers' call. So, instantly they turned the helicopter and flew north in support of the other Watchers.

No sooner had Jonah warned them about the other boat's speed, than it rounded the bend in the river and was on them. At first sight of the Watchers' boat, the Spetsnaz opened fire. As soon as the first shot rang through the low hanging trees, the Watchers' boat guide knew something was wrong. The guide could not guess why his oilfield survey party was taking fire, but he knew that he needed to escape. Easing every last bit of power from his propeller, the guide pushed his airboat hard. His boat was not as fast as their pursuers' but the guide had spent his whole life in the swamps. Using all of his skill, he swung the boat left and right, avoiding the automatic fire of Dimov's men.

Stone, Skull and Harris tried to return fire, but their guide's evasive action was also throwing off their aim.

Seeing a small island, the guide pointed his boat straight towards it. The powerful aircraft propeller threw the flat bottomed boat up the bank and along the top of the island. With his boat behaving like a hovercraft, the guide flew along the length of the small island, rejoining the water at its far end. The former Spetsnaz troops were obviously much less skilled, as their nerve broke on approach to the island. Rather than fly over the land, they turned away and sailed around the island.

The Watchers had now regained some of the advantage they lost to the faster boat, and were pulling away. Shots still rang across the bayou, but the increased distance had thrown the accuracy even further off.

Then, just as the guide was planning his next manoeuvre, a greater threat than the Spetsnaz started to appear.

The guide could see gas bubbling to surface of the water and there was a strong smell of diesel wafting across the bayou. The guide had only seen this once before, and despite the high humidity, the phenomenon was enough to cause him a cold sweat.

Desperately the guide's eyes darted around, trying to spot the centre of this disturbance in the river. The Watchers were still returning fire, oblivious of the greater danger they were sailing towards.

Andrews was the first to realise something was wrong. The bubbles were still rising to the surface, but their ripples were beginning to circulate. Once the circular current became more obvious, all of the Watchers guessed what was happening. They had all been riveted by Andrews' account of the Jefferson Island whirlpool, and now, a matter of hours later, they saw one opening before them.

It seemed only to take seconds for the power of the whirlpool to grow. Full grown trees were pulled into the flow, completing a full circle of the pool, before disappearing into the vortex. The guide's adrenalin was in full flow and his mind seemed to be working at super speed. Swinging his boat hard towards the bank, he tried to escape the pull of the vortex.

The once tranquil river now resembled whitewater rapids, as they sailed ever closer to the fearsome whirlpool.

As well as avoiding the strong current, the guide also had to steer around the many trees being pulled towards the vortex. The centre of the whirlpool had now opened into a sink hole, almost twenty feet across. Still, the guide worked to keep his boat out of the maelstrom, and save both himself and his clients.

Then suddenly, he crossed the widest part of the whirlpool, and was skillfully working his boat around the outer rim of the vortex. Just as the Watchers and their guide were again able to draw breath, they saw that the Spetsnaz had not been so lucky. Without their guide's lifetime of experience, Dimov's men had suffered the same fate as the Jefferson Island barges. The last that Stone saw of their pursuers, was the huge rear propeller disappearing into the whirlpool's centre.

The Watchers were now sailing amongst the dark brown water, which was still flowing quickly downstream. As Stone looked around, he saw scenes of devastation on the banks. The whole area looked like a hurricane had been through. Then as fast as it started, the swamp water returned to stillness and they continued their journey, slowly and quietly towards the tour company's base.

It had all happened so quickly, that Butler and Salt were just reaching them in their helicopter.

They were too late to be of any help, but they kept the boat in sight for the remainder of their journey. The river guide was, by now, sure that the Watchers were not an oilfield survey company. The oil business is cutthroat, but is not known to produce boat chases and shootouts.

"What was that all about?" the guide asked Andrews.

Red Andrews' answer of "if I told you, I would have to kill you", was said with a little too much conviction. Andrews' answer was quickly backed up by a roll of cash from Skull. Together, they silenced any further curiosity from the guide. But they could be sure they would not be retaining his services for any further excursions into the swamp.

All the Watchers had now received Jonah's recall message. They all needed to return to their French Quarter hotel to debrief the day's events. All had something to add to the mix, but it was Barbara and Miguel's story from the Archbishop which was most immediately worrying.

In the hotel briefing room, Jonah had begun to cover a new wall with information about Ellen White and her new Millerites.

Jonah's analytical mind had already made progress in cross referencing the Archbishop's information against what they already knew. They had some information about Ellen White and the two others who travelled with Matthew Saint. But they had only dug deep enough to track their travel plans. Now, much more detailed background information would be needed. This task fell to Amber, through her Embassy connections.

Sending Barbara and Miguel undercover seemed like a given. Such a dangerous assignment would need very careful planning.

But Barbara had another task, which could really only fall to her. Ellen White's teachings needed to be thoroughly considered. If White really was hoping to destroy the world, they desperately needed to know how she planned to go about it.

While Barbara and Miguel started thinking about how to infiltrate the Millerites, the other Watchers debriefed their time in the Atchafalaya Swamp.

"Steve lad, you and Randy are up first", announced Jonah.

"There's not much to tell", replied Steve Butler. "We over flew the whole delta area. There's plenty of scope for smugglers to use the river, but nothing obvious from the air".

Randy Salt continued to explain what they had seen. They already knew the river was navigable all the way from the delta, to the site of their shoot out. But their flight had confirmed their were any number of places O Lobo and Dimov's men could have kept out of sight. There were also hundreds of islands large enough for them to have slung contraband in a cargo net, under a helicopter.

"Well Randy lad", replied Jonah. "We might have been chasing a wild goose in the Port of New Orleans". Jonah was now convinced the plutonium had been transferred from the Portuguese ship, before it entered the Mississippi River. The Atchafalaya now seemed a much more likely point of entry for the deadly cargo.

"You're next Nev lad", said Jonah, looking towards Stone and Andrews. "What did you get from the drill site?"
"We can be pretty sure our boys have been there", replied Stone. He explained the traces they had found at the abandoned cabins. The outline of automatic weapons was a good indication that hunters were not there. The helicopter cargo net also pointed towards O Lobo's organisation. But the clincher was the Spetsnaz showing their hand and getting involved in a gun fight.
"Could we be lucky enough that the plute went down the sink hole, Nev lad?", asked Jonah.
"Nice thought, but unlikely", replied Stone. "With the weight of that stuff, I'd guess it went out in the cargo net". They just needed to work out where, in the enormous haystack of Louisiana, where O Lobo had hidden his deadly needles.

The one Watcher who could not make the briefing was Joao Alva. The huge enforcer was still overseeing their surveillance team at the Evergreen Plantation. Although missing in person, Alva was able to video conference from the motor home. "Sounds like I'm missing all the fun", said Alva.
Not sure about fun", replied Stone. "I can cope with bullets. But that whirlpool scared the crap out of us".
It did not take Alva long to update on the Plantation, as very little had happened. "I'm bored

to tears", said Alva. "No sign of Saint, or radiation. All I'm doing is making sure the guys stay awake". Although Joao Alva thought he had nothing to contribute, Jonah's analytical mind was able to make something of his report. Jonah deduced several things from the lack of activity at the Plantation. "Well Joao lad", he began. "We can be sure the plute isn't there. You haven't detected it moving in or out, and Nev is sure they were keeping it out in the swamps".

Jonah then turned his thoughts to Matthew Saint. "All we know for sure, is that his tracking device is inside. So, is the young fellow in there, or not? asked Jonah, somewhat rhetorically. "I'd wager they still have him there", continued Jonah. "He's a very valuable commodity for O Lobo, and the plantation house is the most secure location the wolf has access to".

"Do they still need Saint?" asked Skull. "How difficult can it be to drop a ball of metal into its housing?" Skull was wondering the former Spetsnaz soldiers could perform the last steps of arming Saint's improvised nuclear devices.

"I'd wager that they do need him Skull lad", replied Jonah. "The Spetsnaz might have handled nuclear warheads before. But O Lobo is cautious". Jonah was sure that O Lobo would want an expert handling the valuable, and dangerous, weapons. "Besides", added Jonah. "The devices were built in Portugal. If Saint wasn't wanted for the final assembly, why risk bringing him to the U.S.?"

"So", said Skull. "We stay on the plantation

186

house. But, the big question is, do we maintain the perimeter, or are we going in?"

"It would be really useful to get inside", replied Stone. "But it's a huge risk. Johnny Johnson has been stressing stealth and discretion all the way through this. If we are caught in there, we risk a diplomatic row".

Jonah chipped in to adjudicate on the dilemma. "I would love to get a team inside that house. But Nev is right, they have it very well guarded, and we can't risk attracting the U.S. Authorities attention with a gun fight at a prime tourist location".

With priorities agreed, the Watchers organised their tasks for the next day.

Joao Alva was to get a break from supervising their team at the Plantation. The giant enforcer would back up Miguel in supporting his sister's undercover mission.

Steve Butler would relieve Alva at the Plantation. The others would concentrate on the plutonium. They had decided to widen their use of radiation detectors. By fitting one to their drone, and the others to motorcycles, they could gradually widen their search area. Needless to say, going out for a ride was the most popular task.

Chapter 19.

Miguel Cuba and Joao Alva were settled into the seats of a hired van. They took turns watching the street and the feed from Barbara's tiny video camera.

Both men were fairly relaxed, even Miguel, who doted on his younger sister, and worried constantly about her safety.

Barbara's first outing was not into the lair of the new Millerites, as they had yet to track them down. She was starting her search in a Southern Baptist church, in the area that Ellen White was said to operate. While she might encounter some of White's followers, overall, the Baptists were good people.

White herself, had come from the Seventh Day Adventist church. But Barbara had learned that many of her followers had also been drawn away from the Baptists.

The only white face among a very black congregation, Barbara stood out a mile. But Barbara was counting on being noticed as a newcomer.

Theirs was a happy branch of the Christian church. Originating from the southern slaves, the church goers had learned to celebrate the good in their lives, not dwell on the many bad things they suffered. Barbara knew that, as a Christian, she would be welcomed into the church. Her tanned, but white skin would just ensure that she was noticed. She was very quickly noticed. The beautiful, slightly Moorish looking, Portuguese woman could not avoid being spotted in a crowd. It took no time at all for members of the congregation to welcome her into their church. Despite her catholic faith and vocation, Barbara loved this type of gospel service, which was so very different from the Catholic mass. The colourfully dressed blacks were clapping, dancing, swaying and singing. Barbara found it all very cheerful. The southern style of gospel worship began with the slaves singing songs to celebrate the end of their working day. The slaves also prayed for God to liberate them. Now, despite it being many generations since the end of slavery, the Creoles just enjoyed their exuberant style of worship.

After their service, many of the congregation were happy to talk to their pretty visitor. Armed with her nun's knowledge of the Christian bible, Barbara was easily able to talk with the devoutly religious church goers.

They were such a close community, that very little relating to church escaped their attention. Many were well aware of Ellen White's Millerite revival. "Child, she's too high an opinion of herself, if you ask me", commented one of the colourfully dressed women. "All her talk of reincarnation and visions. Seems like she wants to be another Christ". The woman went on to tell Barbara that a few of her own congregation had become fascinated with Ellen White's firebrand style of religion. Although the woman had never attended White's sermons, her friends told of very convincing trances, almost bordering on possession. They also told of her certain belief that the world was soon to end in fire and destruction.

"I'd love to see that", replied Barbara. "Do you think you could introduce me to your friends?"

"Child", replied the woman. "That's a dangerous road to be going along. Her preaching tells a very bad version of the bible's teachings. But, they always looking for new converts, I'm sure my friends would take you to a meeting".

While Sister Barbara was winning the confidence of the Baptists, the other Watchers were going about their own tasks. Steve Butler had settled into the camper van at the Evergreen Plantation. He expected from Joao Alva's experience, that he was in for some long and tedious days. He had the feed from their many hidden cameras to watch. He also had to be alert for alarms from Matthew Saint's tracking device, and from his radiation detector. On top of all that, he also had to supervise their team of surveillance operatives who were spread around the plantation. Butler longed to be with the others, riding their motorcycles around Louisiana, in the hope of picking up a radiation reading.

Stone often reminded himself of how much his life had changed since meeting the Watchers. He thought his life was over when he resigned in disgrace from the British police. But, now he was in the employ of British Intelligence, riding his Triumph through wonderful Louisiana countryside. If that wasn't enough to bring a smile to Stone's face, the beautiful British spy who rode alongside him certainly did the trick.

Stone was still, at times, a little sad that Trudy Varley and her daughter's lives had gone a different direction to his own. As he rode with Amber, he could not help smiling at the lovely blonde biker. Here was a stunning woman who lived in the same, murky world that he inhabited. "I wonder", thought Stone, as they ride through their search grid. "Perhaps not, while we still have some stray nukes", he reminded himself.

Sister Barbara was surprised to learn that Ellen White was making no attempt at hiding her Millerite revival. White was still a member of the Seventh Day Adventists, and was hiring one of their halls for her meetings.

Barbara arrived in plenty of time, with her former Baptist escorts. White, she learned, would make a big entrance, right on time. The mood of the congregation was far more sedate than the cheerful Baptists. But this was the south. In the south, sedate did not mean sombre, and this was still a friendly and welcoming congregation.

"The Millennium is almost upon us", boomed a powerful female voice. Ellen White had walked onto the stage with perfect punctuality. At the first sound of her voice, everyone in the hall fell silent. "Paul said that the Lord himself will come down from heaven", continued White. "With a loud command, with the voice of the archangel and with the trumpet call of God, the dead in Christ will rise first". "Thus", she went on. "One of the events to occur at the beginning of the millennium will be the resurrection of the righteous. Righteous, such as you!"

White's powerful, firebrand voice continued, "we know that you, the righteous, will be taken with the resurrected saints, to meet the Lord in the air". "Jesus himself promised his disciples that he was going to heaven to prepare a place for them. Then, at his second coming, he would return to take his people with him".

Ellen White spoke on, convincing her congregation that they were all the Lord's people and they would be taken to the clouds at Christ's second coming. Ominously, White then explained that Christ's Second Advent could not come without the Apocalypse.

"Revelation says that at Christ's second coming the entire world will be shaken by an earthquake so powerful that the mountains will flatten out and the islands in the sea will disappear". Then she added "God will judge the dead according to what they had done as recorded in the books. He will raise the wicked to life after the millennium, so they can be judged for their evil deeds and condemned for ever." "Then, after God has judged the wicked", continued White. "They will be sent to Hell".

Barbara's Catholic faith believed Hell to be a place where the souls of all sinners went to after their death. Ellen White had a different interpretation for her congregation. Peter tells us that, following the judgment of the wicked, they will be destroyed in a lake of fire, where the earth itself will be burned up. "So", she reasoned, "hell is not off in some distant part of the universe, it is not in the centre of the earth and it is not happening now. Hell will be the destruction of the entire planet by fire at the end of the millennium." "Then, good news!" she announced. "God will rebuild our world into a new heaven and a new earth, the home of righteousness, where all wars, natural disasters, pain and weeping will be a thing of the past".

Next came part of Ellen White's sermon that really interested Barbara. White went on to give a date for the apocalypse. But, the way in which White delivered this news was a surprise to Barbara. She had heard of Ellen White's visions, but what she was about to see surprised even the experienced nun.

Suddenly, White gave three shouts of "Glory!" which echoed and re-echoed around the hall. The second, and especially the third, were fainter than the first. Her voice sounded quite a distance from Barbara, despite her being only a few feet away. For a few seconds White swooned, as if she had no strength. Then, she was instantly filled with strength again, rising to her feet and walking about the room. She moved her hands, arms, and head in gestures that were free and graceful.

Two of the largest men in her entourage moved towards White. They demonstrated White's superhuman strength while in a vision. Each man took hold of one of the slight woman's arms. But whatever position she moved a hand or arm, it could not be hindered or controlled by even these strong men.

For the entire period of her trance, the slightly

build woman held her 18 pound family bible in her outstretched left hand.

Barbara noticed that White appeared not to breathe during the 20 minutes of her vision. White's eyes were open without blinking; her head was raised, looking upward with a pleasant expression as if staring intently at some distant object. She appeared utterly unconscious of everything happening around her.

Then, Ellen White began to speak again. Not in the firebrand voice Barbara had first heard, but in the strange distant voice that began her trance. "I hear Reverend Miller and Samuel Snow" said White.

Miller and Snow were the two key individuals who worked out 22nd October 1844 as the date of the apocalypse. This date passing without incident became known as the Great Disappointment.

Now, the two, long dead Millerites appeared to be speaking through Ellen White. "Christ is coming", whispered White. "He will return on the tenth day of the seventh month of the present year".

This prediction confused Barbara, as the 10th July had already passed.

Jonah was watching and listening to the feed from Barbara's hidden camera. As always, he was quick to analyse the information he was receiving. Searching the Internet for the Great Disappointment, Jonah realised that White's words were exactly those spoken by Samuel Snow in 1844. But, Snow was not using the modern day Gregorian calendar.

Despite the Christian calendar being introduced by Pope Gregory in 1582, Snow worked out the date of the Apocalypse using the calendar of the ancient Karaite Jews. The Karaite's began their year with the ripening of the barley crop in Israel, giving a three month difference between the two calendars. "We've got a little over a week Barbara lass", said Jonah through her earpiece. "It's a different calendar. She means October 22nd, just like they worked out in1844."

Then, just as suddenly as her vision began, Ellen White started to come out of her trance. She let out a long-drawn sigh, as she appeared to take her first natural breath. "D-a-r-k." She exclaimed, in her soft, distant voice. Then, just like at the beginning of her trance, White again went limp and strengthless. The men from her entourage again moved forward to support White as she came out of her trance. The men led the weakened White off the stage, and her sermon was over. The congregation was in no hurry to leave. The people stood in huddles, discussing the revelation they had just heard.
Some of White's entourage were on hand to explain the discrepancy between the two calendars. Gradually, a very different mood passed through the congregation. If White's vision was correct, they had 10 days before Christ's second advent and the end of the earth as they knew it.

It was now imperative that Barbara win the trust of the new Millerites and learn what she could from them. Armed with her own broad bible knowledge and Jonah feeding information through her earpiece, Barbara began to discuss theology with anyone who would listen.

Barbara had to portray herself as a believer and become accepted by the group.

As she chatted with the congregation, Barbara became aware that some of White's entourage were taking an interest in her. They had noticed that her knowledge of the Millennium and the Apocalypse was far greater than the other church members.

"Sister", said a voice behind Barbara. A cold sweat came over Barbara, as the greeting took her by surprise, initially thinking that she had been recognised. Barbara was used to being called sister, as it is the honorific title bestowed on all nuns. But in the Catholic Church, the title is not widely used for the congregation in general. However, in this branch of Christianity, brother and sister are pleasantries used extensively between church members. Barbara had not been recognised as a nun, she was just being greeted by one of Ellen White's entourage.

"Is this it? Am I in?", thought Barbara as the young woman approached her.

"I'm Sister Beth", said the woman, reaching out to shake Barbara's hand. "I couldn't help overhearing, you know a lot about the apocalypse".

"I read my bible every day", replied Barbara. "Our world is in such a mess, it makes sense that Jesus would want to do something about it". Barbara had carefully worked out her augments over the apocalypse, and they seemed to be just what Sister Beth wanted to hear. The two women were still talking when the rest of the congregation had drifted away. It seemed that Barbara's tactics had worked. The next day was Saturday, the Sabbath day observed by the Seventh Day Adventists. Beth invited Barbara to her Saturday service.

The New Millerites also kept Saturday as their Sabbath. But, unknown to Barbara, it was to a much more traditional, New Orleans ceremony, that Beth had just invited her to.

"Yes!" exclaimed Jonah, listening to Barbara's video feed at their hotel. It was testament to Barbara's ability that she had gained the Millerite's confidence so quickly. But, sitting in the van with Joao Alva, Miguel Cuba had mixed feelings. He knew the importance of their mission and knew he could not stop Barbara taking the risk. But Miguel always worried for his younger sister. He would be constantly alert while Barbara was in the danger zone.

Chapter 20.

The bleep from his computer screen stirred Steve Butler out of his daydream. After a seemingly endless period of inactivity, Matthew Saint's tracking device had moved.

It had been many years since Butler left the Royal Marines, but he still had his warrior's instincts. Instantly he went through radio checks with his surveillance team and started his commentary.

"Stand by, stand by. Signal North East corner of the house", said Butler.

"Got him, Steve lad", replied Jonah, picking up the feed from one of their hidden cameras. "He's with three Spetsnaz, getting into a black 4x4".

"Unit one, permission", replied the first of the surveillance operatives, who was hidden in undergrowth along the plantation drive. "I have the 4x4. I have a clear shot".

"Take it, unit one", replied Jonah. The old detective was not authorising anyone to be killed. The marksman would use his high powered rifle to place a tracking device on the car.

The suppressed rifle gave a muted crack, as the tiny projectile headed towards the 4x4. The bullet casing was designed to cut through the plastic bumper, and then be stopped by the metal of the car body. The tactic worked exactly as planned and the car travelled on, with its tiny passenger.

"We're live, Steve lad", said Jonah, as the first signal arrived on his monitor.

With Saint on the move, Jonah recalled the

Watchers who were out searching with the radiation detectors. They had the signal from the tracker and their surveillance team to follow Saint's car. But they needed to be ready for whatever happened at his destination.

Barbara, Miguel and Joao Alva were not among the Watchers following Saint. They had their own operation to prepare for. Barbara had arranged to meet Beth at the Seventh Day Adventist's hall. She knew that would not be their final destination, as Beth had already told her they would be moving on in her car.
This meant that Miguel and Alva could not maintain a static observation point; they too had to be mobile.
With the risk that she could be searched, Miguel had been very careful with the bugs and trackers he had equipped his sister with. The tiny trackers in her shoe and jacket were passive; they would only transmit when remotely activated by Miguel. The rest of the time, they sat dormant and immune from detection. They had not dared risk their standard radio kit. Barbara had a tiny transmitter in her watch, but it only sent a signal when she wanted it to.

With Alva in the van and Miguel on his Triumph, the Watchers set off after Barbara, Beth and two of the men from Ellen White's entourage.
As van and motorcycle exchanged position, they started to realise the roads looked familiar. "We're heading back into the French Quarter", observed Miguel. He was right, Beth was indeed taking

Barbara back towards the Watchers' hotel in the historic area of New Orleans.

Before long Jonah had picked up their car on the cameras the Watchers had placed for their own protection. "Bourbon Street, Miguel lad", said Jonah, as he watched Beth's car drive onto New Orleans' most famous street.

It was too early in the day for Bourbon Street to be pedestrianised, so Beth was able to pull up close to their destination. Miguel rolled by on his Triumph, just in time to see the four of them enter a Voodoo Emporium.

"I thought these were religious people", observed Alva.

"This is New Orleans", replied Miguel. "The faiths have all blended a little with the variety of immigrants who arrived from so many routes".

While Miguel and Alva positioned themselves to watch the building, Jonah completed Miguel's explanation of the mystical African beliefs. Voodoo was brought to French Louisiana during the colonial period by workers and slaves from West Africa and later by slaves and free people of colour fleeing the Haitian revolution at the end of the 18th century. French and African cultures began to fuse, as the black Creoles began to associate Voodoo spirits with Christian saints who presided over the same domain. Some leaders of each tradition believe Voodoo and Catholic practices are in conflict, but at the level of street culture both saints and spirits act as mediators, with the Catholic priest or voodoo Legba presiding over their respective activities.

Other Catholic practices adopted into Louisiana Voodoo include reciting the Hail Mary and the Lord's Prayer.

Singing is an important part of voodoo worship. Songs have been passed down orally for hundreds of years. Songs would be accompanied by patting, clapping and foot stomping. Many songs mirror tunes of the Catholic Church, as well as associating the Catholic saints with African deities.

Inside the voodoo emporium, Barbara was surprised to be led out of the small shop, through a beaded curtain and up a winding flight of stairs. Above the shop, the stairs opened into a much larger room. It was a room like nothing Barbara had seen before. But somehow, it instantly said voodoo to her. The whole room was an eclectic mix of Catholic and African iconography. At the head of the room was an alter. In many respects, it was similar to the ones Sister Barbara had worshiped at throughout her life. Thick candles burned and icons of saints hung above the alter. But, African masks also hung amongst the saints. Bones and skulls also sat among the candles. Then, Barbara noticed that one of the skulls wore a top hat and dark glasses. She dug into the recesses of her mind, for where she had seen this image before. "Baron Samedi", she remembered. Samedi was a voodoo spirit, or Loa. The Haitian dictator Papa Doc Duvalier styled himself on Samedi, always seen wearing top hat, tuxedo and dark glasses.

Papa Doc's body guard, the Tonton Macoutes,

were rumoured to be zombies, apparently in a constant state of trance. "I hope I don't meet any zombies here", thought Barbara as she looked around the room.

Gradually the room began to fill, mostly with black Creoles, but Barbara spotted the occasional white face among the crowd.
Barbara realised that Beth and the man who had driven them had disappeared from the room. She looked around the room, for signs of where her hosts might have gone. Her initial suspicions eased by the relaxed way the assembled people were behaving. "This is the south", she thought, remembering that in the southern states, relaxed is their default position. The nun should perhaps have been uncomfortable here. She had been brought to this strange place, where icons of her catholic faith mixed with African mysticism. But Barbara's work with the UN and the Good Shepherd Sisters had taken her to practically every corner of the world. If Barbara was nervous, it was of Carlos Lobo's involvement, not of the voodoo.

Stone and Amber were both well in the zone which comes from riding a powerful motorcycle at the limit of its performance. They were riding towards the Evergreen Plantation, listening intently to Butler's commentary of Saint's journey. With each update, they had to adjust their own route, heading ever closer toward the French Quarter.
Soon, Saint's car pulled onto Bourbon Street and

into the sights of Miguel and Alva.

"Got him", said Miguel. "They're being dropped outside the voodoo emporium. Looks like Barbara will have some company".

With no incoming comms, Barbara was cut off from everything the Watchers were doing outside. It took a huge amount of self control for Barbara to avoid showing recognition for Saint, when he walked into the room. The people with Saint were clearly part of this group, as Barbara watched them talking freely with the assembled crowd. Despite the very relaxed nature of the Creoles, there was a very steady build up of anticipation. Although Barbara had little idea of what was coming she could sense the mounting excitement in the room.

Then, just as had happened before Ellen White's entrance at the Millerite's ceremony, the room went deathly quiet. She was about to find out where her hosts had gone, they walked through a hidden door at the side of the altar. Beth was dressed in colourful West African clothing. By her side, in top hat and tuxedo, was Baron Samedi. Beth seemed very different to how Barbara had known her. Among the Millerites, she had appeared confident, but at the same time she displayed the reserved behaviour common of Puritan Christian sects. This new Beth was wild eyed and extrovert. She seemed almost in a trance. Or, had Barbara believed in such things, possessed by the Loa spirits.

Although Papa Doc Duvalier's version of Baron Samedi was a ruthless dictator, here, it was clearly Beth who was in charge of proceedings. The colourfully dressed woman immediately took control of the room.

Barbara thought hard to remember all she had read about voodoo rituals. As the first song began, she remembered there are four phases to a voodoo ritual, all identifiable by the song being sung; preparation, invocation, possession and farewell. The songs are used to open the gate between the deities and the human world and invite the spirits to possess someone. Barbara also realised why it was Beth who was leading the ritual. Voodoo queens were very important in the Louisiana version of the African religion.

Voodoo queens exercised great power in their communities, and led ceremonial meetings and ritual dances. These drew crowds of hundreds of people. They were practitioners who made a living through selling amulets, and gris-gris charms. Their spells and charms guaranteed to cure ailments, grant desires, and destroy one's enemies". Such was their power and influence that they were recognised by journalists, judges, criminals, and citizens alike.

The voodoo queens emerged in a society that upheld an oppressive slave regime and huge power differential between blacks and whites. But, they were also influenced by a shortage of white women, which resulted in many interracial liaisons. In French colonial communities, a class of free people of colour developed, who were given more rights and, in New Orleans, acquired property and education. Free women of colour had high influence. In particular, those who were spiritual leaders exercised extraordinary power.

Beth appeared to have modelled herself on Marie Laveau, by far the most famous of New Orleans' voodoo queens. Among the fifteen voodoo queens scattered around 19th-century New Orleans, Marie Laveau was known as "The" Voodoo Queen, the most eminent and powerful of them all. Her rite on the shore of Lake Pontchartrain in 1874 attracted 12,000 black and white New Orleanians. Politicians, lawyers, businessman and wealthy planters, all came to her to consult before making an important financial or business decision. She also helped the poor and enslaved. Although her help seemed non-discriminatory, she actually favoured the slaves of her wealthy customers. Many runaway slaves credited their successful escapes to Laveau's powerful charms.
Also a Catholic, Laveau encouraged her followers to attend Catholic Mass as a way to protect their true beliefs. Barbara realised that this paralleled Beth's ability to mix her Millerite beliefs with being a voodoo queen.

Barbara used the distraction of Beth's entrance to briefly activate her communicator. She could not risk a long transmission, but it was enough to reassure Miguel and the other Watchers. Most importantly, it allowed them to position her in the building. The surveillance experts were able to direct a laser microphone at one of the windows. Inside Miguel's van he used sophisticated software to convert the window's tiny vibrations back into speech. It did not take Miguel long to work out that it was a voodoo ritual. What he had trouble with, was how voodoo fitted with the Christian Millerites.

Beth led the room through the four stages of her ritual. As the change of music signaled the invocation, Matthew Saint was called forward. "It's a blessing", thought Barbara. Despite the very African influence, there were enough similarities with her catholic faith, for Barbara to recognise Beth giving Saint a blessing.
Beth danced in front of Saint, holding a large snake she called Le Grand Zombi. With her other hand, she shook a gourd rattle to summon the loa snake deity Damballah. As she danced, Beth chanted over and over, "Damballah, ye-ye-ye!"
In time, apparently coming under her spell, Saint joined in the dance.
The whole room was coming under Beth's influence. Rhythmic drum beat and the heat of the flaming torches, mixed with Beth's chanting to create a heady atmosphere. The crowd swayed with abandonment, seemingly possessed by the voodoo spirits.

A change of music heralded a change in the ritual. The dancing stopped and Beth handed Le Grand Zombi to Baron Samedi. Beth turned to the alter and worked on preparing something. When she turned back towards Saint, Barbara could see that Beth had made a Gris-gris bag. These conjuring bags contain such items as bones, herbs, charms and snake skin, tied up in a piece of cloth. Despite Hollywood's obsession with voodoo dolls, these are rarely used in real rituals. The Gris-Gris bag is the magic charm of choice in Louisiana voodoo. Beth's bag was for Saint. This cemented Barbara's guess that the ritual was some sort of blessing. "A blessing for safe handling of an atomic bomb", thought Barbara. "I've never been asked to give one of those".

Now that Jonah had his information feed restored, the old detective was able to start assessing the new information. Many of the team were puzzled by how voodoo fitted with the Millerite's plans for the apocalypse. Jonah's analytic mind was starting to work out what might be happening. The Millerites were originally a very northern entity. The movement began and thrived in the evangelically Burned Out District of New York State. But their revival was happening in the very different Deep South.
Jonah was starting to realise that what the Millerites were planning must be huge. "They need followers", thought Jonah, "and they won't have much influence in the modern day Big Apple". New York today was such a busy, cosmopolitan city, that building a following for any new idea would be an uphill struggle.
But, in the south, there was a much greater sense of community for Ellen White and her New Millerites to exploit. The southern identity, coupled with the voodoo superstition, would provide a rich source of followers for whatever Ellen White was planning.
Jonah's big unsolved puzzle, was to work out how

O Lobo and Georgi Dimov could benefit from an apocalypse.

Chapter 21.

Miguel Cuba breathed a sigh of relief when his sister walked out of the voodoo emporium.
Most visitors to New Orleans stayed somewhere near the French Quarter. Barbara used this fact to avoid travelling back with Beth and her friends. While the congregation were leaving, Barbara kept up her cover as a tourist, by walking Bourbon Street, taking in the historic buildings, street musicians and the beautifully polished motorcycles which were gathered outside the many bars. Miguel watched intently from his van. But Stone and Amber were able to get much closer. They had ridden their motorcycles into the closed off street and were behaving like any biker couple in this most famous of tourist locations. Stone was now starting to feel quite comfortable in playing the role of a couple with Amber.

Eventually everyone from the voodoo ritual had left the building and either left in cars, or dispersed around Bourbon Street's many music venues.
Saint had been whisked away in the same 4x4 he had arrived in. Steve Butler was still receiving the tracker signal from the car, and he thought it a fair guess they would return to the plantation. But Butler still directed his surveillance team to shadow the car.

The Watchers now needed to return to their hotel to make sense of everything which had happened that evening.

Barbara in particular had to take special care. Their targets had seen her and they could not risk Barbara being associated with the Watchers. As Barbara walked a circuitous route back to the hotel, the team was not just watching her; they were looking for anyone paying Barbara attention. One by one, the Watchers returned to their hotel, and into Jonah's makeshift briefing room.

Throughout the operation, Jonah had been in constant communication with his old friend, and the Watchers' MI5 handler, Jonny Johnson. Jonny's mind was every bit as complex as Jonah's. Both men had the ability to instantly process new information, and analyse it in the context of what they already knew. They had both been struggling with the need to recruit lots of help, when Saint's bombs would be devastatingly destructive on their own.

It was Jonny who saw a potential target which might need an army.

"October 22nd", said Jonny. "There's a huge conference at The Islamic Center of America, in Dearborn on the same date the Millerites prophesied the apocalypse. Ellen White must see that as some sort of sign".

The only fly in Jonny's theory, was that Dearborn was half a continent away from New Orleans".

"Sounds possible Jonny lad. But why would they base themselves here, for a target near Canada?"

asked Jonah.

Jonny had no answer for him. Both men knew they had a lot of research and thinking still to do.

When Barbara arrived at the briefing, she quickly brought them up to speed on what had happened at the voodoo ceremony. Her explanation of how White managed to combine Christian and voodoo beliefs helped fuel Jonny's theory that there might be an Islamic target. She could be taking advantage of tensions between the Christian and Muslim faiths, which pre date the crusades.

Stone jumped in to play devils advocate with Jonny's theory. "I understand how she could build enough fundamentalist desire to hurt the Muslims", began Stone. "But how will that bring about the end of the world?"

"That, Nev lad, is the biggest of questions", replied Jonah.

The Watchers' operation had again entered a stage where intelligence gathering would be vital. Amber was the first to go to work, planning a cover story and feeding it into U.S. Intelligence. Through her role as British Military Attaché to the U.S., she had a direct conduit into their intelligence agencies. She could not let them know about the nuclear threat. But anything terrorist related was enough to send the Americans into a tail spin.

Jonny Johnson would concentrate on Europe. Carlos Lobo's involvement seemed to have gone further than delivering the plutonium. Jonny needed to figure out what, besides profit, was in it for the gangster.

While the intelligence experts were playing their parts, Jonah started to research the potential target of The Islamic Centre of America. The Islamic Centre is a huge Shia mosque in Michigan. The institution itself dates back to 1964, but its new mosque opened in 2005. It is the largest mosque in North America and the oldest Shia mosque in the United States. Dearborn's large, mostly Lebanese, Shia Arab population earned the city its title as the "heart of Shiism" in the United States.

Jonah's research showed that, if their theory was right, this would not be the first time the mosque was threatened by terrorism. Ironically, the last threat came from within the Muslim community. In 2011 a Californian named Roger Stockham was arrested for terrorism after attempting to blow up the Islamic Centre of America. Stockham was a convert to Islam who was targeting the Shi'ite community. He had a history of mental illness and firearms offences.
Jonah could find no link between Stockham and Ellen White, but his attempt might have drawn her attention to the mosque as a target.

Although tiny at the side of the Christian population, Islam in America has been growing steadily. With 0.9% of the population, Islam is the fourth-largest faith behind Christianity with 78.3%, 1.8% of Jews and 1.2% of Buddhists. Jonah read that American Muslims are now one of America's most racially diverse religious groups.

Native-born Muslims tend to be mainly African Americans, making up about a quarter of the total Muslim population. Many of these converted during the last seventy years.

An estimated 20–30 percent of the slaves brought to colonial America from Africa arrived as Muslims. But Islam was stringently suppressed on plantations and it was easy for Jonah to see how the voodoo beliefs would have remained strong in the south. Then, after the abolition of slavery, the Muslim population began to grow, with immigration from the former Ottoman and Mughal Empires.

While Jonah was researching Islam in America, Jonny had been searching Europe's intelligence data bases for any connection O Lobo might have to the Millerite's cause.

Jonny could find nothing linking O Lobo to the Millerites. Neither could he find any suggestion that the catholic gangster shared their literal belief in the apocalypse and the millennium. What he did find made Jonny remember the old saying "the enemy of my enemy is my friend".

Carlos Lobo's organisation had been slowly and secretly funding a number of anti Islamic organisations in Southern Europe. "This could be it", thought Jonny. "If O Lobo wants to hurt Muslims, he has found a heck of a way to do it". But, just like Jonah, Jonny still could not fit everything together. O Lobo's dislike of Muslims could explain his involvement in the plot. But, how could the bombing of a mosque bring about an apocalypse? That was a puzzle which would test the minds of both veteran spy masters.

The Watchers were puzzled by what Ellen White, Beth and O Lobo could be planning with Saint's two nuclear devices.
The date of Dearborn's huge Muslim gathering being on the anniversary of the Great Disappointment seemed too important to ignore. Add in O Lobo's funding of anti Muslim causes, and the odds seemed stacked in favour of that theory. But it still did not answer how murdering so many Muslims could bring about the Apocalypse.

"Should we be thinking geological?" asked Red Andrews. The oilfield troubleshooter had been considering the effect two nuclear explosions could do to America's fragile tectonic geology. "The devices are too big for a bore hole", added Andrews. "But I'm sure there is somewhere on the San Andreas Fault they could be dropped in. It could cause one hell of an earthquake".
This had been an area the Watchers had not yet considered, and it seemed quite feasible.
Jonny Johnson's MI5 analysts had already worked out the expected nuclear yield from the Cuban warheads. Andrews cleverly fed the information through his oilfield scientists, to work out the potential damage. It would have to have been a massive oilfield explosion to match the nuclear detonation, but it was, just, within the realm of possibility.
When Red Andrews relieved the results of his

geological enquiry, he looked more white than red. "Massive damage along the west coast of America", reported Andrews. "That would fit with Revelation saying that at Christ's second coming the world will be shaken by an earthquake so powerful that it will cause the mountains to flatten out and the islands in the sea to disappear", he added.

"I'm not so sure", challenged Barbara. The catholic nun knew the bible in far more detail than any of the Watchers. "Revelation talks about the entire world being shaken by the earthquake", she continued. "Red's calculations only have the western seaboard affected. If they want to bring about the Apocalypse, the earthquake would need to be powerful enough to make a wreck of the Earth, rendering it formless and empty."

Jonah had been quietly taking in all of the debate. Neither of their theories so far could render the Earth formless and empty. His own theory of bombing the Islamic Centre of America would kill thousands, but it would not destroy the world. Red Andrews' geological theory seemed more like an apocalypse, but in global terms, its effects would be quite localised.
Inadvertently, it was ex special forces soldier Randy Salt who provided Jonah with an answer. Like many former soldiers, Salt's choice of T shirts were often of some military significance. Today, he had chosen one with an image from Dr Strangelove. Stanley Kubrick's satirical movie dealt with the consequences of America and

Russia's Cold War turning nuclear.

"They want to start a war", announced Jonah. "There is enough nuclear know how in the Islamic world, for retaliation to be massive". The whole room went quiet as the Watchers took in Jonah's suggestion. If he was right, the Millerites were planning to bring about a global conflict. But they still needed to work out how killing thousands of Muslims in a single American city could bring about something on that scale.

While Jonah was leading the discussion on the Millerite's plans, Steve Butler was controlling the surveillance team in shadowing Matthew Saint. Just as they had on the outward journey, they were relying on the tracker in the 4x4 bumper. The operatives had scattered themselves along the route back to the plantation. But they avoided being in direct sight of Saint's car. One by one they checked in with Butler as the 4x4 drove by their positions.

Butler felt confident as the blinking light of the tracking device was confirmed by each successive operative. He watched the 4x4 arrive, caught by the tiny cameras the Watchers had placed earlier in their mission.

As the occupants disembarked, Butler's confidence disappeared. "He's not there", said Butler, into his headset. "They've done a switch on us".

Somewhere, between the surveillance operative's stations, Matthew Saint had changed vehicles. No matter how carefully Butler scrutinised the camera feed, the nuclear engineer had not arrived back at the Evergreen Plantation.

Butler's outburst caught Jonah's attention and drew him away from the ongoing debate at their hotel.

Aided by Nev Stone, Jonah reviewed the recordings from their cameras hidden on Bourbon Street. There was no mistaking Matthew Saint walking out of the voodoo emporium and getting into the 4x4. "They've pulled a conjuring trick on us Nev lad", observed Jonah, as it became obvious Saint had changed vehicles mid journey. Jonah could not be sure if the switch was a routine precaution, or whether Dimov's men knew they were being watched. What he could be sure of, was that they had lost their nuclear engineer again.

"Your Uncle Jonny isn't going to be happy Amber lass", said Jonah, in what Stone thought was the understatement of the day.

They would maintain surveillance on the plantation house and the voodoo emporium. But for now, the Watchers' best target was Beth, the voodoo queen. Just like her more famous predecessor, Marie Laveau, Beth had a hairdressers shop in the French Quarter. Laveau used the hairdressers chair gossip to guide her clairvoyant powers. More than 100 years later, Beth's clients were still willing to give up the most sensitive of gossip to their hairdresser. This intimate information often resurfaced as evidence of Beth's power.

The Watchers had planted more hidden cameras around Beth's salon. Butler's surveillance team had also been redeployed from the plantation. Cameras would keep Jonah informed of activity at the plantation, but it was now vital that they could follow Beth, in the hope she led them back to Saint.

Chapter 22.

"Stand by, stand by", announced one of the surveillance team. "Off, off, off, I'm two cars behind", he clarified, as Beth left her salon and drove out of the French Quarter. The other operatives started their engines and readied themselves to join the small convoy following Beth. It was the third time they had followed Beth away from her salon. The first time she went home for her lunch. The second time, she visited the voodoo emporium. They hoped this third trip would bring them more luck.

The team already knew it was not the voodoo emporium this time, as Beth was driving out of the French Quarter. But they could not yet rule out another journey home.

"It's not home", announced the operative as Beth turned away from the direction of her home. The team followed a routine surveillance method, of following a car. The small team followed in convoy, continuously changing position, so the same car was never behind Beth for too long. Before long, the Watchers found that their close surveillance was unnecessary. They knew exactly where Beth was heading. She was going back to the Seventh Day Adventist hall, where Barbara had first met Beth. "Is that where they are hiding Saint?" thought Jonah, as he monitored the radio transmissions.

"Nev lad, can you and Amber get over there with a laser mic?" asked Jonah.
The Watchers needed to know who was inside the building, and its many windows provided plenty of scope to use a laser microphone. Stone and Amber lost no time jumping on their motorcycles and riding out towards the hall.
Again playing the role of a tourist couple, Stone and Amber settled onto a bench within sight of the hall. Among their collection of tourist looking cameras and video recorders, they hid the small laser mic. This sophisticated piece of equipment was a regular part of the Watchers' surveillance tactics. We hear sound, because of the vibrations they cause in the air. The sound waves cause very slight vibrations in windows, mirrors or other surfaces which interrupt their journey through the air. Stone's laser mic picked up the vibrations and turned them back into speech.
Other than toilets and a kitchen, there was only the one big room at the Seventh Day Adventist hall, so Stone was confident he would capture anything said inside.

Within seconds of Beth entering the building, Stone started to pick up speech. "That's another batch under my spell", said Beth as she walked into the hall. She talked almost none stop, telling how the numbers attending the voodoo emporium were growing rapidly.

"We're gearing up for a rite to rival Marie's 1874 St John's Eve rite on Lake Pontchartrain", she added.

Finally, the reply Stone waited for came. But it was not Matthew Saint's voice that answered Beth. "Let's hope so Sister Beth. 12,000 people will give us the army we need", replied the distinctive female voice. "It's Ellen White", said Stone, as he listened to their conversation.

No matter how hard they listened, there were no other voices inside the hall.

Just before the two women parted, White asked a question which puzzled Stone. "Will TAG deliver on time?" asked White.

"Oh, you can be sure of that", came Beth's reply.

Stone was still puzzling over this last exchange, when Beth walked out of the building, heading straight towards him and Amber. Fearing compromise, Amber went straight into spy mode, kissing Stone to hide their faces. Her move caught Stone by surprise, but it was a very pleasant surprise. Despite Stone knowing Amber's reaction was necessary, the kiss felt a little too long and too tender to be just business.

Beth seemed in a form of meditation as she walked around the small green space on which Stone and Amber sat.

Whilst holding her embrace, Amber watched Beth over Stone's shoulder. She seemed deep in thought and oblivious to the couple sitting on the bench. It was then that Amber realised Beth was not meditating. She was making a phone call. The tiny Bluetooth headset was hidden by her thick black hair.

"Wish we could listen in", thought Amber, knowing they could not deploy their microphone without being seen.

In time, Beth finished her walk and returned to her car.

While Stone had been listening to the two women talking, Amber had used the time to approach Beth's car. They now had a tracking device which would make following Beth much easier.

Beth drove off towards the south east of the city. The surveillance team was still in position, but Jonah was monitoring the progress of their tracking device.

Jonah watched the flashing light make its way across the map on his computer monitor. He realised Beth was driving away from the affluent areas of the city where she and Ellen White lived. The south eastern area, close to the Mississippi was traditionally where the poorer black Creoles had settled, as historically, the land had been given to the freed slaves. It was also a low lying area which was often badly affected by the Caribbean's regular hurricanes. The 9th Ward, which Beth was driving into, was the worst hit by Hurricane Katrina. Work was still ongoing to repair the devastation caused to the district.

Stone and Amber had followed at a safe distance with their motorcycles. The surveillance team had spread out to enter the 9th Ward by several routes. So, when Beth parked her car, they were all in position to approach, watch and plant their tiny surveillance cameras.

Stone could see the devastation caused by the hurricane in August 2005, when almost every levee on the Mississippi was breached, flooding 80% of the city.

The 9th Ward was by far the worst hit area, where an entire community had died. Entire sections of the district had been destroyed. The city was now slowly rebuilding, but there was still much evidence of Katrina's destruction. Crosses on buildings showed the dates they had been inspected and the number of bodies found inside. Yet, despite the devastation, every lawn on the wrecked plots was neatly manicured. City by-laws meant that owners must cut their grass or risk losing their property for not taking care of their lot.

While Stone, Amber and their team were working their way through the 9th Ward, Jonah was, as always busy with research. From his maps, he saw that this easternmost downriver part of the city is the largest of New Orleans seventeen Wards. On the south it is bounded by the Mississippi River, with Lake Pontchartrain forming the north end of the ward. Through the centre of the Ward runs the Industrial Canal, dredged through the neighbourhood in the 1920s. This now separates the sub districts of Upper and Lower 9th Ward.

Jonah looked at the background and history of the 9th Ward. He knew this was a predominantly black creole area, but he did not realise quite how much black history the Ward held. Development of the area along the river started first, at the beginning of the 19th century, followed by building on high land along Gentilly Ridge. The rest of the area between Gentilly Ridge and Lake Pontchartrain was swamp. It was not drained or developed until the mid 20th century, when an expanding population needed more land.

Just like the rest of New Orleans, the 9th Ward had produced its share of music legends such as Fats Domino.

Lincoln Beach was a lakefront amusement park for the blacks, during the era of racial segregation. The nearby Pontchartrain Beach was the corresponding amusement area for whites. "That's why Marie Laveau picked that area", thought Jonah. After White and Beth had discussed the Voodoo Queen's Lake Pontchartrain rite, Jonah had researched what they meant. He learned that Laveau's largest ever ceremony was held in the place where black and white New Orleans met. The 12,000 that White had mentioned was the estimated number of black and white people who joined in the 1874 St John's Eve rite.

Because it was poor, low lying land, the 9th Ward had suffered more than most in the areas regular hurricanes. Parts of the 9th Ward flooded during Hurricane Flossy in 1956, and the Lower 9th suffered catastrophic flooding in Hurricane Betsy in 1965. But it was Hurricane Katrina that thrust the 9th into the nation's spotlight. Much of the land on both sides of the Industrial Canal was flooded in 2005, with the majority of damage caused by storm surge.

The Lower 9th suffered worst, with storm surge coming through two large breaches in the Industrial Canal flood protection system, creating violent currents that not only flooded buildings, but smashed them and displaced them from their foundations.
Then, to add to the Lower 9th's problems, the Ward, not yet dry from Katrina, was re-flooded by Hurricane Rita a month later.

During the Mardi Gras of 2006, the 9th Ward became a popular spot for visitors. The national attention the area received due to the hurricane and the events following the disaster provided Carnival revellers with an additional destination during their celebration.
Tourists were not the only ones to venture into the area. Locals flocked to the devastated neighbourhoods as well. Hundreds of people gathered on Fat Tuesday, in the celebratory spirit of a jazz funeral. Many residents made their first trip back to take part in this massive block party in their former neighbourhood. "Voodoo rites, block parties, jazz funerals", thought Jonah. "The New Orleanians certainly know how to party".

Watching the camera feed, it was clear to Jonah that the excitement of 2006 had faded from the Lower 9th. It was now a much quieter place. The streets were still largely deserted, but repairs had begun, particularly to the roads and essential infrastructure.
Main roads had already been resurfaced, even those which had been neglected for years prior to

Katrina.

Stone and Amber had remained on their motorcycles, as the helmets would hide their white faces and Amber's blond hair. As they toured the district, they could see that, although the bigger roads were improved, smaller, neighbourhood roads remained a patchwork of potholes, dips and humps.

It was in one of these more neglected neighbourhoods that Beth had parked. The houses were all still boarded up and with no apparent sign of life. But Stone's trained policeman's eye spotted the things that were out of place. Some of the window boarding looked much more secure than others. Roof aerials had been repaired, or renewed. Air conditioning units had been fitted. But most out of place were the Slavic faces of men trying to look inconspicuous. No matter how well trained Dimov's former Spetsnaz fighters were, their white skin would always stand out in the Lower 9th.

Stone had spotted four buildings on the ramshackle street which looked slightly different to the rest. Three of the small houses had been worked on, and among the houses, a disused convenience store also looked more secure.

"Found them", said Stone into his hidden radio. "Plot my GPS, and I'll get the team to plant cameras".

"I'm already on it Nev lad", replied Jonah. "And I'll see if Jonny can find an excuse to task a satellite".

The Spetsnaz had watched Stone and Amber ride by, so they could not risk another pass. But they needed to get in close with one of their radiation detectors. "Skull", said Stone, attracting the MC President's attention over the radio. "I think we need to give the surveillance team more of a briefing. Without black skin, we stand out a mile". The surveillance team were employees of the Watchers MC, not full members. The club's fully patched members were also directors of their global security business. Many of the employees aspired to MC membership, but they rarely knew as much about a job as the members did. This team was on loan to Skull from the Watchers' Texas chapter. Knowing they were going to New Orleans, the Texans had purposely chosen black operatives to make up the team. "Agreed", replied Skull. "I'll head over and give the briefing the authority of the P patch". It was a big risk to their operation's security to bring more people into their confidence. But there were jobs to be done which the English and Portuguese members could not fulfill. Skull knew that any warning delivered by the MC's International P, or President would carry much more weight.

Skull thought about what to tell the team while he rode his powerful motorcycle towards the 9th Ward. There was no option than to brief on the plutonium. But Skull could not tell them that Saint was a rogue British scientist. It was enough for them to know he was part of O Lobo's smuggling gang. His problem was to decide how much of the Millerite plot to reveal.

The ride over had cleared Skull's head and he had his story straight when he met with the team. "The guy you are following is a smuggler. He's brought plutonium into the country", briefed Skull. Skull got exactly the response he expected from the Texan surveillance team. He knew how patriotic they would be and had already worked out how to answer the inevitable "US intelligence should be dealing with this Prez".

"We're hired to save our client embarrassment", replied Skull. "The plute was stolen from a re-processor. If they don't get it back before any governments find out, they will be out of business". The story was not too far from the truth. The plutonium was from Cuba, but the scientist was from Britain, and Britain was a nuclear re-processor. If the US government found out, it would damage a very important relationship. Skull knew it would be difficult for the Texans to reconcile the conflict of country against MC. But they were very well paid by the Watchers and all aspired to full membership one day. A success in such an important operation would help write their ticket to membership.

Chapter 23.

Satisfied that they had an important job to do, the team started to close in on the buildings that Stone had identified. Some were on foot and others rode old bicycles they kept in one of the surveillance vans.

The Spetsnaz would be very vigilant, so the team had to work quickly and casually. Moving through the area, they planted their tiny cameras. One man risked walking closer to the buildings. He was soon moved on by a guard, but not before leaving an audio bug on the deserted convenience store.

The Watchers are the very best in their business and soon, they had video feed of the entire area Stone had identified. Audio was more limited, but they had a bug on the largest building and long range microphones from all directions outside.

Stone hoped it would be enough. Everything in New Orleans had seemed to be one step forward, then another back. They knew roughly what the Millerites planned, but were no closer to working out their plan.

Just getting Matthew Saint back would satisfy MI5. But the Watchers could not settle just for that, they had to stop the bombs.

One of the operatives was listening intently to the bug on the store, but could hear nothing at all inside. "Maybe it's just for ceremonies", thought Jonah, as he got his regular updates. Jonah had hoped the larger building would be their centre of

activity, but nothing was being said inside.
The long range mics were picking up Bulgarian
speech from some of the Spetsnaz. But from what
little Jonah could translate, it seemed only general
chat. Steve Butler would also review the
recordings, as the former Royal Marine had
worked extensively in Bulgaria as an adventure
holiday leader. What puzzled Jonah from the mic
feed was the speech that was missing.
Since Beth's arrival, Creoles had started to
appear amongst the Spetsnaz. From their
bearing, they looked every bit the soldiers that the
Bulgarians were, but they were absolutely silent.
The Creole guards were also dressed the same,
but it was not like any uniform Jonah had ever
seen. They wore straw hats, blue denim shirts
and dark glasses, and were armed with machetes
and guns. The odd look of the Creole guards and
their silence pulled at something in Jonah's
memory, but he could not quite bring it to the
surface.

Jonah desperately needed feed from the smaller
buildings, particularly the one Beth had gone
inside. But with the heavy presence of Spetsnaz
and Creole guards, the Watchers could not get
any closer. With the team now playing a waiting
game, Jonah turned his attention to some
financial work that Jonny Johnson's MI5 analysts
had prepared.
The Millerite's finances were hidden behind a
multitude of front companies and off shore
accounts. But Jonny's analysts were used to this
in tracking terrorist funds. Jonny was sure that his

team had unraveled the Millerite's complex
financing. Money had been flooding in from all
sectors of Louisiana society. There were small,
regular donations from ordinary working people.
But these were not the small numbers that
Barbara had seen at the Millerite's ceremony,
they numbered in their thousands.
Any money which did not originate from Millerite
followers had been paid in through a charity
linked to voodoo Houngan priests. These priests
represent the good side of voodoo and confine
their activities to white magic, such as bringing
good fortune and healing.
There were also much larger donations, which the
analysts had traced back to Louisiana's great and
good. These had been more difficult to follow, but
Jonny's experts had managed it. These huge
donations had flowed through numerous
accounts, before passing through one controlled
by Beth. "They are working the voodoo angle like
the best of the TV evangelists", thought Jonah.
He could see how Louisiana's superstitious
working people could be taken in by Beth's
theatrical voodoo. But the big donations were
from a broad range of very important people.
"Eee Beth lass, what's your hold over them",
thought Jonah.

Jonah was diverted from his reading, as a truck
pulled up outside the convenience store.
He was about to get an answer for why there had
been no speech picked up on their bug.
The strange looking men in straw hats and
sunglasses approached the back of the truck.

Jonah was hoping he might see the bombs, or plutonium moving in or out of the building. But what he saw was much more macabre. The men were unloading body bags, which looked to be occupied by bodies. Then, looking closer at the video feed, Jonah recognised the man directing the unloading. "It's Baron Samedi, Nev lad", said Jonah. He had recognised the Millerite who had acted as Beth's voodoo assistant.

Stone realised quickly what Jonah meant. He started organising some of the surveillance operatives to tail the truck when it moved off.

"Just when you think you have it sorted, the game changes on you", thought Stone.

They had been in a quiet period, waiting for Beth to lead them to Matthew Saint. Now, they seemed no closer to finding Saint, but they had lots of unexplained bodies enter their scenario.

Barbara and Miguel could not afford to be seen. While they were awaiting another opportunity to go undercover with the Millerites, the other Watchers were getting spread quite thin. They needed to keep some people in the 9th Ward. Beth would need to be tailed, if she moved away. Now they also had the added problem of following Baron Samedi's truck.

The truck did move off, but Samedi remained within the wrecked store. "Tag the truck", instructed Stone. He had made a snap decision for a tracker to be placed on the truck as it left. A heavily silenced rifle coughed, as its high tech projectile started its journey towards the truck.

The operative had expertly planted the same type of tracking device they had earlier used on Saint's car. Now they could track the truck remotely and concentrate their resources on the main players.

Activity picked up in the Lower 9th during that evening and throughout the night.

There were increasing sounds of movement within the convenience store, but not a word was said. Jonah was sure there were now many more people inside than just Baron Samedi, but they had seen no one enter the building. At least no one alive.

The truck came and went twice more in the night, delivering yet more body bags. Each time the Watchers tracked it to unremarkable buildings close to the French Quarter.

"Curiousour and curiousour", thought Jonah, as he puzzled on what was happening.

There was also a steady stream of people arriving at the two houses either side of the shop. Barbara was watching the video feed and recognised many of the new arrivals.

"They were all at the voodoo ceremony", observed Barbara.

Then, something even stranger happened. Hired mini busses started to arrive and park along the road, but this time, they were not bringing people into the Lower 9th. Small groups of men began to walk out of the former convenience store. All were dressed in the denim shirts, straw hats and sunglasses, worn by the other guards. There was something oddly distant about them that Jonah could not quite figure out. But the strangest thing was how so many people could have been inside, without the bug picking up their speech.

Each bus left the 9th with four occupants; a driver, one of Beth's inner circle and two of the oddly silent guards.

It was then that Barbara's phone rang, announcing Beth's sing song voice. "We've something very special for you today", she began. "Be ready, transport will be there within an hour". With that short, cryptic message, Beth ended the call. Many people would be getting a similar call, none would know what was in store for them.

Despite Barbara's knowledge of the busses leaving the 9th Ward, she was just as much in the dark.

What was certain was that Barbara would be travelling and the Watchers would have to be close by.

It was a given that her brother Miguel and the huge enforcer Joao Alva would be close by in a van. But they all got a sense that whatever the Millerites were planning, was starting to gain pace, so extra back up would follow Barbara to her destination. Stone and Amber had now become something of a team, so they remained paired. Skull decided to take Harris with him. The Watchers' potential recruit had been showing promise throughout the operation and Skull wanted to keep a presidential eye on him.

While one team was readying themselves to follow Barbara, the others were watching activity increase in the 9th Ward. Mini busses continued to arrive, and leave with their crew of four.

Other cars came and went too, but the Watchers did not have the numbers to follow them.
But one car in particular immediately attracted their attention. A large black funeral hearse, which had been converted to a limousine pulled up. Inside, with a driver, was Ellen White. When she was joined by Beth and two of the straw hatted guards, Jonah knew this was the one that needed their attention.
Jonah and Butler quickly organised their resources to follow the hearse. Although they were to find it would not be a long surveillance. As the hearse finished its short journey at the north end of the 9th Ward, Jonah was quite literally wanting to kick himself.
Beth and Ellen got out of their car and walked to tents pitched on the shore of Lake Pontchartrain. "How could I have missed that?" thought Jonah, as he watched the live surveillance footage. Posters around the site advertised a world record breaking voodoo festival.
The Watchers had been so focused on the search for Matthew Saint, that they had neglected their usual scrutiny of local news. The attempt to better the 12,000 attendees at Marie Laveau's voodoo rite had been well publicised.
People were arriving steadily and the whole site was starting to develop a festival atmosphere. Fires were burning, music was playing and many of the people had started to dance, or at least sway in time with the rhythmic music.
Finding out about the festival did not answer any of Jonah's questions, it just prompted even more. How could this fit with the Millerite plot? Was

Matthew Saint, or the bombs there? Could the bombs be detonated here? If the target was Dearbourne, how could all this fit with a Muslim convention half a continent away?

But most pressing in Jonah's mind, was a question about Barbara's safety. If so many festival goers had made their own way there, why did Barbara and the others get special treatment? There was still something worrying Jonah about the straw hatted guards. Their distinctive clothing and unearthly, far away expressions nagged at Jonah's memory.

Barbara's group arrived without incident and they were led into one of the many large tents. This time Barbara was fitted with a tiny camera and radio, so Jonah could see it was just a drinks reception.

But more of the straw hatted guards circled among the guests. "Tonton Macoutes!" exclaimed Jonah, as his memory returned. The distinctive style of dress was worn by the special operations unit of Papa Doc Duvalier, the Haitian dictator. Haitians named this feared, paramilitary force after the mythological Tonton Macoute bogeyman, who kidnapped and punished unruly children by catching them in a sack, or macoute and carrying them off to eat for breakfast.

Most hated of the Macoutes was Luckner Cambronne who led them throughout the 1960s and 1970s. His cruelty earned him the nickname as "Vampire of the Caribbean".

Some of the most important members of the Tonton Macoute were voodoo leaders. This religious affiliation gave the Macoutes an unearthly authority in the eyes of the public. From their methods to their choice of clothes, voodoo always played an important role in their actions. It was also rumoured that the Tonton Macoutes were zombies. They appeared to be in a constant state of trance, and they unquestioningly followed every order Duvalier gave.

Voodoo seemed to be playing an increasing role in the Millerite plot, but Jonah still could not work out how it all fitted together.

The crowds arriving at the festival made it easy for the Watchers to mingle and they began to work on getting closer to the tents. The straw hatted guards stood between them and the tent that Barbara had entered. Stone noted that the festival seemed wholly the preserve of the New Orleanians, Dimov's East European thugs were nowhere to be seen.

"I'm guessing there are no bombs here Amber", said Stone. "They wouldn't trust that sort of security to the locals".

"Probably the same for Saint", added Amber, who had seen how closely the Spetsnaz had been guarding him. So, the question was, if there were no bombs and no engineer, what was the significance of the festival?

The Watchers continued to circle the tents, trying to get closer. Stone and Amber concentrated on one side, while Skull and Harris covered the other. The ever growing crowd seemed constantly on the move. As new people arrived, they moved as a mass, this way and that, around the various displays and attractions. Always, the steady rhythmic music and bonfire smoke filled the air. Then suddenly, Beth appeared on a stage behind her tent. The entire crowd surged, pushing for a position where they could see the Voodoo Queen. The surge happened so quickly, that Skull and Harris became separated. Harris was pushed much closer to the side of the tent. Much too close, for the straw hatted men.

A face appeared in the tent flap, staring directly at Harris. It was a face like nothing Harris had seen before. The eyes were the worst. They were like the eyes of a dead man, not blind, but staring, unfocused, unseeing. The whole face, for that matter, was vacant, as if there was nothing behind it. It seemed not only expressionless, but incapable of expression. Harris was frozen to the spot. The only time he had seen anything like it before had been in a zombie movie. But zombies are not real, are they?

Most people consider zombies only to be the stuff of horror movies, but they do exist in Haiti in the present day. Thousands of people in Haiti are considered to be zombies, some of whom lead normal lives with families and jobs. It's even considered to be a crime to make a zombie in Haiti.

Then, while Harris was transfixed by the zombie, he felt a sharp puncture in the back of his neck. He suddenly became lethargic and could feel his breath and heart slowing, to the point that he must have appeared dead. But Harris was aware of everything happening around him. He just could not make any movement or sound. Harris saw and felt the two straw hatted men lift and carry him into the tent. But much as the terrified biker tried to scream out, not a sound passed his lips.

The men lay Harris down among a row of bodies. He looked around as best he could, with his unmoving eyes. The bodies all looked dead, but so, he guessed, did he. Every ounce of mental strength went into moving. But try as he might, nothing moved.

Harris had never been more frightened in his life. The bikers were always in control, always in charge. Yet here he was, helpless. All he could hope for was that the Watchers would come for him.

Chapter 24.

While the Watchers were at the voodoo festival, or staking out the 9th Ward, Jonah and Jonny were trying to figure out the Dearborn connection. The basics were easy to find. Dearborn is in the State of Michigan, near Detroit and close to the Canadian border. Although nearby Detroit became famous as America's Motown, Dearborn possibly has a better claim as the birthplace of the US automotive industry.

The city was the home of Henry Ford and is the world headquarters of the Ford Motor Company. The city's residents are primarily of European or Middle Eastern heritage, descendants of 19th and 20th-century immigrants. Those with Middle Eastern ancestries make up the largest of the city's ethnic groups, with Lebanese, Yemeni, Iraqi, Syrian and Palestinians. It also has the largest proportion of Arab Americans in the United States.

"Perfect", thought Jonah, if the Millerites really did want to target Muslims.

The first Arab immigrants came in the early-to-mid-20th century to work in the automotive industry and were mostly Lebanese. Since then, Muslim Arab immigrants from Yemen, Iraq and Palestine have joined them.

After the Arab Muslim community built the Islamic Center of America and the Dearborn Mosque, Iraqi refugees came, fleeing the wars in their country since 2003.

Dearborn's Muslim credentials strengthened further in 2005, when the city opened its Arab American National Museum. "Another potential target", thought Jonah.

Jonah also found a large number of potential targets among the city's political leadership. The city council president is a Muslim Arab-American and the majority of the council members are Arab.

If Jonah was right about the Millerites wanting to stir up religious tension in Dearborn, he found plenty of previous examples. In 2010 members of the Christian group "Acts 17 Apologetics" were arrested and prosecuted for handing out Arabic-English copies of the Gospel of John.

Then a Nevada Tea Party Senatorial candidate, Sharron Angle, suggested that Dearborn was contributing to the "militant terrorist situation," by enforcing Islamic law.

In 2011Preacher Terry Jones planned a protest outside the Islamic Center of America. He cancelled the protest when the Local Authorities required him to post a $45,000 "peace bond".

Then a week later, Jones led a rally at the Dearborn City Hall, designated as a free speech zone. Riot police were needed to control counter protesters.

Terry Jones managed to lead a protest in front of the Islamic Center of America in 2012, speaking about Islam and Free Speech. The mosque was placed on lock down and 30 police cars were needed to prevent a counter protest.

Jonah also read that the city has a small African

American population, whose ancestors came from the rural South during the Great Migration of the early twentieth century. "Well, there's the link to New Orleans", thought Jonah. "There's probably some family connections".

As Jonah dug deeper, he found more reasons to choose Dearborn as a place to stir religious tension. Both of Islam's largest denominations are prominently represented in the city. The Sunni and Shia branches of the religion are both present in very prominent ways.
The Sunnis, through their American Muslim Society, have Dearborn Mosque. This huge mosque, built in 1937 was only the second mosque built in the U.S. The building is three stories high and covers almost an entire city block.
Although the Sunnis represent almost 90% of the world's Muslims, the Shias have a disproportionately large presence at Dearborn's Islamic Center of America. This is the largest mosque in North America and the oldest Shia mosque in the United States.
With its large, mostly Lebanese, Shia population, Dearborn is often called the "heart of Shiism" in the United States.

Tensions, of varying levels between the two denominations, date back to the death of the prophet Muhammad in 632. The disagreement was over who should succeed the prophet as the first Caliph.
Adherents of Shia Islam favoured Muhammad's

son-in-law and Cousin Ali ibn Abi Talib.

Ali's rule over the early Muslim community was often contested. He constantly struggled to maintain his power against the groups who betrayed him. This eventually led to the First Fitna, or civil war within the Islamic Caliphate. The Fitna began as a series of revolts and ended with Ali's assassination in 661.

Many countries consider Sunnis the orthodox version of the religion. The Sunnis favoured Abu Bakr as Muhammad's successor. Although they did not completely reject Ali ibn Abi Talib, they consider him the fourth Caliph rather than the first.

Jonah was not sure how the differences between the two denominations could fit into the Millerite's plans. But he did know that O Lobo was an expert at turning any tensions or disagreement to his advantage.

Jonah also knew that there was another, potentially more explosive factor to American Islam. The racial tensions of the 1930s and the Black Power movement gave birth to the Nation of Islam.

The Nation of Islam was created in 1930 by Wallace Fard Muhammad. It taught a form of Islam, promoting black supremacy and labeling white people as "devils". The movement's message caused great concern among white Americans, but it was effective among blacks, especially poor people, students and professionals. At its peak, there were estimated to be over 20,000 members.

The Nation of Islam has received a great deal of criticism for its anti-white, anti-Christian, and anti-Semitic teachings, and is considered a hate group by many people. Two of the most famous members were Malcolm X and Muhammad Ali. Malcolm X was one of their most influential leaders and advocated the complete separation of blacks from whites. He left the organisation after controversial comments on the John F. Kennedy assassination. Eventually Malcolm X converted to Sunni Islam and started a movement among African Americans towards Sunni Islam.

The Nation of Islam adding racial, as well as religious tension to the mix interested Jonah. Particularly when he learned about the scope of conversion to Islam inside U.S. prisons. Muslim inmates comprise about 20% of the prison population, or roughly 350,000 inmates. Many of these inmates came into prison as non-Muslims, with 80% of prisoners who find faith in prison converting to Islam. These converted inmates are mostly African American, giving Jonah yet another link to the New Orleans voodoo community.

Always the logical planner, Jonah habitually challenged his own thinking.
They had linked a massive Muslim conference in Dearborn, with the anniversary of the Millerites' Great Disappointment.
He had also found links between Dearborn and New Orleans black Creole people. Many former slaves headed to Chicago and Dearborn during

the twentieth century's Great Migration.
Couple these with the draw of Dearborn's huge
mosques to former prisoners converted to the
Nation of Islam in prison. Jonah was starting to
see Dearborn as the ideal target for the Millerites.
But he could still not figure out the need for
nuclear weapons, and how they might hope to
draw others into a world destroying nuclear war.

Of all the states who consider themselves Muslim
countries, only Pakistan was officially a nuclear
power. Jonny led Jonah through what British
Intelligence knew of Pakistan's nuclear
programme. They began working towards their
own bomb in the mid 1970s, in a continuing arms
race with neighbouring India. Problems obtaining
enough weapons grade fissile material delayed a
viable test detonation until 1998.
Once they had a reliable source of material, their
weapons development gathered pace.
A source in Russia's foreign ministry leaked that
there are somewhere between 120,000 to
130,000 people directly involved in Pakistan's
nuclear and missile programmemes. Jonny's
intelligence analysts considered this figure
extremely large for a developing country.
The size of the programmeme's workforce
seemed to have paid off.
Jonny explained that the actual size of Pakistan's
nuclear stockpile is hard to gauge owing to the
extreme secrecy which surrounds the
programmeme in Pakistan. However, in 2007,
retired Pakistan Army's Brigadier-General Feroz
Khan told a Pakistani newspaper that Pakistan

had 80 to 120 genuine warheads. "If they managed that in nine years, what have they got now?" thought Jonah.

Jonny had some information, although what he could access was a little old. By the time of their first tests in 1998, Pakistan had at least six secret locations, and by now may have many more secret sites. In 2008, the United States publicly admitted that it did not know where all of Pakistan's nuclear sites are located. "This isn't sounding good", thought Jonah.

Although British Intelligence did not know where the Pakistani missiles were hidden, they did have a good idea of the types they had developed. Jonny knew that Pakistan had built Soviet-style road-mobile missiles. These were useful for moving around and concealment measures, but they were built to defend against India. They were no threat to the U.S.

It was their longer range missiles that worried Jonny.

They have a wide variety of nuclear capable ballistic missiles with ranges up to 2500 km. They also have nuclear tipped Babur cruise missiles with ranges up to 700 km. none of these could reach the U.S. mainland, but they could hit many of America's interests around the world.

More worryingly, from a strategic point of view, they have the Hatf-4 Shaheen-1A, which is capable of carrying a nuclear warhead and is designed to evade missile-defence systems.

The Pakistan Air Force presented the greatest threat for direct retaliation against the U.S. Jonny knew they had perfected a tactic known as toss-bombing. This is a method of bombing where the attacking aircraft pulls upward when releasing its bomb load, giving the bomb additional time in flight by starting its ballistic path in an upward direction.

This compensates for the gravity drop of the bomb in flight, allowing the pilot to distance his aircraft from the blast effects of a nuclear bomb.

"So Jonny lad", began Jonah. "We know the Pakistanis are capable of nuking the US. But would they? They are a mainstream country, with a reputable presence on the world stage".

"It's not so much the country", replied Jonny" "we're more worried about their technology and tactics". Jonny explained that, with 130,000 people involved in Pakistan's nuclear programmes, there were plenty of opportunities for radical groups, or rogue states to obtain their technology. Leakage from Pakistan began very early in their programme. One of the key scientists is already known to have widely disseminated Pakistan's secrets. Abdul Qadeer Khan, better known as A. Q. Khan, was responsible for bringing gas-centrifuge uranium enrichment to Pakistan's atomic bomb project, thus solving their fissile material shortage. Allegedly, this technology came from Khan's previous employers in Holland and he was convicted in absence of espionage by the Dutch. He also founded the Kahuta Research Laboratories, Pakistan's key nuclear research facility, serving as it's Director-General until his

retirement in 2001
In 2004, Khan confessed to his government over his suspicious activities in other countries after the United States provided evidence to Pakistan.

When Libya was forced to give up its weapons-related material in 2003, their gas-ultra centrifuges were early models that Khan developed in the 1980s.
Pakistan and North Korea maintained some level of trade and diplomatic relations.
Khan admitted that he had exchanged secret information on uranium enrichment with North Korea in exchange for ballistic missile technology.
In 1987 Pakistan turned down Iran's offer to purchase fuel-cycle technology. But Khan gave them a sensitive report on centrifuges. This came to light in 2003 when the Iranian government came under intense pressure from the Western world to fully disclose its nuclear programme. On 4 February 2004, Khan appeared on state-owned Pakistan Television and confessed to running a proliferation ring, and admitted to supplying technology to Iran, North Korea and Libya.

"So, you see Jonah", concluded Jonny Johnson. "It's not just established States we have to worry about. Khan's technology is widely spread through some very unstable countries. And we have no idea what weapons grade material has been squirreled away. Improvised nuclear devices could come from, literally anywhere".

Chapter 25.

While Jonah and Jonny were talking politics, Harris was fighting for his life inside the voodoo tent. Or, at least his mind was fighting. His body was immobile as a result of the cocktail of drugs delivered into his neck by a blow dart. As Harris' mind silently screamed out for help, the bodies piled up around him. Logic had long since left Harris. All his terrified brain could process, was that he was surrounded by the dead. But the bodies were not dead. Just like Harris, they had been paralysed by the same ancient recipe of drugs. All of them were going through the most terrifying experience of their lives, in absolute silence.

Away from the tented area, Stone and Amber had started to wander towards the extremities of the festival site. The main focus of the festival was around the tents and huge bonfire. But there were other, much smaller fringe events happening around the edges of the site. Many of these were individual voodoo sorcerers plying their trade of spells and charms.
Others were souvenir stalls, aimed at the tourists. But it was another, very animated group that attracted Stone's attention. Not least because there was a TV crew among them. Stone recognised the voodoo queen who was the centre of attention. She was one of Beth's entourage, who left the French Quarter voodoo rite which Barbara had attended.

"What's catching the TV attention?" asked Amber.
"Only one way of finding out", replied Stone, as
he started moving towards the group.

When Stone saw what the cameras were filming,
his blood seemed to chill. In the light of what they
suspected the Millerites of planning, the events he
was watching took on a very dangerous
significance.
The queen held a large voodoo doll, which she
waved about to emphasise her words.
All of New Orleans souvenir shops sell that most
stereotypical of voodoo items, the voodoo doll.
Stone knew that in the days of Marie Laveau you
might occasionally see a little wax doll stuck with
pins. But, despite their frequency in fiction
Voodoo dolls were rarely used in the practices.
Nevertheless, today they are sold everywhere.
Most are made-in-China souvenirs, but a local
variety are sold at Marie Laveau's House of
Voodoo, Rev. Zombie's Voodoo Shop and the
New Orleans Historic Voodoo Museum.
The use of a voodoo doll suggested to Stone that
the gathering's purpose must be to attract the
attention of people outside of the Creole
community.

The voodoo doll was most frightening, not for any
occult significance, but for the image it depicted.
The world has many personalities, both living and
dead, whose representation as a voodoo doll
would cause outrage. But none had the explosive
potential of the figure this sorcerer was using. The
image was one that Stone had seen in caricature

many times before. Every time such an image appeared, it caused outrage and violence. The bearded doll, wearing turban and Arab dress, was unmistakable. Also unmistakable, was the intent of its use, as the caricature bomb in its hand could only be there as an insult.

Stone knew that violence over insulting images of the prophet Muhammad went back at least to 2005, when a Danish newspaper printed a cartoon of Muhammad with a bomb.

Tension over the subject grew when Dutch politician Geert Wilders showed the cartoons on Dutch television, earning critical condemnation.

Violent reaction to publishing the cartoons peaked in 2015 when Charlie Hebdo's Paris offices were attacked by armed gunmen, killing 12 journalists and artists.

The U.S. did not escape the violence, as later that year two people were shot at an exhibition in Texas, where the cartoons were displayed.

Amber recognised the news crews present. None of them were mainstream news media. They were all from the sort of channel which delighted in creating controversy.

Under the glare of the TV lights, the news anchors worked the crowd into a frenzy, as the voodoo queen pushed pins into her doll. Stone was in no doubt that this would provoke a violent backlash from Islam's more radical factions. But the most that had been killed over Muhammad caricatures so far, were the 12 Charlie Hebdo staff. It was hardly going to be enough to trigger a nuclear war.

Back in the tent, the bodies continued to pile up around Harris. His apparently lifeless eyes took everything in and inwardly, his silent screams grew stronger. Between his attempts at screaming, Harris' mind was working overtime. "What's happening to me", "why do they need all these paralysed bodies", how can I escape", have the Watchers missed me yet?"

Skull had missed Harris. The two got separated by the crowd surging and Skull had been searching for him ever since. The MC President would not easily lose one of his team. Harris was an employee of the Watchers, not part of the inner circle of full members. But, when on a job, Skull treated all his team with the same respect. "Nev, Amber, get back here and help me find Harris", said Skull over the radio. He was starting to worry a little now. Harris was a capable operative, but with radio and phone, he should have made contact by now.
Harris' phone buzzed silently in his pocket and he heard Skull's every word through his earpiece. But still, his paralysed body could not react. Gradually, Harris was comforted that the Watchers were searching for him and the panic began to subside. Logic started to regain control of his mind, as Harris tried to take stock of what was happening to him.
As Harris' mind cleared, he remembered seeing the zombie Tonton Macout, just before his neck was punctured.
Often, DVD movies come with a documentary

film. Harris had seen such a documentary, after watching a zombie movie. Slowly, he began to align parts of the documentary with his own situation.

Belief in zombies is unique to voodoo. The Creole word "zombi' came from Nzambi, a West African deity but it only came into general use in 1929, after the publication of William B. Seabrook's The Magic Island. In this book, Seabrook recounts his experiences on Haiti, including the walking dead. The legends tell that Haitian zombies were normal people, who underwent zombification by a voodoo sorcerer, through spell or potion. The victim dies and becomes a mindless automaton, incapable of remembering the past, unable to recognise loved ones and doomed to a life of miserable toil under the will of the zombie master. But the documentary had told Harris that in reality, only a part of their mind had died. The process also had much more to do with potions than spells.

The film gave many examples of zombies in modern day Haiti. The dictator, Papa Doc Duvallier's Tonton Macoutes were said to be in trances and followed every command that Duvallier gave them.

There were also many stories of people who died, and then many years later returned to shock and surprise their relatives. A man named Caesar returned 18 years after he died, to marry, have three children and die again, 30 years after he was originally buried.

Another case involved a student who had been shot in a robbery. Six months later, the student returned to his parent's house as a zombie. At first it was possible to talk with the man, and he related the story of his murder, a voodoo witch doctor stealing his body from the ambulance and his transformation into a zombie. As time went on, he became unable to communicate, grew more lethargic and died.

Harris remembered the film saying that zombies, are created by the use of drugs. A blow dart administers tetrodotoxin, a powerful neurotoxin found in puffer fish. And a cocktail of hallucinogenic drugs, which allow the sorcerer complete control over their victim. "That explains the puncture to my neck", thought Harris, remembering the dart that hit him.

This causes severe neurological damage; primarily affecting the left side of the brain (the left side of the brain controls speech, memory and motor skills). The victim suddenly becomes lethargic and then slowly seems to die. In reality, the victim's respiration and pulse becomes so slow that it is nearly impossible to detect. The victim retains full awareness as he is taken to the hospital, then the morgue and finally buried alive. Again Harris knew that what he had seen in the documentary was now happening to him, and the people around him.

Harris took some comfort from remembering that the victims were revived. The sorcerer must dig up the body within a few hours, before they asphyxiate. Then, they use a concoction called Zombie Cucumber to revive them as a shell of their former self, with no speech or memory.

Zombie cucumber is a part of voodoo which did not come out of Africa, as it is native to the Americas. The plant Datura Stramonium, or Jimson Weed, is a plant in the nightshade family, thought to have originated in Mexico. It has long been associated with witchcraft and the occult, as its many colloquial names show. Datura is also known as hell's bells, devil's trumpet, devil's weed, devil's snare and devil's cucumber.
The ancient inhabitants of California ate the small black seeds to commune with deities through visions. Across the Americas, other indigenous peoples such as the Algonquin, Cherokee, Marie Galente, and Luiseño also used this plant in sacred ceremonies for its hallucinogenic properties.
Harris guessed he would taste Zombie Cucumber before too long. But he hoped the Watchers would find him in time to administer the drugs needed to revive him.
The plant's active agent is atropine. For centuries it has been used to relieve asthma symptoms and as an analgesic during surgery or bone-setting. Atropine is also used by the armed forces as a nerve gas antidote. It is the plant's powerful hallucinogen properties that make it useful in voodoo and witchcraft, but Harris was counting on a clinical dose of atropine to bring him around.

The documentary had told Harris what to expect if the Watchers did not come to his rescue. Most zombies were expected to become slaves, a commodity of the zombie master. At one time it was said that most of the slaves who worked in the sugar cane plantations of Haiti were zombies. In 1918 a voodoo priest named Ti Joseph ran a gang of zombie labourers for the American Sugar Corporation, who took the money they received and fed the workers only unsalted porridge. The relevance of the unsalted porridge was that a zombie will remain in a robot-like state indefinitely, until he tastes either salt or meat. "So much for The Night of the Living Dead", thought Harris, remembering Hollywood's flesh eating zombies. But salt or meat did not bring a cure; it returned the zombie to the grave.

The reality behind the zombie has only been taken seriously by medical science within the last ten years, since the use of CAT scans of the brain, along with the confessions of voodoo priests, explaining their methods. Previous to that, zombies were considered mentally defective or explained as stunts to confuse scientists.

Skull and the Watchers were desperately trying to find Harris. But their efforts were hampered by increased activity at the festival. Everything seemed to be happening together. The shock journalists around the voodoo doll were working their audience into a frenzy. At the main bonfire, the heat, flames, music and hallucinogenic smoke were driving the dancers wild. Then, the Tonton Macoutes around the tents seemed to dramatically increase their security presence. Skull wanted to get closer to where he had last seen Harris, but the security and the crowds were pushing him further away. As the security cleared a trail to the tents, two huge refrigerated trucks backed up to the entrance. "What are they bringing in now", thought Skull.

He was soon to see that it was actually things going out, not in. "Coffins", exclaimed Skull. "Why on earth would they be moving coffins out, while the rite is still going on?"

The men in straw hats still wore their sunglasses, despite the dark. Yet they seemed to move effortlessly between the tent and the lorry, with a seemingly endless parade of coffins. It was the ease with which the security zombies carried the coffins that convinced Skull they were just empty boxes. Had the biker president known that one of them carried his friend, he would have fought like a tiger go get through the crowd. As it was, Skull thought the lorries' cargo warranted only an electronic tracker. Rather than physically follow the lorries, Skull tasked an operative to tag the trucks with their state of the art devices.

Jonah was, as always, monitoring everything that was happening with the teams in the field. He watched the lorries' two tracking lights move north, in tandem along his computer screen. He had no idea of their journey's purpose, or just how long a drive they had just begun. More importantly, just like Skull, Jonah had no idea of their human cargo, or that Harris was aboard. Also unknown to Jonah, was that another lorry had begun a similar journey, on a parallel course to the coffins. This truck carried no tracking device and its military markings would have given the Watchers no cause to link it to the Millerites.

Other than its pair of drivers, the military truck carried no human cargo. But its cargo had the same destination as the paralysed bodies and was crucial to Ellen White's plot.

The lorries leaving the festival site seemed to trigger a gradual winding down of activity. The Muhammad doll had been packed away, leaving the shock journalists nothing to excite their audience about. As the flames from the bonfires gradually subsided, the volume of the rhythmic music reduced with it. The voodoo sorcerers were no longer pumping out the hallucinogenic smoke into the crowd, so their frenzy began to pass.

Skull and his team had turned their whole attention to the search for Harris. As the crowds of revelers reduced in size, their search became easier. But their was no sign of the biker anywhere. Eventually, Skull conceded that Harris must somehow have been taken from the site. His lack of communication suggested he was taken against his will, but Skull had still not connected the coffins to his friend.

Chapter 26.

Voodoo Queen Beth had slipped away early from the festival. She had been instrumental in setting up and running it, but she now had another task vital to the plot. Had the Watchers been able to follow her, they would have found out about the mysterious TAG they had heard Beth talking about. But she had avoided being seen in the crowd and Jonah would have to wait for that particular piece of intelligence.

Beth had learned much from studying her role model, Marie Laveau. Most important to the Millerite's plot was her Machiavellian intelligence machine. The way that both Beth and Laveau gathered information and used it to manipulate people would have impressed even J Edgar Hoover.
Beth had followed Laveau's lead and opened a hairdressing salon. She had built up an impressive client list, comprising the wives and staff of New Orleans' most prominent residents. There is something about a hairdresser's chair which relaxes their occupants. The hairdresser becomes a trusted confidant, who the client feels compelled to tell practically anything.

Like Marie Laveau, Beth represented herself as a seer and used fortune-telling techniques such as palmistry. There is no evidence that Marie's clairvoyant abilities were any more successful than those of any other fortuneteller. Many people attest to the accuracy of a reading because they do not understand the clever techniques involved, like cold reading. So called because it is accomplished without any foreknowledge, this is a skilful method of fishing for information from the sitter while convincing him or her that it comes from a mystical source.

Actually, many of Beth's readings were not truly "cold". Far from lacking prior information about her clients, she used her position as a hairdresser for gossip collecting, discovering that her women clients would talk to her about anything and everything and would divulge some of their most personal secrets to her. She also developed a chain of informants in most of the prominent homes and businesses.

Much of her work for the ladies involved love predicaments. Beth knew the personal secrets of judges, priests, lawyers, doctors, ship captains, architects, military officers, politicians and most of New Orleans's other leading citizens. She used her knowledge of their indiscretions and blackmailed them into doing whatever she wanted. She was then paid by her wealthy female clients. Most of the time, this was how her love potions and gris-gris worked, which is apparently 100% of the time.

It was through these methods that the man who sat opposite Beth fell into her influence.

Major General Richard Stirling was a career army officer. He had served in most of the conflicts his country had become embroiled in throughout his long career. Stirling had been decorated for service in the Balkans, West Africa, Iraq and Afghanistan, along with other, less public campaigns. But now, Stirling headed up Louisiana's National Guard.

Many combat soldiers have difficulty adjusting to a more normal life back home. Stirling had probably accepted at least one promotion too many, as a desk job back on US soil had not suited him at all. Peace time bored him, and like many bored men, his attentions turned to sexual indiscretions. These indiscretions became known to Beth, and they allowed her to exert significant influence on Stirling.

As a senior army officer, Stirling was well paid, but he had married well and much of his comfortable lifestyle was funded with his wife's money. His life would be very different indeed, were his wife to learn of his infidelities.

Beth had begun by extracting small favours from Stirling. They were little things, which seemed to have little significance. But each favour broke a rule and the more rules he broke, the deeper Stirling became bound to Beth. The more that Stirling fell under Beth's spell, the more significant the favours became. Each bringing greater risk, should Stirling be found out.

Now, Beth's influence over Stirling was so complete, that he was diverting significant army resources to the Millerite cause. Although, Stirling had no idea of why he was being instructed to take the actions he had put in place.

259

The lorry being driven north by two National Guardsmen had been deployed by Stirling. He knew not the purpose of his lorry's cargo, but it was a cargo he was compelled to dispatch, on fear of exposure.

Likewise, the training exercise he was soon to initiate was a mystery to him. The exercise itself was part of the National Guard's routine training schedule. It was the relocation of the exercise which Beth had instructed General Stirling to do. Stirling felt bad about how he had let himself fall into Beth's power. He knew the history of the National Guard went back to the British colonial era, when they were simply known as the Militia. It was the Massachusetts militia which is credited with starting the American Revolutionary War at the Battles of Lexington and Concord, and provided the majority of soldiers during the course of the war.

The National Guard of the United States is a reserve military force, organised into units based in each of the 50 states and operates under their respective State Governor, except in Washington, D.C., where the President of the United States is their commander in chief.

The Governors delegate control to their State Adjutants General. Major General Stirling was the Louisiana Governor's TAG.

The majority of National Guard soldiers hold a civilian job while serving part-time as a National Guard member. All members of the National Guard are also members of the militia of the United States. Because of this dual State and

Federal role, National Guard units fall under the dual control of both state and federal government. State governors, through their TAG, are free to activate the National Guard to respond to domestic emergencies and disasters, such as hurricanes. Stirling had activated the Louisiana Guards many times to assist in hurricanes, riots, civil unrest, or terrorist attacks.

When deploying the Guards for State purposes, governors can utilise the Guard's federally assigned aircraft, vehicles and other equipment so long as the federal government is reimbursed for the use of supplies such as fuel, food stocks, etc.

Although there were many reasons that Stirling could have used to activate Louisiana's 10,800 Guards, their most common deployment is the traditional weekend a month and two week summer training periods. It was this which Stirling had used as cover for deploying National Guard assets to the Millerite plot.

General Stirling's exercise fitted perfectly with New Orleans' risk profile. He had planned a flood recovery exercise, and the area chosen had suffered during Hurricane Katrina.

But it was the area's demographics, not its geography, that interested the Millerites.

The working class area to the south of Lake Pontchartrain was where the city's Muslim population had settled. In a comparatively small area, there was; the Muhammad Mosque, run by the radical Nation of Islam, the Islamic Centre of New Orleans, two Islamic schools and the Masjid

Al-Islam mosque. The Islamic Centre of New Orleans was particularly affected by Katrina, being flooded with around six inches of river water. It was to this location that Stirling was sending his troops.

As Stirling's troops were deploying, Beth was contacting the Shock Journalists who attended the voodoo festival. Still fired up from the use of a Muhammad voodoo doll, the TV crews were eager to cover National Guard troops deploying into such a heavily Islamic area.
They were just the type of journalists to loudly question the official story that the troops were on hurricane practice. It made a far more exciting story to allege that the U.S. Government was keeping down Muslim unrest.
"Texans have died for daring to display cartoons of Muhammad," began the TV anchor man. "After these scenes at the New Orleans Voodoo Festival, are we next?" he asked as footage of the Muhammad doll played on the screen. "The Governor seems to think so", he said, as the pictures changed to jeeps and personnel carriers rolling into the Muslim quarter. "Official sources say the exercise is part of New Orleans' hurricane preparedness", said the anchor. "But we say, it is too big a coincidence that the day after a voodoo sorcerer insults Muhammad, almost the entire Louisiana National Guard deploys into the Muslim population".

The troops were doing all the right things for flood prevention. They piled up sand bags, set up rescue centres and erected public address systems. But somehow, the message from the shock journalists was gaining strength. Many of the mainstream news channels had deployed TV crews into the area and were already questioning the location of the exercise.

Jonah had learned his lesson about failing to follow local news, when he missed the Voodoo Festival. So now, he had several news channels playing on monitors in his hotel suite. He was quick to pick up on the developing National Guard story, and equally quick to link it with what the Watchers had seen at the voodoo rite.
Jonah had already guessed that part of the Millerite plot would be to cultivate unrest in Muslim communities both in the US and overseas. "But how does New Orleans fit with Dearborn?" he thought to himself. Had Jonah known about the lorry which General Stirling had sent north, he might have been able to answer his own question.
But, while the National Guard lorry and the two lorries of coffins drove parallel routes towards Dearborn, Jonah would be kept guessing.

Baron Samedi and his assistants were already in Dearborn, as they had flown north. Ownership of the warehouse they were in was thinly disguised; there could be little doubt who had named their company Wolf Imports and Exports. The building was part of O Lobo's global smuggling network and had been leased to Ellen White as part of his expensively funded package of support. The large open space had been set up as a rudimentary clinic. The edges of the floor were ringed with foam mats. Each mat was equipped with intravenous drips and basic patient monitoring equipment.

Harris and his fellow passengers would soon be lying on the mats, where Samedi would administer his second cocktail of drugs.

Eventually the two refrigerated trucks arrived at Wolf Imports and Exports. Harris, though in the dark, could feel his coffin being lifted from the lorry and the temperature gradually rising. As he was lifted from his coffin and laid on the mat, Harris could see just how tightly packed the two lorries had been loaded with coffins. "How many of us have they taken?", thought Harris.

Baron Samedi's assistants hooked Harris to an IV drip and the Zombie Cucumber cocktail started to flow though his veins. It was a very strange experience for Harris. In his paralysed state, he could feel the drug flowing into his body, but he could still not react to it in any way.

Steadily as the drugs worked their way around his system, Harris felt a slow transition. Very gradually, he began to make slight movements. Nothing big, just the flicker of an eye lid, or the twitch off a finger. Harris began to get excited. "They're bringing me out of it", he thought.

But something else was happening inside Harris. The more control he regained over his body, the less focused his mind became. Slowly but surely, paralysis was replaced with fog. In time, Harris had regained all of his movements. But whatever was left behind his eyes, it was not Harris.

The assistants disconnected Harris and the others around him, from their drips. But all of them remained on their mats, waiting for instructions. As the assistants completed their medical tasks, they moved to a more practical duty.
A pile of cardboard boxes and wooden crates had appeared in the warehouse loading bay. This was the cargo that General Stirling's troops had driven to Dearborn. The assistants were walking back and forth between the men on the mats and the boxes. With each trip, a pile of equipment was steadily growing at the side of each man.

The men on the floor lay still, connected to blood pressure and heart monitors. Now though, their stillness was different. Rather than a pseudo death, it was just a relaxed, almost sleepy state. When Baron Samedi was happy with the vital signs of each man, he unhooked the cables and put them to work carrying equipment. They worked tirelessly and robotically, with the piles of equipment now growing much faster. Once each man had his own pile of equipment, each settled back onto his mat to await further instructions.

The Watchers were now in the air. It had been a difficult decision for Jonah, about how to deploy the team.
Much seemed to be happening in New Orleans. The Millerites and their voodoo offshoot were very much centred in the city. Mathew Saint had been

265

positively identified as being there. Then, there was the added, but as yet unexplained factor of the National Guard deployment.

Together with Jonny Johnson, Jonah had to balance this against all the evidence pointing at Dearborn as the target for the nuclear weapons. So many Muslims would be gathered in Dearborn for their festival, in addition to the large existing community. Couple this with their festival opening on the anniversary of the Millerites' Great Disappointment and Jonah was certain that would be the target.

With a relatively small team to work with, Jonah decided he could not split their resources. Their convoy of vans, cars and motorcycles had again rolled up the loading ramp of Red Andrews' Hercules aeroplane. The atmosphere was tense inside the huge air craft. The Watchers knew they had left loose ends in New Orleans, but they were flying towards the most powerful weapons known to man.

Chapter 27.

The Watchers divided the necessary tasks between themselves and went to work.
The Sergeants at Arms, Steve Butler and Joao Alva had their specialist weapons to prepare. All of them cleaned and checked their personal weapons.
Stone and Skull took charge of the radiation detection equipment, making sure they were all tested and had fresh batteries. Finding Saint's deadly weapons was the most important part of their mission.
Miguel, Barbara and Randy readied their cameras, microphones and other surveillance equipment.
With the stakes so high, everything had to be working perfectly.

While the Watchers prepared, Amber was monitoring every intelligence feed that was available to her. As an MI6 operative, she had the whole range of British Intelligence systems open to her. But, through her role as a Military Attaché in the British Embassy, she also had a great many sources in U.S. Intelligence. If there was something to find, Amber was determined to find it. But so far, the Millerites seemed to have remained under the Intelligence Agencies' radar.

Only two of the team were missing from the Hercules flight. Jonah had decided that his control centre in the hotel suite was too well developed to move. As he would run the operation through cameras, radios and computers, he could perform his role from New Orleans.

The other missing member was the one who sat heaviest in the Watchers' minds. They hated leaving one of their own, and Phil Harris had last been seen in New Orleans.

They had left the Texas chapter's surveillance team to continue the search. But they were employees, not club members and it did not sit well with the tightly knit bikers. This was the second reason for Jonah keeping his control centre in New Orleans. He knew the Watchers would take some comfort from him being close to the search for their missing member.

None of them could know that they were all flying towards a reunion with Harris. Although it would not be the Harris that any of them knew.

Jonah used the time the Watchers were in the air to plan and prepare. They had hoped to intercept the bombs long before they were ready for detonation. But, as the anniversary of the Great Disappointment drew closer, Jonah had to consider the risk of them being too late to prevent a nuclear holocaust. The Watchers were flying into the greatest danger of their careers. As their planner, Jonah needed to minimise the risk for them. To do this, he needed to understand the risks of a nuclear explosion.

As a Detective Inspector, Jonah was given some awareness of radiological and nuclear weapons as part of his counter terrorism training. But until now, he never considered nuclear terrorism as a viable risk. The only part of the lesson he could remember was an amusing pneumonic the instructors used to explain what happens when during a nuclear detonation; Fred Flintstone Hates Barney Rubble's Electric Car. The initial letters also stood for Flash, Fireball, Heat, Radiation, Electromagnetic phenomenon and Cloud.

Just knowing the headlines was nowhere near enough detail. Jonah had some fast studying to do. He learned that between 40 and 50% of the explosion's energy is dissipated in the blast, with another 30 to 50% felt as heat.
This left around 10% of the energy to produce radiation, the hidden danger from an atomic bomb.
With the exception of the radiation, the physical damage caused by a nuclear weapon is identical to that caused by conventional explosives. However, the energy produced by a nuclear explosion is millions of times more powerful per gram and the temperatures briefly reach tens of millions of degrees.

The blast was the first thing Jonah had to consider. The heat and blast causes gas to move outward in a thin, dense shell called the hydrodynamic front. The front acts like a piston compressing the surrounding air to make a spherically expanding shock wave.
This shockwave piston causes most of the destruction resulting from a nuclear explosion. Most buildings, except reinforced or blast-

resistant structures, will suffer damage. The blast wind can exceed 300 miles per second, which is approaching the speed of sound. It can also exert forces many times greater than the strongest hurricane.

Heat would also cause massive damage to buildings, by igniting combustible materials in the buildings. But the blast from the Hiroshima Bomb also set fires through electrical shorts, gas pilot lights and overturned stoves, creating the possibility of widespread fires in Dearborn.

Jonah was less concerned about damage to buildings, than he was of injury to the Watchers. He paid special attention to the physiological dangers of an explosion.
The blast sends pressure waves through human tissue. These waves mostly damage the join between bone and muscle, or the spaces where tissue and air meet. Spaces like the lungs and abdominal cavity, which contain air, are injured by hemorrhaging or air embolisms, either of which can be rapidly fatal. Most eardrums would also be ruptured by the pressure.

Flash was also of concern to Jonah. The detonation would produce large amounts of visible, infrared, and ultraviolet light, which could injure the Watchers eyes. Flash blindness is caused by the brilliant flash of light produced by the detonation. This is where more light is received on the retina than can be tolerated, bleaching the visual pigments and causing temporary blindness for up to 40 minutes. Retinal burns were more dangerous, causing permanent damage by scarring the retina. It only occurs when the fireball is actually in the individual's field of vision and is a relatively uncommon injury, but one that Jonah did not want the team to suffer.

Electromagnetic pulse was less of a concern to Jonah, as it was much less likely to injure the team. It could, however, make their communications very difficult. Comms were always vital to the Watchers' method of working. Gamma rays from a nuclear explosion produce an electromagnetic pulse. The pulse is powerful enough to cause metal objects to act as antennas and generate high voltages. These voltages can destroy unshielded electronics and disrupt radio traffic. Jonah read that this could be a relatively easy fix, as electronics can be shielded by wrapping them in aluminium foil. "Looks like you'll be going to the supermarket Nev lad", thought Jonah.

Other than an explosion itself, Jonah's biggest worry was the radiation. About 5% of the energy released in a nuclear explosion comes as ionising radiation: neutrons, gamma rays, alpha particles and electrons moving at the speed of light. 5% did not sound much, but considering the intense energy from a nuclear explosion, it was still a huge danger.

Jonah had to consider all of these factors in giving the Watchers their best chance of survival.

Survivability is dependent on factors such as if you are indoors or out, the size of the explosion, the proximity to the explosion and the direction of the wind carrying radioactive fallout.

Jonah could calculate the size of the explosion, as he knew the size of the Cuban plutonium spheres, which were designed for a 2.3 megaton thermonuclear warhead.

What he could not know was whether events in Dearborn would be inside or outside.

There was also a fair chance the team would get close to the weapons, since finding the bombs was their prime objective.

What he could control was their standby location. Jonah planned to ensure their base was outside the hot zone and in a well constructed building.

The text books say that death is likely, and radiation poisoning almost certain if the Watchers were caught in the open, with no buildings to mask the radiation, within a radius of 3 km from a 1 megaton blast, and 50% chance of death at 8 km.

But Jonah could also take account of variability for real world conditions, and the effect that being indoors, or shielded by buildings can make.

Akiko Takakura survived the effects of the Hiroshima bomb at just 300 meters from the hypocenter, due to her position in the Bank of Japan, a reinforced concrete building.

In contrast, the unknown person sitting outside, on the steps of the bank, received lethal third degree burns and was killed by the blast, within two seconds of the explosion.

Jonah settled on 20 km for the Watchers's hotel, positioned to take advantage of prevailing wind blowing away any fall out. He also located a diner from the 1960s, built with thick concrete, which was close to the Islamic Centre. This would give them a bolt hole with some degree of protection.

The Watchers' last task before the Hercules landed was to practice with their CBRN suits. They had obtained British Army equipment, designed to give some degree of protection from Chemical, Biological, Radiological and Nuclear attack. The lightweight charcoal lined suits and filtered respirators would give short term protection against particulate fallout. But the Watchers would need to be clear of any direct exposure to ionising radiation.
For those with military experience, or police in Stone's case, the drills were just a refresher. But the bikers, with their irreverent brand of humour, could not help laughing at those new to the equipment. In particular, the drill to put on a respirator in nine seconds caused the most amusement. It sounds a simple task, but under pressure and with those who have completed, shouting the countdown, it became almost impossible.

Soon the massive aircraft was on the runway and the Watchers' convoy of bikes, vans and cars rolled down the loading ramp. This time, as the flight had only been from New Orleans, there was no immigration red tape to deal with. It had been easy for Amber's Embassy colleagues to oil the wheels of airport security, and have the convoy waved straight through the gates.

Stone and Amber took the lead, with the military grade sat-nav on Amber's Buell leading the way to their hotel. The two of them were becoming very comfortable in each other's company. The other bikers could tell from the synchronisation of their riding that there was something more than team work developing there. Stone knew that too, but he also knew they both had to remain professional while such a high risk operation was underway.

Barely had they unloaded their gear at the hotel, when Jonah had them on high alert.

The old DI had been monitoring news channels, which showed film of the National Guard deployed into Dearborn. The strange thing was the Michigan State Governor, who was the unit's Commander in Chief, claimed to know nothing of the deployment.

Jonah was worried because of the sudden change in the Louisiana Guard's exercise plans to work in a heavily Islamic area of New Orleans. Now, in a different state, at the opposite end of the country, the National Guard was unexpectedly on the street in a Muslim area. Jonah could not see how it all fitted together, but he was convinced the deployments were linked.

The Watchers worked together with the efficiency of a Special Forces unit. They quickly settled on key tasks suited to their particular skills.

Steve Butler and Randy Salt headed for vantage points on the roofs of tall buildings. Their military service made them ideal for providing top cover as snipers.

Barbara and Miguel went undercover, posing as religious scholars, interested in learning about Islam.

Skull, Joao Alva and Red Andrews took the van, so as to have weapons, computers and other equipment close at hand.

Stone and Amber headed out on their motorcycles to scout the area and plant their cameras.

It did not take long for Stone and Amber to find the National Guardsmen.

Neither did it take long for Amber, who had spent many years in the States, to notice that the Guards looked wrong. All of them had the same far away look they had seen on the straw hatted security men in the 9th Ward and the Voodoo Festival.

The other thing that looked out of place was their uniforms. At first, Amber could not quite decide what was wrong. Then Stone spotted the insignia on the Guardsmen's uniforms.

"This is Michigan, not Louisiana", said Stone.

"Why would The Louisiana National Guard be deployed so far from home?"

This was one of the things that Beth had obtained through blackmailing General Stirling.

The military lorry that the General had sent to Dearborn had been full of Louisiana National

Guard uniforms and equipment. It was these uniforms that the zombies resurrected by Baron Samedi were now wearing.

The zombies could patrol for hours. They obeyed their instructions unquestioningly, walking round and round the two main Islamic buildings. Despite their hours of walking, they neither tired, nor became bored.

Many of the Muslims visiting the area tried to ask the soldiers why the National Guard was there. But the zombies had neither the speech, nor the reasoning ability to answer them. They just patrolled on, ignoring the pubic around them.

Many of the younger Muslims were suspicious of authority. This was not helped by the soldiers being around their holy sites with apparently no good reason. The soldiers' unwillingness to engage with them further antagonised the young men.

This was beginning to create tension and the young men were beginning to shout at the soldiers.

Chapter 28.

Word spread quickly about the unrest in Dearborn. Stone could not believe how quickly placards had been painted and taken onto the streets. Their messages varied from a simple "why?" to much more violent messages about the U.S. Government. Stone could not know that the placards and banners had been prepared long in advance, as part of Ellen White's meticulous preparations.

As the Watchers placed more of their cameras, Jonah started to get a bigger picture of the trouble that was brewing in Dearborn. Also receiving the video feed was Skull in his more local command post inside the Watchers' van. "At this rate they won't need a bomb, Skull lad", commented Jonah.
"It all seems to be happening too smoothly", replied Skull. "There has got to be some bigger plan that we aren't seeing yet."

The piece of the plot that Skull could not have seen was Major General Stirling's involvement. Beth's blackmail of the Louisiana Adjutant General was crucial to the Millerite plot. Without his help, Matthew Saint's bombs just amounted to a terrorist attack. It would probably be the most destructive and most significant terrorist attack the world had ever seen, but it could not bring about the apocalypse that the Millertites hoped for.

It could be said that the 9/11 attack on New York's Twin Towers did start a war. But it was not the apocalyptic war that could bring about the end of the world. The Millerites needed to trigger something much bigger than the U.S. War on Terror.

While Skull and his team were watching developments in Dearborn, the Texas Chapter's surveillance team continued the search for Phil Harris in New Orleans. They had concentrated on the break down and removal of the voodoo festival's infrastructure. But despite tracking every contractor who left the site, they had no leads on Harris' whereabouts. This was hardly surprising, as Harris had left the site, in a refrigerated lorry, long before the surveillance team began its work.

What did become apparent to the Texas team was the similarity in what was happening on the streets of New Orleans and Dearborn. All the Watchers employees had ambitions to prospect for the MC and hoped to become full members and directors of their global security business. So each made it their business to follow what the MC members were doing in Dearborn. They saw that protests against the National Guard presence in New Orleans was growing in exactly the same way as Dearborn.

Not everyone in the U.S. takes an active involvement in politics. But those who do tend to be polarised between the two ideologically different main parties. Supporters of the Democratic Party tend towards a left wing, liberal or socialist agenda.

But it was the extreme right wing of the Republican Party that the Millerites had exploited. The Republicans are in general, a Christian, Conservative organisation. But in recent years, a much more extremist faction had developed at the far right of the party. These were passionately opposed to anything they saw as threatening Americanism. A particular target of their venom was any suggestion of creeping Islamification of America. It was from this extreme right that many of the shock journalists came. Ellen White had worked hard to bring key media people into her congregation. Now, as Muslim protests grew, the Millerite controlled media was on hand to fuel the flames.

Across America, groups of Muslims began to protest outside National Guard bases. In each case, TV cameras were quickly there to spread the news.

The U.S. President at the time was too young to have first hand experience of the Cold War with the Soviet Union. But the tension in the phone calls into the Oval Office was just what he imagined of the hotline calls his predecessors shared with Moscow.

The political leaders of many different countries had been put through to the President. All of them were leaders of very different regimes to that of Soviet Communism. But the theme of their calls were the same, reducing hostilities which might escalate to war.

The leaders of the world's Islamic states were among the first to phone the White House. Their reasons for calling were much the same, to reduce tension among the world's Muslims. In many cases, their immediate concern was to prevent conflict which could damage trade. Despite ongoing conflicts in their own countries, many of the Arab leaders were engaged in thinly veiled sabre rattling with the President.

Allies of the U.S. were also quick to call the White House. With increased migration away from conflicts in the Middle East, the Muslim populations of many countries were growing. Each of the world leaders was concerned about what they saw as provocation in the deployment of the National Guard into Muslim areas.

No matter how much the President reassured them, they did not believe his protestations of innocence.

The shock media had been doing an excellent job of alleging Federal involvement in what they saw as "the Muslim problem". No one had yet learned that it was blackmail of the Louisiana TAG which had put soldiers onto the streets.

America's President could not guess how appropriate his comparison with the Cold War Hot Line would become. Presidents Kennedy and Kruschev initiated their direct line in the wake of the Cuban missile crisis. Its purpose was to quickly resolve misunderstandings and prevent either of the superpowers starting a nuclear war. Unknown to the President, remnants of two of

Cuba's nuclear warheads were now in one of his cities.
At least one of the leaders he spoke to was capable of nuclear retaliation. But no one outside of the Watchers and British Intelligence had any idea that there may be a nuclear threat to the current unrest. The threat of nuclear weapons was never far from the President's thoughts. But, for now, it was not an immediate threat.

Very quickly Jonah's capacity to keep up with the growing media storm was becoming overloaded. What had started on the shock media channels had now spread to the international media.
Jonah could not help but think he had joined the police in a very different world. Almost 40 years ago, the young constable had little idea what was happening outside Britain. 24 hour satellite news and the Internet were not yet even the subject of science fiction.
Yet the old DI had grown with the changing world. In his chosen field of counter terrorism, the Internet and social media had been the terrorists' fastest growing propaganda tools.
It was no surprise to Jonah when campaigns both pro and anti Muslim took hold on the Internet. With everyone present having a camera phone, video of any perceived bad behaviour by soldiers or protestors, instantly went viral. The nature of the posts ranged from destroying the U.S. Government, to outlawing Islam.
There was a huge amount of inaccuracy and misinformation amongst the digital media.
Jonah had learned this was always a danger with

digital content on the Internet. Stories and opinions could be shared, and then shared again within seconds. With the friend list of each sharer multiplying its audience. If an incorrect or misleading caption had been attached to a photograph or video clip, this would be shared on as factual.

Mainstream digital news sites added to the inaccuracy of some of the stories. Few of their journalists spend the necessary time checking the stories and verifying sources. Instead, they prefer to use hedging language in reporting viral stories. They use words like "reportedly", or "claims", to indicate a level of uncertainty. They will often pose their headline as a question. Jonah saw many such headlines, like "Is the U.S. Government suppressing Muslim rights?" The journalists see such language as a way of avoiding claims of defamation, but the average reader will often read the question as a statement of fact. Then forward the post to all of their friends.

The Millerites were taking advantage of the public and the media's willingness to distribute stories without verifying facts. Ellen White had put together a team of skilled social media users to fire up tensions on both sides. The same young fanatics used multiple Internet identities, one minute condemning the President for putting the army on the streets, the next, calling for Muslims to be thrown out of America.

Thanks to the information superhighway, the misinformation circled the globe many times over.

In countries around the world, advisors hurried to brief Presidents, Prime Ministers and Heads of State.

As the official state leaders read their briefing packages, they could be sure that the leaders of a multitude of fanatical terrorist groups would be receiving similar briefings.

Most people have heard of terror groups such as: Islamic Jihad, Hezbollah, Boko Haram, Al-Qaeda and the various incarnations of Islamic State. But such was the anger fuelled by the Millerite campaign, that many smaller groups were banding together to make their plans.

The list of proscribed organisations around the world is a long one. The group of organisations on the list professing an Islamic ideology is by far the largest. Despite their many differences, most viewed America as the Great Satan, for its military role in Iraq and Afghanistan.

Snippets of intelligence were beginning to reach Jonny Johnson at MI5. It was precisely this joining together of terrorist organisations which had concerned he and Jonah.

With resources and, more importantly money, pooled, their collective danger was multiplied many times over.

Jonny's biggest fear was in not knowing the extent of AQ Khan's proliferation of nuclear weapons technology. The United Nations were keeping a close watch on the world's rogue states. But the stateless terror groups were much harder to monitor.

The U.S. President and other Heads of State were concerned mostly with conventional weapons, as none knew of the Millerite devices. But Jonny Johnson knew only too well. He also knew that MI6 sources in North Korea were becoming increasingly concerned about activity in the North's suspected nuclear sites.

North Korea's nuclear programme is a source of deep concern for the whole international community. In 2006, 2009 and 2013, they conducted successful nuclear tests in a show of arrogance. The last was soon after they were sanctioned by the UN for launching rockets. Jonny knew the North was believed to possess enough weapons-grade plutonium for at least six bombs.

However, the intelligence community never believed Pyongyang was fully disclosing all of its nuclear facilities. Both the US and South Korea believe the North has additional sites linked to a uranium-enrichment programme.

Jonny knew this was significant, as North Korea had depleted its stocks of reactor-grade plutonium, but the country has plentiful reserves of uranium ore. Uranium enrichment uses small centrifuges that can be hidden away much more easily than the plants needed for plutonium.

Always keen to boast, North Korea made claims about its capabilities in the wake of its last test. They claimed to have miniaturised a device, small enough to fit a nuclear warhead onto a missile. Pyongyang also said the 2013 test had a much greater yield than the plutonium devices it

detonated in 2006 and 2009.
Jonny's analysts suggested that boasting of a high-level test could have been code for the use of highly enriched uranium rather than plutonium. Although both present roughly the same level of threat, a uranium bomb would signify a huge technological achievement because the process of enriching natural uranium ore to weapons grade is significantly more difficult. But Jonny knew that North Korea was among the states to have benefited from AQ Khan's technology proliferation.

Although the word's leaders had not yet grasped the significance of the intelligence from North Korea, Jonah and Jonny were only too aware. If a none Muslim state, with nuclear capability, was considering conflict, the Millerites dream of global nuclear war was drawing closer.

Chapter 29.

International politics were a long way from the thoughts of the Dearborn citizens. Tension seemed to be growing minute by minute on the city's streets. Extreme groups from both sides of the political divide were growing both in their numbers and the level of their hate. Muslim fundamentalists grew stronger in their condemnation at the National Guard being in Dearborn. While the right wing nationalists objected to the very existence of the Muslims. Peaceful Muslims were trying to go about the business of the conferences they had travelled great distances to attend.

Stone began to realise that, although the numbers on the streets were growing, they were all in some way linked to the growing tension. It was noticeable that there were very few ordinary Dearborn citizens going about their daily lives. All of the surrounding streets had growing mobs of fanatics, hurling abuse and more solid objects at each other. Around them patrolled the oddly silent National Guard, who in turn were being scrutinised by the Dearborn Police.
In the middle of all this were the peaceable Muslims, trying to enjoy their religious gathering. But Stone could see that, gradually, tempers were starting to rise among this group too.
The biggest crowds gathered around The Islamic Centre of America on Ford Road.
It was easy for Stone to see why it was such a

draw, as the huge, elaborate building was America's largest mosque. "I've never been here before", said Amber. "But it seems strangely familiar. A bit reminiscent of the Taj Mahal too, but that's the wrong religion".

While Stone and Amber were watching the angry crowds grow, Barbara and Miguel were inside one of the nearby exhibitions. Coincidentally, the exhibition was on Islamic architecture, and could have answered Barbara's confusion over the mosque.
Signs between the exhibits explained that what today is known as Islamic architecture owes its origin to buildings in Roman, Byzantine and Persian lands which the Muslims conquered in the 7th and 8th centuries. Further east, it was also influenced by Chinese and Indian architecture as Islam spread to Southeast Asia. This explained the familiarity of the building to Barbara. Not only did it contain some of the same influences as the Taj Mahal, but much was drawn from her own Christian heritage.
Barbara saw the Christian influences in a model of The Dome of the Rock in Jerusalem. This is one of Islam's most important buildings, but its design was patterned after the nearby Church of the Holy Sepulchre.

Nearby was a huge model of another mosque with obvious Christian influence. The model seemed slightly out of place to Barbara. Had she known the model had been donated days earlier, she would understand how space had hurriedly been made for the beautiful exhibit. The large scale model, donated by an anonymous benefactor, was of the Great Mosque of Damascus, completed in 715 by Caliph Al-Walid I. The mosque was built on the site of the basilica of John the Baptist after the Islamic invasion of Damascus and bore great resemblance to 6th and 7th century Christian basilicas.

Outside, in the mosque's huge paved area, angry crowds were still building around Stone and Amber. The same square had seen many protests over the perceived islamification of Dearborn, but none had been anything close to the scale that Stone was now witnessing.
In quieter times, Stone might have enjoyed spending time in the beautiful spot with Amber. But now, with anger and tension growing around them, they were both starting to feel a little afraid. As the numbers grew and the volume of the chanting grew louder, missiles started to be thrown between the protestors. At first they were small things, like drinks cans or plants from the flower beds. But as the anger grew, the objects became larger, with stones being smashed from the surrounding structures. Then, more worrying for the tension levels, a large group of skinheads began to throw bacon towards the Muslims.

"Heads up Nev", said Skull, through Stone's earpiece. "The National Guard is here".
Samedi's zombies, who had been patrolling the whole area, were now gathering in the square.
The zombies, dressed in the Louisiana uniforms

from General Stirling, started to surround the protestors. But it was noticeable that they were concentrating on the Muslim group. As they came face to face with the angry group, the zombies cold, lifeless eyes stared at the protestors, antagonising them further.

Around the world, TV screens showed the National Guard surrounding the large group of Muslims, apparently ignoring the other protestors.

Then, amidst the crowd, something familiar caught Stone's eye. Just as Stone was taking notice, Skull caught the same thing on the van's monitors. "It's Harris", exclaimed Skull, looking at one of the Guardsmen.

"It can't be", replied Stone. "How would he have got here?"

As always, Jonah was watching and taking in everything happening on his radios and monitors. He too had spotted Harris, then zoomed the image in close to be sure.

"It's Harris alright, Nev lad", said Jonah. Harris had the same far away look as the other zombie guardsmen. Slowly, step by step, and in line with the others, he edged closer to the Muslim protestors.

Amber tried to attract Harris' attention, but his dead eyes looked coldly at the protesters, and still he paced slowly forward. Unable to catch Harris' eye, Stone and Amber pushed forward through the crowd. They desperately wanted to reach their friend and were scattering people as they forced their way closer.

Then, as they reached the line of Guardsmen, a

whole group of them turned in unison.

Baron Samedi was controlling his zombies by radio. Each of them had a radio earpiece, with each small group working on a different frequency. There were no individuals in Samedi's army, each group moved to a collective instruction.

Moving as one, the Guardsmen raised their rifles towards Stone and Amber. As they did so, Jonah saw that other small groups were starting to move and flank Stone. Jonah did not yet know how Samedi was controlling them, but it reminded him of a chess master moving his pieces into position.

Protestors scattered as the first of the zombie's shots rang across the square.

Stone and Amber dived for cover, simultaneously drawing their pistols as they fell behind a flower bed.

Steve Butler and Randy Salt reacted just as quickly. Zombies began falling in pairs, as the two snipers steadily shot, reloaded, then shot again.

Stone and Amber's pistols now added to the square's gunfire. Covering each other as they raised to fire, they too began to reduce the numbers of zombies walking towards them.

Despite the bodies falling around them, the zombies showed no fear and continued walking slowly towards Stone and Amber. Their drug ridden brains knew only the orders of their master and moved on with their task.

Each of the Watcher's bullets found a target, but neither the sniper rifles or the pistols were suited to rapid fire. It seemed that as each zombie fell,

more arrived to take their place.
Harris was still well within the main body of zombie Guardsmen.
Butler and Salt were being selective with their targets, trying to clear a path between Stone and Harris. But as each group of zombies moved in unison, the gaps were quickly filled.

Then, Stone had an idea. "Skull. Bring all of the auto injectors", he shouted into his radio.
Stone had remembered the suits of protective CBRN equipment the Watchers carried in their van. Each respirator haversack contained three Antidote Treatment Nerve agent autoinjectors. These devices, used by both police and military, are medical devices designed to deliver a single dose of life-saving drugs. They are spring-loaded syringes, which are easy to use and are intended for self-administration by patients. The drug is administered into the thigh or the buttocks. The injectors were designed to overcome the hesitation associated with self-administration of a needle-based syringe.
The auto injectors carried by the Watchers provide Atropine and Pralidoxime chloride in a single delivery system.
The device is only intended for extreme cases of organophosphate, nerve agent poisoning. Stone had remembered Jonah's briefing about Zombie Cucumber, the cocktail of drugs used to revive the zombies. Above all, he remembered that atropine was a key ingredient of the cocktail, remembering the name from his police CBRN training.

"The atropine should help bring them round", said Stone, explaining why he needed the auto injectors.

The three auto injectors from each of the 11 Watchers' kit gave them 33 doses of atropine. Nowhere near enough for the whole zombie army, but hopefully enough for them to reach Harris. With Amber and the two snipers providing covering fire, Stone and Skull ran forward, their pockets bulging with auto injectors. With injectors in both hands, needles hit the thighs of the first four zombies they reached. The zombies fell with the same synchronisation that they had been moving with. Then, as the large atropine dose took effect, their heart rate raised, they began to twitch uncontrollably and their dead eyes came to life.

Stone remembered the phrase his instructors had used to describe the effects.

 "Hot as a hare, blind as a bat, dry as a bone, red as a beet, and mad as a hatter". These reflect the warm, dry skin from decreased sweating, blurry vision and central nervous system effects.

More zombies had fallen before the first ones started to rise, recovering from the atropine dose. As they rose to their feet and stumbled about looking more human, Jonah exclaimed "its working Nev lad".

Now, Stone knew that he could safely use an auto injector when he reached Harris. Stone and Skull fought their way through the zombies, the deeper in they got, the harder it became. Knowing they must save at least one injector for Harris, the bikers had resorted to brute strength, using fists and elbows to topple the zombies. Eventually, breathless and full of adrenalin, Stone and Skull reached their friend. Stone instantly injected his thigh with the first dose of atropine, causing Harris to fall forwards into his arms. With Skull, he quickly moved into the evacuation technique used by both police and military. Each man threw one of Harris' arms around a shoulder and moved off, dragging Harris' heels behind them.

Now with only one arm each to fight with, they used fist and injectors to force their way back through the zombies.

Shots continued to ring out from Butler and Salt's elevated positions. Amber had now moved forward to support Stone and Skull. She was now amongst the zombies herself, with each shot hitting its mark, rather than providing covering fire. All three shooters were reluctant to kill any of the zombies. Without their wits and free will, they knew not what they were doing. So, their shots went through the soft tissue of legs, instantly felling the zombies. Only those who recovered enough to point a gun at the retreating Watchers received a more deadly bullet.

With life and personality coming back to Harris' face, the Watchers fell back to their van. Their priority now was to care for Harris. They would leave the zombies to the security forces, while they regrouped and planned their next move.

As soon as she was in the van, Amber fed in the information about the atropine. Her intelligence role as Military Attaché allowed her the cut offs needed to keep the Watchers' involvement quiet. Soon, the real National Guard had broken out their own supply of auto injectors and, with greater numbers, were bringing all of the zombies out of their drug induced spell.

Under the care of the Watchers, Harris was quickly regaining his senses. His memory returned more slowly than his faculties, but their return brought problems for Beth and Baron Samedi. Harris began to remember the warehouse he was kept in.

The memories came in flashes, like short clips of video. At first it was difficult for Harris to make sense of them. But slowly, he began to piece together lying on the mat, connected to wires and tubes, with Samedi leaning over him.

As more snippets returned, they became steadily longer and faster coming. Then, came the crucial snippet. Harris remembered subconsciously noticing the wolf's paw logo as he left with the fake National Guard. With that image as a hook, his mind brought back more of the warehouse exterior and the surrounding street. The Watchers now had the Millerite's Dearborn base.

With the police and real National Guard regaining control at The Islamic Centre of America, the Watchers were free to concentrate on the warehouse.

Jonah was now back into planning mode. Rapidly scanning maps and satellite images of the area around the warehouse.

While Jonah planned, the Watchers were busily preparing to mount an operation. Weapons and surveillance devices were meticulously checked. Their small helicopter drone was sent out to supplement the images Jonah already had with live pictures.

Barbara and Miguel were not involved in preparations to move on the warehouse, but they were just as busy. One of Harris' returning memories had made no sense at all to any of the Watchers. But it instantly registered with Barbara. The huge, ornate model being loaded into a truck seemed completely out of place in the voodoo environment of the warehouse. Although Baron Samedi's choice of accessories was quite eclectic, he had nothing the size and grandure of the model building Harris had seen. "It could only be the Great Mosque of Damascus", thought Barbara. She was thinking about the beautiful, but oversized model mosque she had earlier seen in the exhibition.

Yet again, the Watchers had their priorities split between two important objectives. The model mosque seemed a strong possibility for one of the nuclear devices. But the warehouse also demanded urgent attention. There was little doubt that they would need more manpower. Although it would have to be used in such a way to keep the British involvement secret.

While Jonah planned, Skull made phone calls. As international President of a huge motorcycle club and security company, Skull had plenty of resources to call on. They just needed to decide how to use them.

Within minutes of receiving Skulls call, columns of bikers were riding from all points of the compass towards Dearborn. Some of the bikers were members of Watchers chapters. But many were their support clubs. These were bikers who aspired to become Watchers, but hadn't quite made the grade. They would do pretty much anything to impress the Watchers.

Gradually, Jonah, Stone and Skull got all their pieces in place. The most important case of their careers was working towards a conclusion.

Chapter 30.

The sound of two helicopter rotors cut through the Dearborn air. Red Andrews had pulled in another favour from his oil company contacts. But the corporate aircraft were now fulfilling the most adventurous flight they had ever made.
The rotor sounds, just slightly out of time with each other, reminded Stone of the Apocalypse Now film. Which was appropriate both for the apocalypse they hoped to prevent and the Vietnam origin of the technique they were using.

Former US Special Forces soldier, Randy Salt had given the other seven Watchers a crash course in Spie Rigging. The Special Patrol Insertion/Extraction (SPIE) system was developed during the Vietnam war to rapidly insert or extract a patrol from areas where a helicopter could not land.
Eight nervous bikers watched the helicopters arrive and the crews lower their two SPIE ropes. Each was wearing a harness to clip into a D-ring inserted in the SPIE rope. A safety line is attached to a second D-ring above the first. With the bikers firmly attached, the helicopters lifted vertically until the ropes and their precious cargo were clear of obstructions. Then, the pilots flew quickly towards the warehouse.
The pilots had to treat the ropes and the Watchers as an external load and carefully monitor airspeeds, altitudes, and oscillations. But they were both ex- military pilots and had

executed the tactic many times before.
The eight Watchers were soon on the warehouse roof and the helicopters flying away from any security force attention.

At the exhibition of Islamic architecture, Barbara and Miguel Cuba had received their reinforcements from the support clubs. They could not tell the other bikers the true nature of their mission. So, instead briefed them about being hired to recover a stolen piece of art. While the bikers got into position, Barbara and Miguel worked their way back into the exhibition hall. As they went, they placed miniature cameras, so Jonah could warn them of security activity. Then, once the security was at the furthest part of their patrol, Miguel set off smoke bombs throughout the exhibition hall. As he activated his smoke, Barbara triggered as many fire alarms as she could reach. At the same time, Jonah set a computer programme running which simultaneously phoned police, fire, media and the Islamic Centre of America's security office. All listened to a pre-recorded message threatening to burn Dearborn mosque in "fires as hot as hell".

While the faithful and their visitors evacuated the building, the bikers worked their way against the flow of people, towards Matthew Saint's weapon. With its deadly contents, the model of the Great Mosque of Damascus was too heavy to be lifted. But it had been built with its own wheels. All Barbara had to do was find and release the brakes that held the exhibit in place.

Bikers from the support clubs quickly reached Barbara. They had removed their distinctive back patches and hid themselves from CCTV with their hoods. Together, the powerfully built men had the exhibit rolling quickly towards the fire exit. Long before the building's security had organised the evacuation, Saint's device was on a truck and away. Soon it would be sitting in the cargo bay of Red Andrews' Hercules aircraft.

Jonah breathed a brief, but heartfelt, sigh of relief as his monitor showed the weapon being secured inside the aircraft. But he had no time for celebration, as a second device and a rogue nuclear scientist were still out there.
He turned his attention back to the team at the warehouse. Each Watcher's body camera sent pictures back to Jonah, as the two teams moved quietly down through the warehouse's admin floors.
With so much happening at the mosque, very little security remained at the warehouse. The zombie Tonton Macoutes were all out with the fake National Guard. The few security guards that remained were some of Georgi Dimov's former Spetsnaz fighters. Although undoubtedly good, the fighters were not the cream of Dimov's organisation. The Bulgarian gangster had been careful to distance himself and Carlos Lobo from operations in Dearborn. These were new, unproven members of his organisation and the Watchers, with the benefit of surprise, were making short work of them.

The count of unconscious and tied gangsters grew rapidly as the Watchers moved through the administration rooms. Then, they came across the only room with any sound to be heard. A TV was on, tuned to 24 hour news channel and Baron Samedi's distinctive voice could be heard above the TV.

Stone slid a thin fibre optic cable through the key hole. Its tiny camera first saw Samedi sitting at a desk, covered with monitors and radio equipment. "This is how he's controlling his zombies", thought Stone as he listened to Samedi giving instructions over the radio.

Then, Stone slowly turned his camera to the room's only settee. For once, the fates were smiling on Stone. All their key targets were in the same room. While Samedi worked his zombie army, Beth, Ellen White and Matthew Saint sat watching their plan unfold on international news. They did not understand how the fire at the Islamic Centre had started, but as far as they were concerned, any panic suited their purpose. All four were so engrossed in happenings outside the warehouse, that they did not notice the door quietly opening.

Before the conspirators could do anything, four sets of tazer barbs found their mark. The electricity passing through their bodies soon had them on the floor and wearing zip tie handcuffs. Harris was still slightly weakened from the effects of the zombie drugs, so he opted to guard their captives. While he sat with an automatic weapon trained on the four conspirators, the other Watchers continued their sweep of the warehouse.

Harris was angry at what had been done to him. The helplessness of his paralysis still haunted him. He remembered everything between being injected at the New Orleans voodoo festival, to being revived in the Dearborn warehouse. Most vivid was his time in a coffin, with the terror that he would be buried alive.

Memories of walking with the zombie National Guard were more vague. But they were returning in snippets. The memories all fuelled his rage at the four people on the floor in front of them. "They will suffer", thought Harris. But he had not yet decided how.

While Harris was smoldering at what Ellen White and her conspirators had put him through, the other Watchers were in far better spirits. They had been making short work of the remaining East European guards and moved quickly through the warehouse building.

"Bingo", exclaimed Stone, as he opened a large van in the loading bay. "I've got the second device".

Acting without thought for himself, Red Andrews pushed passed Stone, heading for the van's cab. The first bomb was already aboard his company's Hercules. He knew time was against them to get both devices airborne and away from the city. With no idea when the bomb could explode, he set off towards the airport. With a small crew of volunteers, Andrews' huge plane left Dearborn with the most dangerous cargo it had ever carried.

In mid-Atlantic, at the ocean's deepest point, the Hercules' cargo ramp slowly opened. Red Andrews and his small team pushed the two crates to the edge of the ramp, all the time unaware if a timer was set on Matthew Saint's devices.

Andrews drew a huge breath, as his pilot turned the nose of the Hercules upwards and the crates slid down the ramp.

The pilot pulled the huge aircraft into the tightest turn it had ever made. The entire crew thought they were on a suicide mission, dropping two nuclear bombs from low altitude. But he was going to give them every chance he could of outrunning the expected blast.

As the Hercules levelled out, a huge plume of water exploded from the sea as the high explosives within the device detonated.

All those in the crew who had any fragment of religion prayed, as the pilot coaxed every ounce of power from the giant plane. Maybe their prayers were answered, as the expected flash and fireball did not follow them. Or, maybe it was just the physics of the bombs. The shaped high explosive charges need to be detonated in a specifically controlled sequence for a nuclear weapon to reach criticality. Without tight control over the firing sequence, they were just conventional bombs, with insufficient explosive power to reach the retreating aircraft.

After seeing the device away from the warehouse, Stone and Amber returned to check on Harris and his prisoners. "Shit Phil, what have you done!" exclaimed Stone, looking at the four bodies on the floor. "They need to stand trial" he added.

"Oh, they still can", replied Harris, glancing towards the open medical bag beside Baron Samedi". It was then that Stone realised his friend had exacted a fitting revenge on his tormentors. Harris had turned their own zombie drugs on them.

Stone saw only the irony in what Harris had done to the conspirators. Amber's mind was computing ways the intelligence services could manipulate the situation to their advantage. Within minutes, she was on the phone to her Uncle Jonny with a plan.

They now had a way of bringing in the Americans, with no loss of face for the British and no damaging press revelations.

With relative calm restored to Dearborn, their Chief of Police addressed a press conference outside the warehouse. While he spoke, body bags were being loaded into coroner's vans behind him. The Chief told a story of an attempt to discredit Islam in the face of rising fundamentalist tensions. The whole plot, from the corruption of the Adjutant General, to the kidnap of revellers from the voodoo festival was explained as turning international opinion against Islam. Nowhere in the Police Chief's speech was a single mention of the Millerite's Apocalypse. The Chief was equally unaware of any risk from nuclear weapons.

Ellen White was named as leading her fundamentalists against the Muslim population.

The story of Beth and Baron Samedi's voodoo practices brought colour to the press conference. The three were all named as being killed by security services, while taking their headquarters. Amber, through her MI6 role, had negotiated with US intelligence to take credit for raiding the warehouse. The Watchers' part in it would remain a closely guarded secret, as would any suggestion of nuclear terrorism.

The media frenzy continued up to the funerals of those involved. Members of the police and military received the full honours their services could provide. Members of the zombie National Guard who died in the fighting were also laid to rest with dignity. They may have fought against the security forces, but their minds had not been their own.

The biggest media storm surrounded the funerals of Ellen, Beth and Samedi. The media had built all three of them into monsters, in the same way they had unified the world in its hatred of Osama bin Laden.

Among the funerals, one coffin went into the ground with much less ceremony. Members of Matthew Saint's church attended a quiet service in Aldermaston. The sealed coffin had been transported back to England for burial, his injuries reportedly too severe for an open coffin. No mention was made anywhere of Saint's profession, or the part he played in plotting the end of the world. In time, few would remember the quiet engineer who had few friends outside of his small congregation.

Halfway across the world from Matthew Saint's funeral, the sun rose in the Caribbean. But, deep inside thick concrete walls, the warmth of its rays was yet to penetrate.
Guards and medics were hard at work on their new captives. The staff were American military personnel, and the facility had been in US hands since 1898 when US marines first took the tiny peninsula. But at the tip of Castro's Cuba, it was a very unlikely place to find an American prison. Now infamous for its detention of mujahedeen extremists, the world knew about Guantanamo Bay. Only a very small group of people knew about these prisoners held deep within the facility, out of contact with daily life in the prison. No one was looking for them, or protesting for their release. Even their closest family and friends had resigned themselves to the loss of their loved ones. The reason for this apparent apathy was four recently held funerals, where mourners were still grieving the loss of these four prisoners.

Deep within the Guantanamo Bay prison, Ellen White, Matthew Saint, Beth and Baron Samedi moved about the tasks they had been set by their captors. They worked without complaint, their emotionless eyes fixed on the task at hand.
US Intelligence had eagerly grabbed the information passed to them by Britain's Military Attaché. When Amber described Baron Samedi's zombie technique to them, they were eager to assess the potential for military purposes. The gift

horse of four subjects on which to test the chemistry was too good to pass, so the four conspirators, who appeared dead on leaving the warehouse, were allowed to remain dead.

In the weeks that followed, US security forces had the clean up well in hand. Any remaining conspirators were rounded up in a series of low profile raids.

General Stirling was quietly court marshalled for his part in the plot. The Adjutant General would not see the outside of a military prison until he was a very old man.

Carlos Lobo had learned from his mistakes in Morocco. He had lost many of his key people to the Interpol action which followed the Watchers' information. This time, O Lobo had sent much less valuable employees to New Orleans and Dearborn. Those that were killed or arrested in America could be easily replaced and had known little about his organisation.

Jonah had returned home to his job within MI5. He and Jonny Johnson would sit through weeks of debriefing at increasing levels of management and government. But the Watchers involvement would remain a closely guarded secret. The bikers had been paid from a covert MI5 account, set up to fund just this type of Black Operation. The Security Service needed a certain mystique in order to stay effective in the shadows. With the Watchers secure as a covert asset, the spymasters were free to use them again.

Enjoying a break from work, Stone and Amber powered their motorcycles along an empty desert highway. Both had fought to keep their feelings for each other hidden while on mission. But now, with the potential apocalypse a recent memory, the two bikers enjoyed testing each other's riding skills and shutting off from the murky worlds they both inhabited.

Occasionally Stone's attention drifted from the road and his beautiful leather clad companion. He smiled at the irony of how their mission had ended. Ellen White and Matthew Saint's dreams of ending the world had started in Cuba. Now, thanks to the weird zombie science they had employed, their own worlds had ended in Cuba.

Printed in Great Britain
by Amazon

36321125R00175